Tom —
I've apprec
ongoing support.
blessing to you and your family.
Walt

1-6-21

DRINKING WITH DEAD FRIENDS
and Other Stories

by Walter Lockwood

Chapbook Press

Schuler Books
2660 28th Street SE
Grand Rapids, MI 49512
(616) 942-7330
www.schulerbooks.com

Drinking with Dead Friends and other stories

These are works of fiction. Characters, names, places, and incidents either are the product of the author's imagination or are used fictitiously. Any resemblance to persons living or dead is purely coincidental.

An earlier version of "The Lion" was published in *Accent Magazine.*

An earlier version of "Cocktail Piano Player" was published in *For the Time Being.*

Layout and design by Magda Phillips

Cover art by the author. Cover design by Vivian Kammel

ISBN 13: 9781948237635

Library of Congress Control Number: 2020921508

Printed in the United States by Chapbook Press.

For Jim Cash, Marinus Swets, and Chuck Chamberlain,
dead friends still misbehaving in my head

Special thanks to my wife Pam and daughter Katie for reading and advice throughout the process; to daughters Susan and Alison, son Matt, Hal and Betty Porter, David Wygmans, Barbara Saunier, Dick Welscott, Jeffrey Petersen, Mike VandeBogert, Jonathan Swets, Dave Hendrickson, and Linda Chamberlain for their time and thoughts.

CONTENTS

SNOW DAY

The phone rang just as her mother's alarm went off. Daisy opened her eyes to a frigid January gloom. She heard a flurry of movement in her parents' bedroom next door to her own, a phlegm-cracked "John Evans," as her father, still mostly asleep, answered and put a halt to half the ringing.

"Shut off your alarm, Isabelle," he barked. "It's the school."

Daisy, dreading the day for a dozen usual reasons but mainly a report she hadn't finished for history, buried her head under her flannel comforter, closed her eyes, trying to find again the warm nest of sleep she'd just been jolted from. Six-thirty a.m. was a cruel time, and eighth grade was a cruel destination. How relentless and unending school was: five days on, two impossibly short days off, and homework dogging her through all seven. With pain, she thought of Lochrin's first hour English class--its endless busywork word lists and mechanical writing assignments that drained all feeling out of her love for the English language. She found joy in reading and learning, but school seemed to be systematically destroying it. She contemplated the blur of school years already behind her and shuddered at the endless, trudging years yet to come, a death walk.

Jerking as she felt a hand brush her head, she opened one eye. The cedar outside her window was heavy-shouldered with white. She heard the faint babbling in the background of a television weather lady.

"Snow day," her mother whispered. "Go back to sleep, sweetheart."

Daisy shrieked, reached up and hugged her mother, who laughed quietly. Was it possible? A day of grace—a blessed snow day, the only one so far the entire winter—and coming when she so desperately needed it! Burrowing back into the warm flannel, she felt giddy with deliverance.

The only discord arose a moment later from her sister Rose's room—a cry of dismay bordering on anguish. This *couldn't* be a snow day—it was the day of Rose's AP math test, her retake of the ACT, and tonight her basketball game for league lead. Rose was a junior, a star of everything, and at the moment she was awake, fuming, stomping around the house like a diva and cursing the injustices of life. Daisy closed her eyes and didn't open them again until sun shone brightly through her window two hours later.

She got to her feet, sliding into slippers, and looked outside to a world of dunes and towers, domes and minarets fashioned by twenty-one inches of snow. Their road was drifted over, their long driveway impassable, her father's Durango a small mountain of white. No cars passed, no school buses, no sound of plows, no sound at all. The snow and wind had stopped, and the world at rest breathed quietly. Out in back, near the west boundary of the large, fenced pasture, the windward side of the stable had gathered a giant drift that swept from the ground to the peak of the roof where a running-horse weathervane balanced white filigrees on its edges. Their two horses, predictably, were out plowing around in the thigh-deep snow looking for shreds of hay. She laughed at them, imagining them standing stoic in the snow storm, haunches to the wind, instead of inside in their sheltered walk-in stalls. Why did they always prefer to be out?

Two male cardinals, like Christmas decorations, dislodged small avalanches as they fluttered in and out of cedars. Squirrels were leaping and disappearing, struggling comically to reach the softly rounded bird feeders. Her cat Chloe sat on the upholstered chair beside the window, chattering at the cardinals and now and then baring her teeth.

At nine o'clock, her mother, full of good cheer, called them into a breakfast of bacon and strawberry waffles, the sharp aroma of sizzling fat transfiguring the house. Her father appeared, dressed in his one-piece flannel-lined barn outfit and a navy blue flannel shirt. He was a builder with his own small company—he stored his heavy equipment in a large steel shed out beyond the stable. Among the equipment was a John Deere tractor with a plow blade to keep the driveway and the horse pasture cleared. Rose came to the table, already showered and dressed, and flopped down in her usual place. Even in jeans and a lumpy sweater, she looked like a model from some magazine.

"Rosie, why are you worried about retaking the ACT?" her mother asked. "Your first score was the highest in the school."

"For heaven's sake, mom, it was only a 32. 32 is a minimum to get into Harvard."

"But you aren't going to Harvard."

"Do I have to take an ACT?" Daisy asked.

"Everybody going to college has to, dummy," Rose snapped. She turned back to her mother. "31 is just the *average* for getting into University of Michigan."

"Then you're above average. Besides, they want you to play basketball. They'd take you with a 25."

"You don't understand. It's the *principle* of the thing."

"She wants to dazzle them, honey," her father said.

"Of course I do," Rose said, nodding to her father.

Daisy watched the eye contact between the two. They were close, much closer than they were to Daisy. Her father went to every one of Rose's games, even the ones in other states with her travel teams. He was her cheerleader and long-time coach, a perfectionist and workaholic himself. Thank goodness Daisy had her mother. Neither of them was much concerned about perfection. Neither was very competitive, particularly since Daisy had long ago given up any hope of competing against her rock star sister.

After breakfast, while Rose complained to one of her boyfriends by cell phone, Daisy helped her mother clean up, and then put on an old coat and snow pants over her pajamas, pulled on her barn boots and pointed knit stocking cap, venturing out to muck stalls and feed the horses. It was a job she loved to do. She called out to Charlie, her chunky bay quarter horse. Charlie raised his head from his snuffling in the snow, heard her voice, and began plowing toward the gate. It made her oddly happy that he came whenever she called. Apollo, on the other hand, her sister's chestnut Arab, continued his nosing around the empty hay crib, refusing to acknowledge her. She cared deeply for both horses, but Apollo was high-strung and full of himself. She shoved the gate against the piled snow, opened it enough to squeeze inside the pasture and throw herself into Charlie's neck, hugging him hard, kissing his nose. Charlie patiently allowed it, his large, chocolate eyes softer and kinder even than her mother's.

She followed tracks he'd already made toward the stable, and Charlie followed her. Snow had blown inside the entrance but not far because it faced away from the wind. Their stalls were always open, side-by-side, the one on the right claimed by Apollo, the alpha; Charlie seemed perfectly content with the other. Daisy quickly raked the few manure clumps into a bin—the horses had obviously spent most of the night outdoors—and spread some new wood shavings, stuffed two flakes of hay in each hayrack, and refilled water buckets at a hand pump. When she bent to scoop feed from a plastic bin, Charlie began to nicker impatiently. Daisy knew the routine well, laughed, and gently scolded, "Charlie, what's your hurry? It's a snow day." She set the shallow feed dish on the floor of his stall, and his muzzle was in it before she could straighten up.

Apollo entered nonchalantly, his princely Arab head held high; he seemed unconcerned about his conical beard of ice and snow. She put a half scoop in his feed dish and set it down.

"Your feast awaits, highness," she said with a curtsy. He snorted once and walked around her.

Her father kept a small office at the back of the stable with an adjoining tack room where saddles and bridles, halters and lead ropes hung haphazardly on the walls. Her father had installed a space heater to take the chill off the area. Daisy switched it to high and sat down in the worn, dusty office chair. Though this was hardly an elegant display room, walls and shelves were lined with ribbons, trophies, and photographs of both Rose and Daisy on their horses. Most of the ribbons and trophies were Rose's, of course. Daisy had done some barrel racing with Charlie, but Rose had gone in for the fancy Arab shows, the elegant costumes, the high-level competition (they'd trailered Apollo all over the Midwest, never seeming to question the cost). Though Daisy didn't admit it, she loved riding a trail and caring for horses far more than competing on them, even in something as unfussy as barrel racing.

Horses were good for her soul, she knew, and at this buoyant moment her history report seemed as distant as a star. She would probably work on it tonight, but that was hours and hours away. There was something else faintly nagging at her—something Lochrin had asked for. Was it a poem? The man was a grammar fanatic. Poems were like math problems to him, but maybe she would surprise him with something. She felt full of poetry today, whatever that meant, and her heart ran free as a horse.

When Rose entered the office, Daisy was filling her father's yellow legal pad with words.

"What in the world are you doing?"

Daisy looked up, startled. She put down her pen and covered the legal sheet with both arms. "Trying to write a history report."

Rose sighed dramatically. "Well, I have a research paper due next week. It's a third of my grade. I'll use this wasted day to catch up on it, I guess." Her ire grew. "Oh, I hate these dirty tricks of nature. Do you think there's a chance they'll get the roads cleared for the game tonight?"

"I hope not. I hope tomorrow's a snow day, too."

"God, you're weird. Snow days drive me nuts." Her cell phone rang, and she turned abruptly to go out. "Oh. Thanks for doing the horses."

Daisy shrugged. "Sure." She loved her sister but sometimes wished she would flunk a grade, come down with a serious skin disease, or break her legs playing basketball. From their common gene pool, Rose had gotten all the talent, beauty, and competitive drive. Daisy had gotten whatever was left, which wasn't much.

She folded her handwritten paper and stuffed it into a coat pocket, shut off the space heater and went back outside. Words and images still danced in her head—accompanied by an excitement that was new. Her father was up on the tractor just starting to clear a path through the frozen tundra. Before leaving the pasture, though, she built two snowmen and used carrots for noses, one for each horse.

That afternoon, Daisy and her mother baked peanut butter cookies and then sat down to play a board game. Her father wouldn't play—he was catching up on some remodeling estimates. Rose said no, claiming board games bored her silly, until Daisy suggested Monopoly. It was a game Rose played like a demon, and, true to form, she bankrupted them within the hour. In the midst of play, she tried on earrings, as if to demonstrate her dominance by being half attentive. Her ears were small and perfect, of course, and made every earring look glamorous. Daisy's ears were noticeably larger and slightly pointed, like a faun's--more animal-like, wilder, less tame than Rose's. She was glad for her pointed ears. She had no plans to have them pierced.

They ate a pot roast for dinner, and her parents drank a bottle of red wine. Her father, in the right mood, was a storyteller, and wine usually put him in the mood. When they'd finished, Daisy asked him for the honeymoon story.

"You've heard it so many times," he said.

"Come on, Dad, I love it."

"Naw, I've still got work to do."

"Honestly, John, it's a snow day. Relax for a minute, would you?"

"I wouldn't mind hearing it," Rose said.

So he told the tale of their wedding in Maine in mid-February, how the snow had started during the small ceremony in a Farmington JP's office and continued hard through the rest of the day and all through the night. They'd rented a room in a bed and breakfast ten miles outside of Farmington, and when they got up in the morning, they thought it was night because snow had buried the place to the top of their first floor windows. He laid on the details, telling how he had to spend much of that first day helping the innkeeper tunnel to the cars, and how no one was able to leave for a week. They were down to coffee and a ring of baloney when the plow and a fire truck finally arrived.

"And nine months later I was born," Rose said.

"And four years later I was born," Daisy added.

"And that is why I'm not thrilled about snow days," he concluded.

Her mother shook her head with a smile. "You're forgetting all the essentials, John. I wouldn't trade that time for anything."

"Well, we certainly got to know each other."

"I hope that happens to me when I get married," Daisy exclaimed.

Rose just stared at her and shook her head. "You're such a romantic. Such a Pollyanna."

"Just like me," her mother said, casting a disapproving glance at Rose.

Daisy helped with dishes and then went to her room, hiding the folded paper she'd dug from her coat. She returned several hours later with a crisp, unfolded white sheet balanced in front of her like a Christmas gift. The other three sat watching weather reports on television. Roads, the weather lady said, would be cleared and schools most likely open by the morning. No more snow in the forecast. Daisy was disheartened by this news and thought about the unfinished history report. Oh well. The sacrifice had been worth it.

"I've written a poem," she announced.

Rose reached over and snatched it from her hands. "This I've got to see."

Daisy was horrified at this sacrilege. Her mother pointed at Rose. "If you're so interested, why don't you read it aloud to us? Is that all right, Daisy?"

"I don't know. I haven't even read it aloud yet."

"Poems are meant to be heard," her mother said gently.

"Okay…I guess."

So Rose lifted the sheet, cleared her throat, and read, not daring any mockery:

"Snow Day, a poem by Daisy Whitfield Evans

Mom's alarm was like a sin,
I hated it so.
I heard a howl of wind,
And gleeming heeps of snow.

Then a hand brushed my head.
"Snow day, dear,"
my mother's voice said.
It rang sweet and clear.

Frost curved on the window pains,
Trees were domes of white,
No sound of trucks or planes,
Nothing but snow everywhere in sight.

The stable was just a drift,
The horses plowing like trucks.
I felt my heart lift.
I couldn't believe my luck.

I sank into my nest,
And stopped the daily race,
The fight to be the best.
It was a gift of grace."

Daisy glanced nervously at her parents. Her father nodded uncertainly. Her mother seemed dazed--touched perhaps by the deep beauty of it.

Rose broke the spell. "Why did you rhyme it, for heaven's sake?"

The question surprised her. "So it sounds like poetry."

"Rhyme has been out of style for half a million years. Anyway, you've made it too sing-songy. Your lines are all end-stopped so every rhyme clangs like a bell. It's cute overall. I mean I like 'gleeming heeps' even though your spelling sucks. But how can you hear gleaming heaps of snow? 'The horses plowing like trucks' is your best line. Rhythm is very inconsistent, but it's not bad for a first try. I wouldn't show it to Lochrin. He'll murder it. What do you think, Dad?"

He stood, shook his head, backing away. "Don't ask me about poetry."

"I think it's very nice, Daisy. It shows a lot of promise."

Daisy hated the word "nice" almost as much as she hated the word "cute." Her heart had shrunk suddenly and tumbled into her stomach. She'd created a vision of this day, pushed the words until they told the truth, but her family had somehow missed it. The joy of the process had turned into an agony of failure. Somehow she kept her voice steady as she took back the crisp, white page onto which she'd poured her soul.

"It was my first try. I guess I'm not very good yet. Thank you for your comments." And she went up to her room in a cloud of bleakest despair. Later, when the red was gone from her eyes, she read the poem over and over and slowly began to see some problems. She recalled how the demands of rhyme had kept her from including important things like church towers of snow, her mother's strawberry waffles, her father's story of the storm, the cardinals and the cat, the carrot noses of snowmen. She loved the word music of rhyme but it imposed so many limits on her thoughts.

In the morning Daisy grimly rode the bus to school, deciding to risk it all and hand in the poem (with a few corrections) to Lochrin. It came back in a week with comments that might have been Rose's, sporting a large red B-, his favorite grade. How much wiser it would have been, she thought, to spend her snow day finishing her history report.

****

Rose Evans opened her apartment mailbox and forcibly removed a too-large, book-like package she could see was from her mother. Communication from home always lifted her spirits. Rose had been away for six years, now in her second year of med school--overworked and weary of the non-stop intensity. She needed the release of horses, of basketball, of hard exercise and the rush that came with it, but that was all in the past. She'd done well enough at hoops, though perhaps not quite as well as hoped for. The level of play in the Big Ten was higher than she'd ever expected. There'd been no championships during her tenure, and no individual honors. But her family, especially her father, had remained faithful, endlessly encouraging.

She shared her apartment with a piano performance major, a Chinese girl named Li who spent most of her time in practice rooms, so they rarely saw each other. Li was so driven to succeed in her fiercely competitive field that she rarely had time even for a glass of wine. Rose knew something about being driven. She remembered the hundreds of hours in the practice ring with Apollo, fine-tuning their mutual connection until they moved and thought as one. Now she only saw Apollo a few weeks in the summer. Daisy was happy to take care of him and keep him in halfway decent shape, but Rose hadn't found a way to fill that emptiness. She would for certain become a doctor, perhaps even a top surgeon, but the years of effort came at a price.

She tossed the package on the cluttered kitchen countertop and poured herself a coffee. A photograph of Apollo and Charlie, inseparable companions, sat propped on the mantle above their small, fake fireplace. She sat down on a stool, took a sip of coffee, and began tearing open the mail. From the padded package she removed a book, actually a magazine...a literary magazine called *Visions* from the community college back home. A short note from her mother was paper clipped to the cover. It read:

"Dear Rose. Look on page 37 to see what your sister is up to. Hope you are well. I'm sending cookies in a separate box. Love, Mom."

She fanned through the modest publication, noticing pages with photographs of some fairly interesting art. Poems and short stories occupied most of the space. On page 37, she saw her sister's poem; she was half amused that Daisy had found the courage to continue writing them. Rose's first silent reading surprised her. She next read it aloud:

"SNOW DAY

By Daisy Evans

For Charlie

She'd listened to the wolf-like howl of wind
the night before, and snuggled down deep within
a flannel comforter to shut it out.
Only half ready for a class report about
some civil war, she shivered once and was asleep.
The next sound she heard was the beep

of her parents' alarm, followed soon
by the local weather man's deep baritone.
A moment later a hand brushed her head.
"Snow day," her mother softly said,
and then "Go back to sleep, my dear."
On each window pane a curved veneer
of frost framed a half-lit scene outside.
She raised her head and peered out bleary-eyed
at a fantastical world of slouching trees, of towers,
of domes and forms of massive flowers
blooming overnight where common things had stood:
a deck chair, a slide, a picket fence once wood,
now transformed to gleaming mosques and minarets,
to swells and dips of bleached and endless coverlet.
No car went by, no sound of struggling truck;
even the plows were silent somewhere, stuck
In muffled paralysis of snow. A smile, a sigh—
she sank into her nest, heard a cry
of joy from her sister's room. The world had stopped,
all schedules canceled, appointments dropped.
A winter holiday, simpler than any other:
strawberry waffles for their waking; she pictured mother
orchestrating cookie making at noon, then
father being pushed to read aloud or spin
a tale of the quintessential storm which buried
cars, entire houses the week they married.
It was a day of nothing at all to do
but simple, undemanding things—and true
exemption from the grind, the daily race--
a gift, a haven, a miracle of grace."

The poem was not quite--she suspected--of professional quality, yet the overall competence of it was stunning. Not everything was accurate. Rose's cry had hardly been one of joy. It was a weather lady, not a weatherman. But that was literary license. Daisy still clung to rhyme, yet now it wasn't doggerel. The music was subtle, the images crisp, and a heart pulsed at the center of work. She could guess why no horse appeared except in the dedication. Eight months ago Charlie had died suddenly of an aneurysm. Both Daisy and

Apollo were still grieving deeply. Their father was talking of buying another horse, but Daisy wasn't ready. She'd gone to work for him part time and enrolled in college classes just to keep occupied.

Rose had always written well, better than Daisy, at least where mechanics and grammatical precision were concerned. At that moment she felt strongly driven to write poetry herself—if she could ever find the time. And next she discovered she was cruelly depressed. Her once incandescent life began to feel colorless as dust. How in the name of everything just and right had lackadaisical Daisy stumbled into a wondrous world to which Rose had no key? She loved her sister, for certain, but she found herself wishing for Daisy to go off, marry a fool, raise a dozen cantankerous children, and never write another poem.

LIGHT BEARER

The gardens doubled themselves in the swimming pool, flowers reflected beneath the surface, growing upside down and dancing as the water moved—the hot pink of petunias and yellow heads of zinnias flashing like tropical fish on a reef. When he swam among them, the sun shown in shimmering geometries of light on the pool's bottom, and the light made him think of the woman.

Throughout John Emerson's life, he had served beauty, loosely planning the English disorder of his gardens and letting God do the rest. How wildly prolific were those creative powers! He couldn't keep them in check, though he tried mightily, fighting off the wild morning glory's strangling vines, the endless variety of weed life leaping up amid his own laughable efforts to control. Most mornings he weeded, but it was never enough. His brother, a pastor, had once remarked, "What a glorious place you and God have created here." John had laughed and replied, "You should have seen the place when God had it alone."

The pool had been there when they'd bought the house years ago. A swimming pool wasn't something he'd desired, yet he'd learned to take pleasure in it, especially once he'd replaced chemicals with natural filtration and begun imagining the gardens. Now he'd enclosed the long concrete deck with flowers and laid out the spacious back lot with plant architectures, changing shows week to week.

In early spring the first crocuses pushed through snow, then explosions of bright blessings as the earth awoke. Burgeoning perennials followed--poppies and peonies, dazzling for a mere handful of days, bowing out to stargazer lilies with their heavy perfume, climbing roses, clematis vines and orange honeysuckle. He invited intriguing rogues to spring up unplanned: sunflowers planted by the birds, and the wild, groping, tenacious moonflowers with their huge white trumpets. He often sat in the evening and watched those giant blooms open in spasmodic little jerks. When his children were small, they had sat in fascination beside him, for they loved the gardens, too, loved the rhythms as he did.

He remembered his small daughter standing frozen in place for an hour to coax a chickadee onto her hand for a seed. His son, two years younger, fearlessly pressed nuts into the paws of squirrels he called by name. Each year these two, along with his wife, helped enrich the soil with compost and plant a patchwork of annuals they chose for wildly clashing colors.

Vegetables and herbs had their own sunny corner. Hydrangeas formed a soft buffer below the cedars enclosing the property. There were stone walls, fences, and trellises eccentrically arranged as entrances into hidden hollows and serene private spaces, his havens from an academic world in which he had been passionately embroiled—for years as a professor of architectural design, then as president (now retired) of the college. Two buildings of his sustainable design stood on campus, built to be disassembled and reused when the time came.

He had worked to be a steward of his small piece of the planet, yet he was aware of growing deficits, especially extremes of weather he'd never seen before. The cardinals that had regularly nested in the tight cover of the weeping cherry had not returned this year. It was a loss. As he'd worked beside them, they had become trusting, almost friendly.

Pollen counts were rising, and his wife's allergies, especially now that the pandemic virus had weakened her lungs, made it difficult for her to work alongside him in the gardens. The two were in their 70s already, and he wondered how long they could maintain this place they loved. Their daughter now lived in New Zealand, their son in western Canada—places less desecrated. Neither had married, so there were no grandchildren, and though the family usually met yearly, the separation was a difficult loss of companionship and support.

His mind, he hoped, was still good. He read for hours each day and wrote. If he forgot certain names, he remembered concepts, design principles, dozens of complete poems, and long passages of scripture. Lists of prayer concerns stayed intact in his memory and daily received his attention during early mornings in the rose hollow as he settled with his coffee on a weathered maple bench.

It was on that bench several days previous he'd seen (or thought he'd seen) a woman of unusual beauty with dark hair to her waist and liquid mahogany eyes, a stranger to him, sitting in his spot. Shaken, he'd greeted her with an apprehensive hello. A wind had blown across her gauzy green skirt, and just then he'd been startled by a jay as it raucously burst from a cedar. When he looked back, the woman was gone.

Puzzled, he'd followed a path to the rear of the yard, to an arch in the cedars with a gate. The snap hook lock was still in place. He carried his coffee back inside, hoping his wife Anna would be out of bed. He found her in the den, wrapped in a robe and curled in a leather chair, sipping coffee, her long, still-youthful auburn hair hanging loose about her shoulders.

"Good morning," she said, and then, "Are you all right?"

"I guess so. The strangest thing just happened," and he told her about the woman in the rose hollow. "It startled the hell out of me. I managed to say hello, I think. When I looked away for half a second, she'd disappeared."

"Was she a neighbor?"

"Never saw her before."

"She must have used the back gate."

"I checked. The lock was still on it."

"Well...she was obviously admiring your gardens."

"I don't mind that. I'm just curious about how she got in and out."

"I'm sure there's an explanation, John. Maybe she'll come back."

But when she didn't, John began to wonder if he'd imagined it. How trustworthy **was** his mind at this point? He'd begun to notice minor episodes of a sort of vertigo, times when the ground seemed to waver beneath him. He would have to sit down until the dizziness passed. Perhaps because he spent so much time alone these days (they were still avoiding crowds, masking in public places), his imagination had become unnaturally active. Too often he found himself envisioning the destructiveness of recent presidential policies and those of other careless, short-sighted world leaders. John caught himself mumbling angry words aloud, startling himself, surprising Anna when she was near.

Yes—these could well be early signs of a slow disconnect from reality, a malady common enough at his age. Yet wasn't reality itself the problem? There were days when, to maintain equilibrium, he avoided news altogether. Knowing he was among the world's most blessed and fortunate only increased his distress. Though he daily found moments of peace in the gardens, hope had become as elusive a phantom as a hummingbird in flight. Someone had coined the term "solastalgia" as a way of describing the loss he was feeling, the loss his children would feel even more deeply, the legacy left by his self-serving generation and others before it. Was there time to repair? Had he even begun to do his part?

One evening he sat with Anna on the patio near the pool, having white wine and a salad. Two hummingbirds buzzed the honeysuckle vine nearby. There was no restaurant on earth that offered this ambiance.

"The Blakes are buying a condo in the Ravines," Anna told him.

"On the golf course? Good grief, Jerry plays three or four times a week as it is."

"They don't want the hassle of a big house and yard any more."

"Don't you hate the thought?"

"I do."

"I can't imagine having to ask permission from some association to plant a flower."

She nodded. "I worry, though. I'm not much help to you, and there's so much to do out here. How long can you keep it up?"

"No condos--promise me, Anna. We'll manage until we can't any more."

"Then what?"

"Hell, I don't know...hire it done. Maybe the kids will come back."

"The kids aren't coming back. And we can't ask them."

"Of course we can't."

She poured them both more wine. "A day at a time then?"

He touched her wine glass with his. "Until we drop."

John swam a half-mile nearly every day, the best and most benevolent exercise he'd ever done. Weight fell off him through the pool season; his paunch disappeared, and his stamina improved. Closing the pool was always difficult for him, as tinged with regret as watching the gardens blacken with the first frost. Though they hiked and skied on local trails, winter no longer held the magic it once had—often milder and muddier now, but also affording longer hours for reading and writing, for fires and cribbage. He grew more outgoing in winter and spent better time with Anna. As they had for many years, they would cut a Frazier fir near Christmas and put it up, and on good years one or the other (on rare occasions both) of their children blew in for the holidays.

He was nearing his sixtieth lap when he noticed Anna standing beside the pool. He stopped, puzzled, and removed his swim goggles. She almost never interrupted him while he swam, even for important phone calls. He did the same for her. She looked a bit pale, befuddled.

"I just saw her," she said.

"Who?"

"Your lady. I saw her from the kitchen window. She was standing in the garden beside the autumn clematis watching you swim. I hurried out here, but she's gone."

"Describe her."

"Long, dark hair, willowy body, a wispy green summer dress. You never told me she was beautiful."

"Then I **didn't** imagine her!"

"Who said you did?"

"This is strange, Anna."

"I agree."

"What should we do?"

"Why do anything? She's not the least bit threatening. She seemed as serene as the garden she was standing in."

He calmed at that. "Well…apparently I have a secret admirer."

"I think your gardens do."

In later August they helped their friends move to their new condo. The smaller residence required epic downsizing. Dismayed at all they'd accumulated, the Blakes hired an agent to run a week-long estate sale. John and Anna were guilty of similar excesses. If they died, what would their children do with it all? The books alone required several rooms. What was the reason they owned five sets of china?

Young people lived modestly these days, paying exorbitant prices for small apartments. They couldn't accumulate. John immediately began making a list of their most expendable possessions, including books unread for years, though he vowed never to begin reading on a screen.

The two celebrated a wedding anniversary in early September. They had a few friends over, dinner by the pool, and a bonfire in the rose hollow. The night was turning chilly by the time the guests went home, and John neglected to put the solar cover on the pool. Though the next day reached the upper 60s, the water had turned cold. John disliked swimming in a frigid pool, yet he was determined to do his laps until the season came to an end.

He stood on the wide coping at the pool's deep end. His usual routine was to descend into the shallow end, adjusting to the water by slow degrees. Today, his plan was to dive in and absorb the cold shock all at once. He took a deep breath and leaped forward, cutting the water crisply and swimming as hard as he could. The plunge took his breath away, but his body was already adjusting on the return lap. As he passed into the deep end, he saw the bottom drain, nine feet down, the wavering hexagons of light on the pool's floor, and he counted the sixth of his usual nine strokes. In the seventh stroke, as he extended fully with his left arm, a vise seemed to clamp on his chest and intense pain radiated to his neck, his jaw, his back. He'd more than once imagined a heart attack in the pool, where he was nearly always alone and without help. How stupid and unthinking not to heed his own premonitions! Overcome by a nauseating dizziness, he realized he was too weak to reach the pool's edge. His arms were dead. He felt his body sinking toward the drain. His mind cried out for Anna, but he knew she was gone--a doctor's appointment that morning. God, what a stupid way to die!

He held his breath beyond endurance, long beyond what he ever had before. He screamed in panicked silence, his body an agonized, useless semi-corpse. His life sped by in a blur--until, desperate to breathe, he suddenly gave up all struggle, slipping away into a dark, quiet peace.

He drank into his lungs the smothering water.

As consciousness drifted away, he felt dimly aware of a presence, of arms reaching to embrace. He felt long hair, a woman's hair, swirling about his face.

The woman pressed her mouth tight to his, drew the water from his lungs and then breathed back into him. He felt consciousness returning. The vise in his chest loosened. She gripped him tighter, holding him like a lover. They began to move through water of the most stunning blue he'd ever seen. He realized her green summer dress was not cloth but long strands of seaweed. Her hair and the writhing weeds twined about his arms and legs, holding him fast, and as the two began moving together, he felt them becoming one. His vision sharpened to laser beams. Her eyes had become his.

They moved more and more swiftly, passing through pods of humpback whales with many calves, rising into the air to a sky full of pelicans gliding on massive wings. The sky was the same intense blue as the water. John saw land below, the shifting, gleaming greens of forests, rivers gliding through deep grooves in the earth, waterfalls plunging into gorges. He could see bees exploring the depths of moonflowers, a cricket singing on a floating leaf, bacteria swimming in a drop of rain.

He heard her whisper, "Light Bearer," naming him.

He awoke staring up at a streaked sky, lying in his gardens near the pool, his bathing suit still damp. Above him loomed an avalanche of white blooms, his massive, trellised autumn clematis. He slowly raised himself on one elbow. He felt no pain. He saw Anna open the patio door, glance in his direction, and head out to find him.

SERENDIPITY

At eight p.m. a squall moved through like an aerial attack, shaking windows and blasting trees, and then passed away as abruptly as it came. The evening in its wake was enchanted. The street was a river of rose. The air was cool and pristinely clear. The leaves glowed a deep, vibrant green—a hundred times greener than normal. Things seemed to have more depth and dimension. Birds rhapsodized. As if inspired, Jack's two parrots commenced whistling noisy arias he'd never heard before, stirring him to put aside his student papers and escape the house. In the yard he could see the lacework of every leaf of a fern, the intricate spiny traceries of the honey locust. Everything was wet and washed. He walked streets that he never ordinarily walked—but a new direction wasn't necessary. It was a changed world all over. Even old things were new.

He ambled on, drinking it in, the rose light by slow degrees fading, yet the grass continuing to glow like luminescent coral. The moon was rising, nearly full, for a few moments balancing on the dark horizon like a giant wheel of Brie.

Jack reached a street corner and stopped as a car passed in front of him, struck a huge puddle, and drenched him to the waist. He cursed loudly and stood with his arms outstretched in shock and dismay. To his surprise, the car slowed, edged to the curb and stopped. The door opened and a woman got out.

"I'm so sorry!" he heard her exclaim. "I honestly didn't see you."

For Jack, the magic of the evening had died abruptly in a cold, muddy drenching. "I'm a mess," he growled.

As she came closer, he saw that she was perhaps his age or a bit older, and though dressed in jeans and a baggy flannel shirt, quite pretty. His anger began to melt away. Beauty, he knew, always had its way with him.

"My house is just a block from here. Come by a minute and dry off."

Jack looked down at his soggy khakis. "It's really not that bad." His tone had softened.

"Jump in the car. You're a mess, and it's my fault."

He thought about it, shrugged, went to the car and climbed in the passenger's side...a thing he would never do except for a palpable magic still lingering about them. Serendipity was in the air. Something momentous seemed imminent. She slipped in behind the wheel, put the still-running car into gear, smiled at Jack, and in less than a block turned up a gravel drive that wound back at least a quarter mile to a ramshackle farmhouse set deep in a surprisingly large wooded lot. Some small outbuildings leaned precariously behind the house, as if once part of a farm around which a neighborhood had sprung up.

"This place was my grandfather's," she said, as if reading his mind. "It used to be an eighty acre farm."

"I never knew it was here."

"Bit of a surprise, isn't it? You can't see it from the street." She pulled up in front of a porch that ran the entire length of the house. When she shut off the engine and the headlights, darkness and silence engulfed them, though the silver of moonlight came drifting through the trees. She reached across Jack's legs, opened the glove compartment, and grabbed a flashlight.

"I'm Ava Green," she said.

"I'm Jack Hawking." He offered his hand, and she shook it with a smile. "I was on a walk," he said. "I live a mile or so south of here."

"I was at the airport. I fly a glider, but the storm kept me on the ground."

"Were you out after the storm?"

"On the ground, yes, but it still was magical…the most gorgeous light I've ever seen."

He grew excited. "That's what I was doing! The world turned into Oz…into the Emerald City."

She gave him an odd look. "I had exactly that thought. I've never seen colors as intense as that. Something crazy happened to the light. And did you hear the birds?"

"Yes! I've been walking around spellbound."

She laughed. "Until I came along."

"No, it was worth it to find someone sharing this… this miracle."

The narrow beam guided them up the uneven wooden steps, and Jack held the flashlight as she found her key and got it into the lock. The door swung open, she switched on a light, and Jack followed her in.

"I should throw those pants in the dryer. Do you mind wrapping up in a towel? I think it's all I have." She took down a folded towel from a nearby closet and tossed it to him. "My bedroom's right there, if you want some privacy." She turned on the bedroom light for him, and once he'd entered she shut the door. He looked around. The antique double bed was a heavy oak four-poster covered with a handmade quilt tossed loosely in place. Everything was plain, simple, uncluttered. A bra and blouse hung over the back of a spindle chair. A dresser with a mirror held a few bottles of cream and make up; a night table stood beside the bed, stacked with books.

A noisy flutter startled him. On a windowsill at the far side of the room, a small owl perched, staring at him. White droppings marked the sill. Jack quickly removed his wallet, keys, change, and belt, and slipped out of the pants. His underwear was damp too, but he stayed in them, securing the towel tightly around his waist. He returned to the living room.

"Umm, there's an owl sitting on a windowsill in your bedroom," he said. She was across the room, turning on an aged gas stove to heat water.

"Oh, I forgot to mention it." She pointed across the room to a massive upright piano. "There's a crow on my piano, too." And so there was, a large ebony creature with gleaming black eyes. Ava took Jack's pants from him, frowning as she looked them over. "They really need washing before we dry them. Do you have time?"

"I believe I do."

"Someone expecting you at home?"

"No. I live alone."

"Living alone works best."

"You, too?"

"Well, I have my birds. The owl isn't great company. I'm just nursing her back to health. But the crow—his name is Bill—is a friend."

"I have two parrots."

She stared at him. "We seem to have some things in common."

"They're characters. Sometimes they yammer like old ladies. At bedtime, they always tell me goodnight--even when I forget."

Smiling, she went to a washer and dryer in a back hallway and tossed in his pants, added detergent, and set the cycle in motion. "I think birds are brilliant things. Bill is very clever musically." She went over to the piano and slid onto the bench. "You choose...Bach, Mozart, Beethoven..."

Jack sat down at the kitchen counter. "Bach."

"My favorite." As she began playing a French Suite, the crow fluttered into the air and landed on her shoulder. While the bird listened, he chattered "Bach...Bach..." and rocked in perfect time to the rhythms of the suite. She closed her eyes as she played and finished with a graceful diminuendo.

Jack was charmed, delighted. He laughed and Bill echoed it, leaping from her shoulder to the floor. Ava rose from the piano and sat down next to Jack at the counter.

"Ava." It was the first time he'd said her name. "You fly gliders? Why?"

"Simple...I want to be a bird. My loveliest dreams are flying dreams. Whenever I have them, I float happily through the whole next day."

"A glider...I've never done it."

"There's room for two. You're welcome to try, if you dare."

"I'd like it."

"I believe you."

The kettle began to whistle, and they were silent as she prepared tea.

"I teach English," he said. "At the public high school. But writing is my first love."

"I knew it was something like that. I'm a wildlife biologist. My specialty is birds. Right now I'm working at a bird sanctuary and doing some research for the university. I write, too--papers on bird behavior."

"I'm 28." He wasn't sure why he said it.

She shrugged. "I'm 29."

They looked at each other and quietly laughed.

He glanced around her kitchen, at the old-fashioned laminate countertops, at the clean simplicity. The gas stove caught his eye. "Your oven door is screwed up," he said.

She looked over at it. "It is. I've tried to fix it but no luck."

"You'll lose oven heat. Let me take a look." He got down on his bare knees in front of the stove. One hinge appeared to be broken. He pulled open the door, saw the problem, and asked her for a screwdriver.

"Phillips or flat head?" Her question pleased him.

"Phillips—but this will take both of us, if you're willing."

She knelt beside him, holding the hinge in place while he put in new screws she'd dug out of a drawer. The fix was a success, and they returned to their tea.

"You surprise me, Jack. Who'd ever guess an English teacher would be handy?" It was the first time she'd used his name. "It's interesting--birds work pretty much like we just did," she went on. "I've studied them for years. Couples bond and solve difficult problems together. Two are smarter than one. Some of them have amazing cognitive functioning."

"I've seen it. When my parrots work together, they can open up their cage door and get out. They outsmart me all the time. It's exasperating."

She laughed, seeming to understand perfectly. They sipped tea, talked about what his house was like. He liked hers better, he told her. This old farmhouse needed some work, but he loved the old wood, the openness, the privacy. His house had only two bedrooms and neighbors too tight beside him--one with teenagers who played basketball and rap music in the driveway until long after dark. When his tea was gone, she poured more. The wash cycle finished; she tossed his pants into the dryer and sat down beside him again. She seemed to sense him watching her--actually staring at her, and she turned to look him in the eyes.

"I know what you're thinking," she said quietly.

"I wouldn't be surprised. You seem to have some sort of wiretap into my brain."

"Odd, isn't it?"

He went silent. After a moment, he asked, "Well, what am I thinking?"

"You'd like to marry me."

Shocked, he looked quickly away from her. Several moments went by as he settled himself and then finally turned back. "Listen, Ava, I hardly know you. I've never even kissed you..."

"Does that matter, Jack? Does it make any difference?"

He took a deep breath and exhaled. "No. Actually not any at all."

"Well, then my answer is yes."

And three days later his house went up for sale. The following week they were married in the simplest of ceremonies. The adjustment took them almost no time at all. Their birds, on the other hand, came around by and by.

THE BEST SHE EVER HAD

For Marinus Swets

The train was passing out of Louisville, and things were looking more and more like the South. It was March, the end of spring break, and hedges of azalea were burning everywhere. Hills began to appear and then rocky passes carved out for the rail bed. Meese was relieved to be going back to Tallahassee and school after the unexpectedly taxing week with his girlfriend and her family in Indianapolis.

The trip had been monumental in several respects. After a year of determined trying, he'd at last won over Sarah in her childhood bed; they were virgins no more. Her awkwardness had convinced him of the truth of her words: she'd saved herself for him and only him. Yet there was a caveat: she thereupon assumed (it hadn't been in his mind at all) that they were now formally engaged. Still gloating and grateful, he didn't have the heart to disagree. And from there everything had spun out of control. Her parents quickly arranged a family party for them. There was talk of a ring, talk of Meese joining her father's advertising firm once they'd married. Meese tried to explain he was an art major with some plans of his own, but his self-assured father-to-be insisted there was plenty of art in advertising.

In Nashville, he had a ham sandwich and a Coke in the club car. When he returned to his seat, an old man and a girl occupied the seats directly facing him. Though the man was dressed nattily in an aging blue suit and pink, polka-dotted bow tie, his head waggled in an unnerving way. The girl—he guessed in her mid-20s--had lush lips painted pink, blonde hair permed into kinky curls, and a short print dress that rode up her graceful legs whenever her knees parted, which was often. She was careless about her knees and kept trying to catch Meese's eye.

"Where you headed to?" she asked at last.

"Tallahassee," he said.

"On vacation?"

"No. Headed back to school."

"Oh. You're a college boy. He's a college boy, Randall."

"Ain't that nice," he said. His hands waggled like his head. "Eloise and me are on our way to Birmingham to get married."

Meese glanced at her, unable to hide his surprise.

"Don't go bragging about it," she snapped at the old man. "I'm only doing it on a bet."

"You say that, but it don't matter."

The girl folded her legs up underneath her and closed her eyes to shut him out.

"Go out for a smoke with me," she said after a few minutes. Meese looked up. She meant him.

"Sure, I'll have a smoke."

They made their way to the platform between cars. The sun had set, but the sky still glowed. He tried to light their cigarettes, but it was too windy.

"Oh, hell," she said. "I don't care about smoking anyway." She suddenly moved against him and pressed her full lips hard to his. He felt her hot tongue opening his mouth. She jammed her pubic bone against him. He got hard, and she felt it and laughed.

"Want to meet me in Birmingham?" she whispered in his ear.

He took a step back, out of breath. "I better not. You're getting married."

"I don't care anything about that old boy. I'm just doing it on a bet." She stepped forward, rubbed her belly against the front of him once more, smiled, and went back through the door into the car.

Lights were on inside now; twilight was fading to black. Rocky cliffs flashed by just outside the windows. Meese looked at the old man. He must have Parkinson's or something to make his head waggle like that. The girl Eloise sat directly across from Meese. She put her feet up on the seat beside him.

"What's your name?" she asked.

"Meese."

"Ever been to Birmingham, Meese?"

"No, never have except for passing through."

She spread her legs a little, pointing to one bent knee and then the other. 'There's one mountain on one side, and one mountain on the other side. And…" pointing up her skirt, "Birmingham is right there in between. Want to go to Birmingham?"

The old man's head waggled faster. "She's a lively one," he said.

Meese felt his face flushing. "You're really getting married?"

"She'll get a house in Birmingham and my old age pension to live on. She could do worse."

"He's my sweet sugar daddy," she said with a grin.

"What do *you* get?" Meese asked him.

"I get laid. It'll be worth the price, even if I die trying. You never get laid without paying the price." He chuckled merrily at his own joke.

Meese smiled, though the thought of the two of them made him squeamish.

"Don't go getting ahead of yourself, old boy," she said, her grin fading away.

"It's a marriage vow," the old man said. "No dancing around it, a deal's a deal."

"Please just shut your wobbly old mouth."

Meese thought he heard a faint tremor in her voice and also thought he understood it.

Night settled in and the sound of the wheels on the track hypnotized all of them. The old man fell asleep, and the wobbling in his head and hands diminished a bit. Meese glanced at the girl. Her eyes were open, staring into his.

"I'm going to the bathroom," she said. "Come with me."

"What for?"

"Oh, you know."

What he knew—the moment he stood up and followed her down the aisle to the ladies' room—was that he was mentally no more engaged than she was. She glanced about furtively and quickly shoved him into the tiny restroom, pressing in behind him and locking the door. What happened between them in the next twenty minutes would serve his fantasies into old age. She did some things he would never feel a woman do to him again—as he'd discovered after decades of looking and hoping. Sarah's passion, by comparison, might have come from a Florence Hartley etiquette book.

The old man was still asleep when they returned to their seats. Meese sat down facing her and was surprised to see she was quietly weeping.

"What is it?" he asked.

"I thought I knew what love was supposed to be, but I didn't--not until you came along," she whispered. "I've made a stupid mess of things."

"What's the trouble?"

"It's you, Meese. It's what just happened. It was the best I ever had."

"I know." He was gratified, but speaking more for himself.

"I can't marry that old man now, not even on a bet. Now I know what it's supposed to feel like, and it breaks my heart. All I want to do is go back home."

"Do it, then. Get off at Birmingham and go back home."

"Will you go with me?"

He hesitated. "I can't. I have to finish school."

"Well, then I can't either. I got myself in a fix. I don't have any money at all. The old boy won't give it to me if I'm going back."

He struggled a moment, wanting to be honorable. "I can give you fifty."

"That's sweet of you, Meese. But I need a hundred for the trip."

He took a deep breath, pulled out his wallet, and emptied all his cash into her hands. Her eyes were still teary, and she looked at him with love.

He sat alone, feeling a confused kind of regret, as the train pulled out of the nightglow of the Birmingham station. It had rained earlier, and dark shapes of cars and buildings gleamed black and slick. His eyes swept over the lines of vehicles as they inched through congested city streets. It was a scene he wanted to paint—suffused with a bittersweet sense of loss.

Though it was only for a fleeting moment, he saw the two of them in the street. Her arm was laced through the old man's, and they appeared to be smiling about something. The train lurched ahead, and the two vanished into a bar called Cap and Bells. The train whistle sounded a lonely, hollow cry as they passed down between mountains and out of Birmingham.

It would be many years before Meese would file away his acrimony and come to see his Birmingham passion as among the best and least expensive of his life.

THE LAST SELFIE

The sunset of that evening in Monterey is burned into my memory—strange clouds on the horizon like a herd of mustangs lifting their heads and galloping across the edge of the world. The clouds shifted on a west wind, a strip of blue sky appeared above the water line, and the sun began to drop clear. The effect was dazzling. Sunlight now rode on the tips of the waves, and each wave became a rampaging grass fire reaching toward the cliffs on which we stood. Clarice chose that moment to scramble up the highest rock (surf crashing far below) with her cell phone in hand to get a picture. She took shots wherever she went, and this would be her most unforgettable.

Smart phones with cameras were relatively new and the word "selfie" even newer when I'd bought an iPhone for her, thinking that she wouldn't have to haul her heavy Nikon everywhere we went. I was right. But I didn't expect her to develop a mania for selfies—one or both of us in nearly every shot she took. You could buy a postcard of the Taj Mahal, she maintained, but not one with Jake and Clarice in the foreground making everything more intimate and meaningful. Shooting in reverse was odd to her at first, but she quickly adjusted. Some of her hundreds of photographs were genuinely impressive. Her face—auburn hair, emerald eyes, milky skin—was eminently photogenic. But the self-absorption of her selfies eventually got on my nerves. Clarice did what she wanted, of course, and I rarely complained. She was my wife of three years; we were still honeymooning, traveling at every opportunity, visiting vineyards around the world (she was a viticulturist), putting off children, sharing everything—everything, that is, except that last selfie.

It would take a rescue team a day and a half to find her body a mile out and well down from the point, carried off by a rip tide. I'd rushed down like a deranged man to try to save her, nearly drowning in the wild water where surf pounded the rocks. I'm not sure what saved me beyond a supernatural rush of adrenaline. Later the police found the cell phone lying in a crevice on the rock where she'd dropped it. She'd got the shot an instant before she took the step backward: Clarice at sunset.

Life is woven tight with irony.

Once I was cleared of any wrong doing (police can be brutal), I wandered home to northern Michigan, driving alone against the better judgment of family, arriving safely after a week to spend the rest of spring and summer in a benumbed haze in the small rural home we'd bought together. With Clarice there, I'd considered it a small paradise: in the distance, on a clear day, we could see a gleaming slice of Grand Traverse Bay.

In our wills, she'd chosen cremation, so I was spared the stress of a memorial service until August. Her mother, a Detroit lawyer, still strikingly glamorous in her fifties, handled most of the details. Sheila was a take-charge, no nonsense woman who put her grieving somewhere that I couldn't get to. After the service, she asked for the ashes (taking me by surprise), so I gave her the urn, minus a small plastic bag of them to spread in our vineyard. For Sheila, I also dug Clarice's iPhone from the unpacked suitcase and showed her the sunset photograph. She stared a moment, shook her head, and handed it back. I appreciated her, but found no comfort there.

My parents were conservative, well-meaning evangelicals who fortunately lived in Phoenix and had no reason to come to Michigan except to see their black sheep son. They flew in for the service, hung around three days in a Traverse City hotel, and got no encouragement from me to stay longer; I thanked them, however, for putting me on their prayer list at church.

Lucille Stone, my English department chair, stopped by often that summer. Lucille had short silver hair that looked whipped with an eggbeater; the story was she'd spent her childhood in Romania with missionary parents who cared for orphans. Now in her mid-50s, long divorced, eccentric without trying to be, she treated her department like family and wrote obscure poetry I tried hard to like. She'd usually find me in the gardens Clarice and I had planted together—work that kept me mindlessly occupied and blessedly solitary.

I owed my job to Lucille. She'd read my single published work, a thin book of stories, and gotten me hired into her department at the community college. On her first stop after Clarice's death, she brought a growler of craft beer into the garden where I was planting tomatoes. I pulled off my gloves and hugged her, and then washed off at the hose and poured the beer into wine glasses I kept in a cupboard near the grill. The beer was almost black, rich with coffee and chocolate. We raised glasses in a sort of toast, and drank.

"Are you staying sane?" she asked, nodding approval at her beer choice. "I worry about you. You and Clarice were so insular, such a little island of two. Now you're a little island of one."

"I'm sane enough. My life just feels…well…pointless. If I manage to sleep for a few hours, I wake up with no sense of what to do next."

"Well, of course. Clarice organized your life for you."

"I think we sort of did that together."

"Sort of. How's her vineyard doing without her?"

My wife's small vineyard had already begun to suffer for the lack of her intelligent care. She could nurse a grape until rich and bursting, but it was a fine art. We grew vinifera varieties, especially Riesling, her favorite. She'd pruned before we'd left for Monterey. But pests and viruses had already begun to make inroads. I needed professional advice but lacked the will to ask. The Mission Point vineyard she'd worked for was scrambling to make do without her. My concerns were too puny to bother them.

"I think I need some help."

"Then ask. I probably know more than you do. Forgive me for saying this, Jake, but I can't imagine a dumber way to die than your wife came up with."

The remark caused me pain, but I couldn't disagree. It was actually embarrassing explaining the circumstances to people. "Selfie demise is getting very popular," I said to her with deadpan irony. "Especially involving trains, high voltage wires, cliffs and mountain tops. I see something online about it nearly every day. I bought her the stupid phone. If she'd used her Nikon, she'd still be here."

"Maybe so. But don't beat yourself up. She did the deed, not you."

I refilled our glasses, and we wandered the vineyard. She asked me to dinner but I said no, not yet. She was a good enough friend not to push. "I hope you're keeping a journal," she said. "Just to make sense of what you're going through."

I said I was--when I had the courage. I was telling the truth.

So I returned to work in early September—teaching as effectively as any empty vessel could. The student papers—always the ditch digging part of the job—got me back into familiar terrain. My mind wasn't ready to focus again on badly written sword and sorcery tales. But somehow the mechanical deficiencies of the writing engaged me enough to feel I was gaining some ground.

When a new student named Cloris Apple suddenly appeared on my class list two weeks into the semester--a late drop-add who was upset about a colleague's course requirements—I thought little of it beyond the similarity of her given name to my wife's.

Cloris Apple came in ready for a fight. She was a thin, hard-edged, scrappy woman of about 40, tattoos showing here and there, cigarette breath, dressed in a black halter top and jeans ripped at the knees. I was trying to prep for my next class. She sat beside my desk with one leg crossed over a knee like a man, short western boots with traces of manure at the heels.

"All I want is some advice about a story," she bristled, glaring at me. "Nobody seems to get it. I don't want to write some personal journal. I don't give a damn about a grade. I just want help with my story."

"Well, I assign a personal journal," I said calmly. "It's just a log of your daily thoughts. It's good writing practice."

"Excuse me, Dr. Allen. Why the hell should you have access to my daily thoughts?"

I sat silent, my energy draining away, staring at her. "Okay, I see your point. Sure. Just do it, and I won't read it."

"I won't do it." She raised her jaw in defiance. I could see clearly the kind of child she'd been.

Something began to unravel in me. "Jesus. Who the fuck cares?"

It startled her. She frowned, shook her head, and stood up. "What's your problem?"

I took a deep breath. "Nothing that concerns you. I'm not myself right now. Sorry. If you don't write a journal, I really don't give a damn."

It was language she understood. "Okay," she said with a small, slanted smile. "Good enough. Thanks, Dr. Allen."

"Cloris," I said as she was leaving. "I'm not a doctor. I'm Jake Allen. Mr. Allen, if you need to be formal about it."

She shrugged, snorted what seemed like a laugh, and headed out.

Watching her go, I felt a wave of exhaustion just imagining months spent with her and whatever tale festered in her head.

The community college sat at the southern end of the bay in Traverse City, twenty minutes by car from my house. It took five minutes to get out of the city, but once I started winding up the peninsula between east and west bays into cherry country and vineyards, my muddled mind would usually begin to clear. It was a Friday, the day after I'd met Cloris Apple. My deceased wife had, within weeks of our wedding, steered me into eating whole foods, wild-caught fish and free-range chicken, drinking our own wines made with minimal preservatives. We'd cooked our own meals most of the time, seeking perpetual health and youth, I guess, but I'd already fallen off that wagon by the trip home from Monterey.

I daily passed a funky-looking burger bar called Chico's as I went to and from school. In good weather with windows down I could smell deep fried onion rings from the road. If it wasn't the aroma that drew me in, it was some sort of predestined astral confluence. The lot was full of pickup trucks and motorcycles, mostly locals, I figured, which spoke well for the food. Inside, the place was jammed and clamorous; there was a long bar with no empty seats and a line of draft beer tap handles. Flat screen television sets seemed to be everywhere with football and baseball analysts cross-pollinating.

In a corner near me, a heavy, bearded guy in a sleeveless tee shirt and hairy shoulders shouted, "Hey, Cloris! We need another round! Get the lead out!"

I glanced from the guy to the waitress he'd yelled at—it was Cloris Apple—shuffling plates of food like a deck of cards onto a table of eight. Without looking away from her work, she shouted back, "Keep your pants on, Buck."

The guy seemed delighted, raised his glass to her. "Okay, Cloris, honey--just wanted to hear the sound of your voice!" There were scattered guffaws from nearby tables.

She got the last plate settled and finally looked toward the bearded guy, her grin a weary one. It was then she spotted me hanging there between the two of them. My heart sagged; her face went pale. At last she took a deep breath, moved toward me as if gathering courage. "Hi, there," trying to sound chirpy. "My English professor. What a surprise."

"Yeah, for sure. Looks like the place is pretty busy."

"There's a table over in the corner if you want. Come on."

I was desperate to get out of there but followed her anyway. It was a tiny café table with two chairs, set next to the path of a half dozen waitresses crashing in and out of the kitchen. I sat down, feeling squeezed, and she took a seat with me.

"Well, now you know what I do."

"Pretty crazy place."

"Yeah--mostly this time of day. In a while they'll be gone." She looked down at her lap, acting shy or something equally uncharacteristic. It took her a little time to figure where to start. "I want to apologize about something. I came after you like Attila the Hun yesterday. Jesus, I can be such a bitch. But last night I finally put two and two together and realized it was your wife that died last spring. Saw it in the paper. Here I am harassing you about a stupid journal and my stupid story while you're going through some kind of hell. I just want to say I'm sorry."

This new tone disarmed me. "It's okay, forget it."

"No, it's not okay."

"Well, you do a terrific Attila the Hun."

I said it lightly, but she didn't smile. "I'm different than that, I hope. I only do it when I have to."

The bearded guy was waving at her again.

"You better get back," I told her.

"I know, I know--impatient bastards. They're pretty good guys, but they test your character on a daily basis." She stood. "Listen, Mr. Allen...Jake. Could I buy you a cup of coffee some time? I mean at school or somewhere—not here."

"Maybe Monday after class."

"Okay. Want a menu?"

The burger and rings were even better than they'd smelled from the road.

She was quiet in Monday's class but seemed alert and interested. She was two weeks behind, so I wasn't sure she was tracking me. That afternoon we met at a Starbucks across from school. She was sitting at an outside table, smoking. She put out the cigarette when she saw me. Today the wind was chilly coming off the bay; she was bundled in a 4H hoodie sweatshirt with a galloping pony express rider printed on it. She told me Pony Express was her 4H group. Most of her kids were barrel racers; she trained them herself because she'd run barrels for years.

"I've got two horses at my place," she said. "I never found better therapy than riding a horse. Come over, if you want. I'm just south of town. I'll show you the trails and you can come out even when I'm not there. There's a key in the top of the porch light. Have yourself a beer and then go saddle up. Do you ride?"

"A little. Nothing to brag about."

"If I'm there, we can ride together and talk if you want. Are you talking to anybody?"

"What's to say?" Actually, there'd been a few times I'd felt like talking, but after that first wave of heartfelt condolences, people pretty much dropped the subject, except maybe Lucille.

"You sound just like me. When I lost my daughter, everybody wanted me to talk about it, but I was too damn angry. Then they all went quiet right about when I needed to start. So I talked to my horse instead." She shook her head, as if remembering. "How long were you married?"

"Three years."

"Were you doing okay?"

"Seemed like we were doing great."

"What was she like?"

I had to take a deep breath at that one. I clenched my teeth, trying to shut down a wave of unexpected emotion. "Don't think I can handle that question right now."

"It's okay. What kind of coffee suits you?" She went in and bought two cups while I struggled to pull myself together. Maybe I did need to talk, yet I doubted that Cloris Apple was the one to do it with. When she came back, I asked about her daughter, but she just said she'd tell me about it some other time. I took a slug of coffee, scalding my tongue, and finally managed to blurt out that my wife was beautiful, better at everything than I was, and pretty close to perfect.

"Lucky you," she said, her voice farther off now. "The men in my life never even came close to being safe."

My feelings toward her began changing for obvious reasons, but I had no plans to visit her at her place, even though I didn't doubt the sincerity of her offer. A few weeks went by. I was puzzled that she hadn't shown me any writing, even though we were now reading student stuff in class. Her intelligence about the writing process, the blunt but insightful comments to people twenty years her junior, made her a rough-edged, improbable guru to the class.

I discovered she was a reader, though with a limited scope. She lived on fantasies, especially the intelligent ones. She'd read and reread *The Hobbit* and *Lord of the Rings,* knew the characters as if they were family members and claimed even to understand Elvish language. The *Narnia* stories were second on her list, and then the Harry Potter tales.

One Friday she came to class with a small boy—the son of one of the waitresses at Chico's who, single and struggling, couldn't afford day care. The kid's presence bothered me: it seemed hugely presumptuous, but Cloris kept him quiet with crayons and her class notebook. No one else seemed to mind but me.

It was nearing time to harvest our grapes and begin wine making. The Riesling grapes were small and not up to Clarice's standards, yet I had to figure out something fairly fast or see the crop go to waste. Unfortunately, there were bigger problems that I was trying to ignore. We'd afforded the house, thanks to combined incomes, but with only one income now (mine the lesser of the two), I was fast burning through savings.

On the last Sunday in September, I got a phone call from Sheila, who'd been lurking in the back of my mind. She'd actually called several times over the months to check on me, never saying a word about the large chunk of cash she'd lent us for the down payment on the house. She told me she planned to be in Traverse City in early December and hoped we might find an opportunity to talk. I feigned enthusiasm while filling with dread. I didn't know Sheila well enough to guess what she intended. I knew her track record with men was spotty—twice divorced—with a romantic history my wife seemed reluctant to discuss. I knew for a fact Sheila's only child was her pride and joy, her princess--and that I hadn't come anywhere near qualifying as a prince.

It was the threat of Sheila, I think, that pushed me toward Cloris. When I called, she didn't seem surprised--gave me the address and directions, though it was difficult to locate even with a GPS. She lived on a narrow, rut-filled gravel road that wound through hardscrabble countryside scattered with undernourished cornfields. I spotted her ancient pickup truck beside a long house trailer so old the siding was streaked with rust. I got out and walked around the yard. The metal barn (I presumed for the horses) looked much better kept than the trailer. The gardens scattered here and there about the property surprised me. Nothing about Cloris would have suggested a green thumb or an eye for beauty. The plots were manicured, some full of flowers (mostly perennials), and others with lines of vegetables. Though the season was fast coming to an end, cabbages, broccoli and beets remained to be harvested, and scattered mounds of chrysanthemums and ornamental cabbages blazed with color.

Cloris suddenly was standing beside me. Startled, I said, "Hey, Cloris. Wow…these gardens."

"Have to do something with the horse manure." She pointed out toward the woods. "I own twelve acres," speaking with pride, "all the way to the back of that stand of woods to the east, and following the creek to the north. We'll ride the trails out in that part."

She took my arm and guided me past a large, fenced arena that she'd obviously spent some money on, with barrels, cones, and poles piled in a corner, and on into a fenced pasture containing the metal barn. She whistled shrilly through her fingers, bringing a white and red Paint and a larger Appaloosa spotted like a Dalmatian ambling toward us. They followed us into the barn where their walk-in stalls and crossties were located. The Paint was the calm one, a gelding, so she saddled him for me, gave me a leg up, and adjusted the stirrups. Soon we were walking side by side through the far field and out into the woods. She was right about horses. I could feel the stress blowing out of my head with every step. I asked her where she'd bought all the unusual perennials in her gardens.

"I don't buy flowers. I thin them out of cemeteries." I laughed, but she went on seriously. "It's not stealing, if that's what you're thinking. I'm doing everybody a favor. People don't keep up the old cemeteries. I consider it a public service."

"It's brilliant. Take me along some time."

She grinned. "I do it at night with a flashlight. Wouldn't want you getting in trouble."

"Oh—*that* kind of public service."

"Well…I figure people don't always know what's good for them."

We rode along quietly for a while, the horses content at a walk, which suited me. What she called a trail was often just a vague, bent over spot in the high grass. When we went single file, she took the lead, saying her mare wasn't a follower.

I asked her to tell me about the story she was writing. She hesitated, looking uncomfortable.

"I feel bad I haven't shown it to you yet--especially after all the crap I gave you. I'm trying to write a myth, I guess. Or a kind of fantasy based on a myth--the story of Demeter and Persephone. You know it?"

"Sure. The goddess of the harvest gets her daughter stolen away while the girl's picking flowers. Hades takes her off to the underworld."

"That's right. Persephone gets kidnapped by the bastard and taken to his underground kingdom, but Demeter searches and searches and finally discovers a way to get her back—at least part time."

"And so the daughter comes home every spring," I continued, "and stays until winter. It's all about the cycle of the seasons…life, death, rebirth. Fantastic story."

"I think so. It relates to my life in a way…to losing my daughter. But I'm having trouble making it say what I feel."

I nodded, understanding. "How about telling the story without the myth--the way it really happened?"

She was silent for the next quarter mile. When she finally spoke, her voice was calm. "Who wants to read about a dumb, drunken son of a bitch who kills his own seven-year-old daughter and himself passing out at the wheel of his truck? Jesus, Jake. The myth has hope, at least. At least she gets her daughter back part time. I want a story that has some hope."

I got the point and stopped suggesting things.

We sat till after midnight in plastic chairs outside her trailer, drinking beer. A few weeks earlier I'd never have believed I'd be doing this. She told me the hardest thing she had to do was give up her daughter's stuff. She held onto it for three years, and then finally passed it on it to friends who needed it. Maybe it was the beer loosening up my tongue, but I admitted I had the same problem with Clarice's stuff, especially her closet full of clothes. I couldn't even look at it, let alone pack it up for Goodwill.

"Don't give it to Goodwill," she said. "What size was she?"

"About your size, I guess."

"Let me get rid of it for you. I could use some better clothes for sure, but I've got girlfriends at work struggling just to make rent and feed their kids."

I told her—and meant it—that I'd count it a blessing if she'd handle that particular business for me.

Before I left she said she'd heard about my book but hadn't read it yet. She asked what I was working on now. I told her honestly I wasn't working on a thing--hadn't worked since I took the teaching job, married Clarice, and got embroiled in buying a house. I planned to get back to it, of course—was just waiting for the well to fill up, as Hemingway put it. It struck her as odd for a writing teacher to quit writing. Though I wasn't losing sleep over the matter, she did have a point.

When I got home, struggling to get a key in the lock in the dark, I found a penciled note hanging on the door:

Jake—You weren't here so I went ahead and picked your grapes, which couldn't wait any longer. I'm taking them home to press. Talk to you later. Sorry to be so presumptuous, but I can't stand waste. Lucille

I laughed hard, went inside and read the note again. I wondered why two such odd, unlikely women were the main ones keeping me afloat.

Three days later, Cloris came by to pick up Clarice's clothes. I was hard at reading papers, so I pointed her to our bedroom, and she disappeared inside. After maybe fifteen minutes, she came out wearing a short black dress my wife liked better than any other.

"Can you believe this?" she said. "Your wife and me are the same size exactly."

My stare must have been strange, because she quickly said, "I think I better take this off." But instead of going back to the bedroom, she pulled the dress over her head right there. She had on Clarice's underwear, too—purple bikini panties and a sports bra.

"That's her underwear," I said.

"You said I could take anything I wanted. This is way nicer than mine. I'll take it off, too, if you want." She turned toward the bedroom.

"Wait a minute," I said. But she didn't. I followed her into the bedroom. She had a slim-hipped, boyish body. There were two tattooed horses running across her tailbone above the waistband. She pulled off the underwear.

Cloris reeked of cigarettes, but I was surprised how quickly I got past that. We were like two people dying of thirst suddenly finding an oasis. We just kept going for the longest time, resting for a few minutes and then starting again. When we finally wore out, she said, "Was it those clothes? Was it her?"

I laughed. "Are you kidding? Nothing like her--way more generous. It was you."

Sheila showed up at the house in December, looking classier than ever. It happened to be the day of my 30th birthday, but she didn't remember. I'd been paying only the interest on the mortgage the last two months, and somehow she knew about it. Since most of the principle was her money, she offered to buy the mortgage, including the value we'd added to it, and rent the place back to me for what I could afford. She'd always wanted a place on the Peninsula. There was a catch, naturally. I'd have to clear out whenever she wanted to vacation there. I'd be a caretaker of sorts the rest of the time. It was a generous offer, though it didn't seem to relieve the anxieties I was feeling. I asked her if I could have a little time to think it over, and she was fine with that.

She held out her hand to show me a thick gold band set with an outsized, perfectly dazzling diamond. "Guess what this is," she said.

"You're engaged?"

She laughed. "God no, Jake. This is my right hand. Guess again."

"Haven't a clue."

"It's Clarice."

I took a step back from her. "You mean the ring is in memory of her?"

"Yes, that. But more than that."

Sheila carefully explained, as if to a child, that she'd sent Clarice's ashes to a Swiss company where they'd extracted the carbon, subjected it to enormous heat and pressure in a special machine, and within a matter of a few months had done what nature took a billion years to accomplish: a perfect diamond. "My darling girl will always be with me." The mawkishness of it seemed so out of character, I was at a loss for words.

I lifted her right hand and looked more closely at the diamond. It seemed lighted by a fire within. "Come on, Sheila. You're kidding me."

"Wrong. It's a perfect memorial."

"It's weird."

She pulled her hand away. "Not at all. I'll treasure it the rest of my life."

By the following spring, I had an apartment close to the college--no view of the bay, of course, but I could still see it from my classrooms. Some days I'd think about that large, perfect, dazzling diamond, essence of Clarice, secure on Sheila's finger, and then I'd remember the rough, uncut luster of other gems I knew.

DRINKING WITH DEAD FRIENDS

Norman Locke had already drunk two tall beers when some old friends began showing up. He was sitting at a small round table at the Last Chance Saloon. The room was nearly full of customers drinking beer and singing hymns. The combination seemed odd, and it was. Beer and hymns on Tuesday (he learned from a waitress with pink hair and a nose ring), accompanied by accordion and guitar, had become the saloon's biggest draw. They were singing *Great is Thy Faithfulness* and other old-fashioned songs of the faith from a blue hymnal stacked near the bar. Of course, Norman had learned all of this only after he'd sat down, drunk a quiet beer and ordered a second, having picked the joint at random on the way home from a funeral.

The first friend entered the bar just as *Great is Thy Faithfulness* came to an end. There was no mistaking Hyde, a fireplug of a man with a wiry explosion of hair, who went over for a hymnal as if he'd been there before, turned and strode directly to Norman's table and sat down opposite him. In his rasping voice (Norman would have recognized it with his eyes closed) Hyde shouted out "*Shall We Gather at the River*, 687," and the musicians flipped some pages in their spiral notebooks and began to play. Hyde's sandpaper baritone led the singing. He handed over the open hymnal to Norman, urging him to join in. But Norman was too stunned to sing. His old friend, as nearly as he could remember, had been dead more than twenty years.

Norman got up to escape before the hymn finished, but Hyde caught his arm and pulled him back into a chair. He finished the last verse, and then said, "You can't leave yet. I just got here."

"There's something in this beer. I'm not feeling well. I need to go."

"Locke, we haven't seen each other in years. Relax. Besides, DeKraker's coming."

"DeKraker? You don't even know DeKraker. DeKraker is dead."

"You get around more when you're dead…meet more people. I see him here Tuesdays. Thursday is Trivia Challenge, by the way. I never miss it--always win, of course. But I'm humble about it."

"You were never humble about it." Norman sat back down and took a long drink of beer. He felt dizzy and out of balance. He was obviously drifting through some very strange dream.

"That was in the old days. I'm changing." Hyde took out a white handkerchief and loudly blew his nose. "You spoke at my funeral," he said with uncommon sincerity. "I've wanted to thank you."

"Of course I spoke at your funeral. You were my best friend. I wrote your obituary, too. Your wife asked me."

"Yeah, I know. Thanks. It was pretty irreverent."

"Well…"

"I know…completely appropriate. You knew me better than anyone."

"Yeah. Why did you go and die so young, you jerk?"

"Just bad luck, man. Sorry."

They both signaled the waitress for beer.

"I don't get this," Norman mumbled.

"You'll figure it out. You're wrong about it being a dream."

Norman laughed uneasily. In the past, back when they were inseparable, Hyde had always seemed to know what he was thinking. "Right. Just a normal day at the Last Chance Saloon."

At that moment their attention shifted to the front entrance, to a booming male voice singing *The Orange Blossom Special*. Norman saw DeKraker plow through the doors, a towering ape of a man with slumped shoulders, seeming to be in his early 40s, though he'd been 83 when Norman last saw him alive.

"DeKraker's here," Hyde said, not looking up. "Always tries to be the center of attention--immature as ever, but he's working on the problem. Not dead as long as me, after all."

"Right."

"By the way, Locke, death is nothing like you expect."

"I'm noticing."

DeKraker spotted them, came over, pulled a chair out to make room for his legs. Norman was struck dumb. This apparition was most certainly the spitting image of his old friend.

"Hello there, Hyde. Hello there, Locke--how is my Boswell? Long time no see."

Norman had once, as a fairly young man, written a mediocre novel with a main character, an educated lunatic, based on DeKraker—hence, the Boswell reference. It hadn't sold past a first printing, but DeKraker had liked it. Norman had written something much better years later, a poem, for his funeral.

"Thanks for speaking at my wake," DeKraker said. "And that poem you wrote me…I was touched. Must have been divine inspiration, Locke. I was shocked you could be that good." DeKraker had memorized poems as a hobby. Colleagues in the English Department, they'd walked downtown to the college together and back, seven miles round trip, for fifteen years. DeKraker had recited Yeats, Eliot, Housman, Hardy, and a hundred others; also sung old country songs during the countless hours of their travels.

Norman had been content mostly to listen and absorb. He hadn't contributed a lot beyond an appreciative audience, which was really all DeKraker needed.

"I guess that's a compliment coming from you," Norman said.

"Take it for what it's worth."

Norman found it strange to see these two together—the two closest male friends of his entire lifetime, whose paths had never crossed in any significant way. Hyde had been his inseparable friend from adolescence on: college roommates, friendly competitors as writers, best men at each other's weddings, support through divorces, losses, nervous breakdowns, and occasional triumphs. Norman had once saved him from drowning. Hyde considered it a life-long debt, which he kept repaying to the end.

DeKraker had come later: his office partner, department chair, mentor and inspiration, his alter ego who said and did things he never dared and repeatedly led him into dragons' lairs. By the time that friendship had developed, Hyde was living across state, teaching and writing, and when they got together, Norman traveled to him because of Hyde's agoraphobia. The two friendships went on in separate worlds. How odd to have Hyde and DeKraker sitting at the same table. Each was larger than life, each commanded the floor in his own extravagant way, each had forced him out of the solitude he craved and dragged him into life against his will. And he cherished them for it. Norman had a close, loving partner in his second wife, children and grandchildren he cared for deeply, yet his life had a large empty spot formerly filled by male friends he'd long outlived.

"About my last few years--" DeKraker said to Norman. "Damned glad you were kind…and patient. Too many years of cheap booze, Locke. I didn't know it was dementia--who ever does? I was like a phonograph needle stuck in the same groove--just kept repeating those tired lines. I imagined if I kept talking, I wouldn't forget who I was."

"I still heard echoes of you," Norman said. "But I wasn't all that patient."

"Well, you fooled me, my friend."

The band seemed to be taking a break from hymns. The pink-haired waitress set down more tall beers and smiled at him as she had each round—actually looking him over. Norman, long accustomed to invisibility, ignored it and drank deep. At this point, beer usually began to have a drugged, depressive effect on him, but this brew was producing a warm, expansive glow. He drank more as his friends watched. "What is this beer?" he asked.

"It's a local. They call it R & R," Hyde answered. "Be careful—it sneaks up on you."

"Good name for beer. R & R...Rest and Recuperation?"

"Repent and Repair," Hyde said.

Norman thought about that. "Well, if it sneaks up on me, I have dead friends to drive me home." He paused a moment. "Do you two drive, by the way?"

"Don't have to," his friends said together.

"Fly?" Norman snickered at his own wit.

Hyde grinned patiently. "No, Locke, better than that. Teleportation. We think it and we're there. No more travel problems for me. Wings are obsolete."

Norman had begun noticing small details he hadn't before. "Ummm...this is very weird. How old are you, Hyde?"

"In my prime, I'd say. How old are you?"

"Ancient."

"I don't think so, Locke. We're all in our prime here."

Norman stared down at his hands. The skin was smooth, the liver spots gone along with the brittle nails and snaky veins. His fingers were pain free, flexible; the arthritic knots had vanished from his knuckles. "What the hell is going on?" he cried. The sticks of his arms, he saw with wonderment, now filled out the sleeves of his shirt.

"You were always slow adapting to change," DeKraker said. "But at least you had an appreciation of interesting people."

"Like us," Hyde chirped. "The truth is, you were pretty boring."

"Screw you, Hyde," Norman answered, though the warm glow of the beer took all the edge out of it.

"He's right, Locke. You were stuck in your quiet little self—writing stories, content with your own company. You put your finest feelings on paper, but *living* them was another matter." DeKraker had slipped into lecture mode. "Always backing away from people…always on the fringe of the circle hoping to escape. I know you charged your batteries in solitude, but, damn, Locke, it took you years to begin to care about people—at least the general run of them. You weren't very giving, you know. Tended to see your accomplishments—you had a modest gift, I admit--as your own doing, too, though you could be fairly humble about your superiority." He laughed at his own witticism.

Hyde jumped in. "And then the problems with that randy imagination--your wandering eyes and indecent thoughts…"

DeKraker nodded agreement.

"Wait just a minute!" Norman blurted. "I don't believe this! Two pots calling the kettle black!"

"Amen, amen to that. We don't deny complicity, Locke." DeKraker's head bobbed, affirming it. "But we've both been working on the problem."

"What in hell are you two up to?

"Just trying to help an old friend."

"I have to go, guys. My wife is expecting me."

"No, she isn't," Hyde said. "Anyway, you can't leave yet. The evening is planned. We're going to a movie."

"I'm not going to any damn movie." Norman rose quickly, finishing off the last of his beer while upright. Both his friends caught an arm and firmly sat him back down.

Hyde leaned in close to Norman's face. "It's a movie you need to see. We're here to make sure you go. It's important."

"Why is it important? What is going on? What is this place, anyway?"

Hyde glanced at DeKraker, who shrugged and said, "A place to rest up."

"Rest up from *what*?"

"Living."

Norman stared into DeKraker's sympathetic eyes. "Then what am *I* doing here?"

"Oh…well…" DeKraker said.

Hyde patted Norman's hand. "The funeral you went to today—someone close?"

"How did you know I went to a funeral?"

Hyde took a swig of beer. "You must've mentioned it."

Norman thought a moment but drew a blank. "Strange…I don't remember who passed. Some poor sap. This pastor officiating didn't even know the guy--did this grim, generic eulogy with an altar call. I was so disgusted I had to stop here for a few beers."

"No friends to pay tribute?"

"None. He looked pretty old--outlived them all, I guess."

"Bummer," Hyde concluded.

"Did he have any kids?" DeKraker patted Norman's arm.

"That was the only good part. The kids said some nice things."

"Well, that's something."

They were all silent. DeKraker poured some of his beer into Norman's glass. Norman stared into the amber liquid, at tiny bubbles rising up. "This is absurd. It just can't be…"

"No?" DeKraker answered.

"It's not possible." Norman watched the musicians returning to their music stands, strapping their instruments to their shoulders.

"Happens to all of us," DeKraker continued, now patting Norman's back.

Norman swilled all the beer in his glass, set it down, and surveyed the barroom. His eyes were tearing up. "This is not what I expected at all."

Hyde smiled. "Of course it isn't."

DeKraker rose and snapped his fingers.

Norman found himself standing in a narrow cobblestone road lined with flower gardens of such spectacular variety and color, so dazzling in the slanted light of a setting sun, that he was compelled to shield his eyes with an arm. And then the fragrance—which he could only describe as heavenly—grew overpowering. He teetered, came close to toppling sideways, but steadying hands gripped his shoulders. When he uncovered his eyes, he saw he was on a high bluff, between his two friends, gazing out at a placid expanse of blue water reaching out of sight. A rainbow path stretched from the orange and peach-colored sun across the glittering emerald surface. The light was still so intense it was painful; he needed his polarized sunglasses but didn't know where they were.

The cobblestone road wound downhill to a great white hotel. On the inland side of the road stood a long line of grand Victorian houses, like candies in a box, with gardens of zinnias, begonias, impatiens, marigolds, petunias, and countless other varieties bordering the green sweep of lawns. He spotted lilac trees heavy in white and lavender bloom, lakes of tulips and daffodils, hyacinths and crocuses, crabapple and dogwood trees in cascades of pink and white, chrysanthemums and autumn clematis—all seasons blooming miraculously at once. The place was deeply familiar to Norman, remarkably like another place, an island he'd visited many times in his life, but this was... infinitely better. A burgundy carriage drawn by two black Friesians came round a corner from the interior forest and stopped. The uniformed driver tipped his top hat to them. The three climbed in, the great hooves echoing hollowly on the stone, as the carriage transported them down the hill, past the great white hotel with a porch stretching for what seemed a mile, and then descended into town.

"Where will I live?" Norman asked as they passed a small stone church.

"In the white hotel, of course," Hyde answered.

"I can't afford it."

"No need to be cheap any more, Locke," DeKraker said. "Either of us. It's free of charge."

"Free of charge? Do you live there?"

"Hyde and I have our own special habitats. This is yours. You fancied this island and gardens—so here you are."

"Will I see you?"

"Any time you want."

"Do I still sleep…and eat…and work…and--?"

"All of it," Hyde said. "But it's different. More intense."

Norman knew he should be a bundle of anxieties, but he felt strangely serene. Maybe it was the beer. "I guess I have a lot to learn."

"You do, indeed," DeKraker said. "And you start here."

The carriage halted in front of a small, old-fashioned theater with a marquee. It stood at the end of Main Street beside a ferry dock lined with passenger boats and, farther down, a harbor of sailboats in slips. On the marquee in large, magnetized letters was the title LIGHT IN THE DARK PLACES.

"Don't know this movie."

"It's premiering tonight…at least this particular remake of it," Hyde said. "No one has seen it—except the film maker, of course."

The three stepped from the carriage into the street. The driver again tipped his hat, and the horses moved on toward the harbor.

"It's hard to understand this," Norman mused. "I struggled with faith. There were times I honestly believed… and at least I went to church. But the waffling…and so many Christians I couldn't stomach..." He shook his head. "DeKraker, you ended up a Unitarian, which is barely a religion. Hyde, you never set foot in a church that I recall. Aren't you two surprised we're here?"

"And not in hell?" DeKraker asked.

"Yes!"

"Well, Locke, my first thought in this place was that very one. But I took a moment—thanks to a friendly suggestion--to consider the parable of the prodigal son...especially the father in the tale. His...I'd have to call it *immoderate*...love and forgiveness are the whole point of the story--for that matter, the point of everything. Why should the rules be any different here?"

"Hell doesn't exist?" Norman was stunned.

"Of course it exists," DeKraker went on, "but you don't go there unless you choose to."

Norman snorted. "What fool would choose to?"

"Lots do. You'll see."

They moved into the theater lobby where an usher dressed in a red uniform with gold stripes on the sleeves met them with three bags of buttered popcorn. Norman wasn't crazy about popcorn, but he took it appreciatively. There was something old-fashioned and joyful about all of this, something deeply comforting about having his two best friends at his side. No tickets were needed. The usher led them down to the front row and seated them, tucking Norman between his friends. The theater, warmed by a half-light, was occupied by a fair scattering of patrons. Norman barely glanced at them as he settled in.

A glaring light suddenly filled the screen, the title LIGHT IN THE DARK PLACES appeared, followed by a single credit: STARRING NORMAN A. LOCKE. Norman's jaw sagged, his mouth gaped, his popcorn spilled on the floor, his eyes burned as if they were aflame. On the screen he saw a dim, jerky eight-millimeter movie, set in the alley behind his childhood home, a circle of children (including himself), boys and girls, playing a naughty doctor game he'd organized; he squirmed with discomfort. The scene shifted to a school playground, a group of older boys (he a willing participant) as they humiliated a classmate for his sissy clumsiness at sports. Shame surged though him just as it had then.

The film quality began to improve. He heard the familiar whine of an armored personnel carrier, saw an adolescent Vietnamese boy, malice in his eyes, leap from behind a burned out tank and heave a rock. He heard the crack of a rifle and shrieked as the boy tumbled to the ground. The sight, to Norman, was unbearable.

He saw his first wife (dead at 50, aided by the stress of divorce) in the kitchen of their home, one of their children coloring at a table. As she stood cooking, he (now 30 something) told her he was leaving to go up north fishing—would return by dinner the following day. He remembered the lie as vividly as if he'd uttered it a minute ago.

The scene shifted to a hotel room, a woman wrapped in a towel, greeting him at the door...her impassioned hug... the towel slipping away. Norman shifted in his seat and groaned out loud. Though he wanted to disappear, his eyes stayed glued to the moving images. More of his life rolled by; he whimpered pitifully when he discovered he could not close his eyes. The movie played on and on and on--a ghastly recital of his lusts and lies, his abominable appetites, his self-absorbed indifference to others, his noxious anger, his willing blindness to injustice. Unable to tolerate more, he turned away, aware now of the audience behind him. Some were yawning, yet certain of the faces appeared glazed and stricken in the film's flickering light. Among them he saw, to his mortification, his long dead parents, his ex-wife, a son lost to addiction, former pastors, beloved teachers, his colleagues, friends and relatives from long ago, all those who had expected so much of him. In the back row on the aisle, a youngish man in tunic and sandals caused him more anxiety than all the rest. Norman leaped up suddenly, intent on running, but his friends yanked him back into his seat.

"Stay to the end," DeKraker ordered. "No exceptions."

And what seemed centuries later, the appalling film concluded with the epilogue: HE WILL BRING TO LIGHT ALL THINGS HIDDEN IN DARKNESS. Norman lowered his head to his lap and wept—wept until there were no more tears left in him. Audience members passed, touching his shoulder as they went out. His friends gently stood him up and led him, broken, from the empty theater. Outside, a crash of setting sun hit him like a truck.

"Oh, God…isn't it night yet?" Norman covered his eyes, wincing in agony.

"Night doesn't happen here," Hyde answered.

"I want the dark. The light is killing me."

"I know how much it hurts, but you don't want the dark, believe me."

"Find me a hole to crawl in and die," he cried.

"We're here to keep you from doing that," DeKraker said. "Dead friends did the same for us."

The two struggled slowly though town, supporting and guiding Norman, turning up the road toward the white hotel.

"Locke," DeKraker went on, "if it's any solace, our films were longer and more despicable than yours. And the three of us are bush league compared to your run-of-the-mill villain. I've seen films take hours, sometimes days. Today we saw the crumby stuff, my friend. It's the hardest part. There's a whole lot more to you than that. Eventually, we sort out the worthy from the contemptible."

"Listen, you bastards--this light is killing me! I'm burning up!"

"It's hot, but it's not killing you, Locke. It's refining fire. It's just the dross burning away."

"I can't stand it!"

"Yes, you can," Hyde insisted. "And your brightest light level—at least at first—will be the setting sun. Lots of shadows and slanted beams. DeKraker and I have been here for years, and we still can't stand midday. It takes eons to adjust."

"Give me the dark! I'm begging you!"

"Interesting…Hitler said the same thing."

"To hell with Hitler!"

"You got that right. He had no one to talk him out of it."

Desperate now, Norman broke away from the two and ran toward the small stone church. He threw open a heavy wooden door and took a dive inside. The light was dimmer, softer; still, he crawled crablike to the front pew and slid beneath it, pulling his shirt up over his head, burying his eyes in an arm and folding into a fetal position. "Lord, help me," he whimpered in agony. "I'm hopeless. Forgive me. I don't belong here. It's no use!"

At that, the room filled with a light so intense he could see bone through the flesh of his forearm. Someone sat down in the pew just above him, setting his heart banging. He could see only a pair of sandals with bare ankles rising out of sight.

"Shall I turn the light down a notch, Norman?" a kindly voice asked.

"Please…" he bleated. The light began to diminish; Norman stayed huddled in a tight ball. Then he felt a warm hand on the crown of his head.

"My son was dead, and is alive again," the kindly voice said. "He was lost, and is found. There's much more work to be done, but you are well loved."

Norman, the words flooding his heart, felt the hand move from his head to his clenched fist, open it, and place something in his palm, something he could faintly see through half-closed eyes—a pair of gold-framed drugstore sunglasses.

"Polarized," the kindly voice said.

Norman sighed, whispered "Thank you," and put them on.

He was back at his table in the Last Chance Saloon. The waitress with pink hair and nose ring set down three beers, smiled at him, and spirited off. Hyde and DeKraker were singing *Amazing Grace* with beaming faces and unsteady voices. Norman, calm in his sunglasses, felt exhausted, burned up, cauterized, purged, cleansed, and loved. He listened to his friends' singing, sighed faintly, and drank his beer.

When the hymn ended, he said, "Wish I could tell my wife."

"Amen to that," DeKraker said. "They've outlived us, Locke. But when they do show up, it won't be marriage any more but something finer. No more 'death do us part.' We'll be youthful and mellow at the same time, and the delights will increase into eternity."

"Into eternity," Hyde declared, and they raised their glasses to such amazing grace.

GARDENS

He looked over the photograph Sylvia had taken of climbing roses massed on the side of a crumbling stone garden house in eastern Romania. The hundreds of pink blooms met at the end of the wall with an arbor adrift in plum-colored clematis against background glimpses of a war zone.

"Great shot. I remember it. The garden was someone's work of art." His enthusiasm seemed to surprise her.

"So you have feelings for gardens?"

"I'm impressed that someone keeps one up with a war going."

Sylvia sat on the arm of his chair, holding the photo. The London flat was his, small and spare except for the gleaming grand piano in the front window. As English as Sylvia was, she didn't look it. When Max first met her two years before, spring of 1988, on assignment in Italy, he thought she was Italian: black hair and flashing dark eyes, honey brown skin. But she was Cambridge-educated, precise and ironic, a bit mannish in her perpetual hiking boots, heavy cameras hanging down, khaki shorts--but surprisingly soft without them. They'd worked together on three AP assignments, faced a degree of hazard, and now were tentatively trying out something more personal.

"Should we use this shot? Is it what you wanted?"

"It's close."

She stood, smiling, and tossed the photo on a coffee table. "There's really no satisfying you, Max darling." She flopped on a couch. "I mean professionally or personally. You're quite exasperating."

She was joking but not. He wondered what there was in him, what imp of resistance that kept her at arm's length? They were fine company with mutual respect and professional rapport. She loved listening to him play, especially Chopin; the music spilled over into their physical relationship. There was no reason they shouldn't deepen the commitment…no reason but the tattered remnants of a thought he'd chased since childhood. It was an old thought and beyond time to give it up.

They had dinner on a tiny balcony overlooking a middle class residential area with a large green space and passenger trains rumbling through close by. Sylvia was already in her silk pajamas. Max refilled her glass with white wine and then emptied the bottle into his own glass. A telephone rang inside.

"Would you mind? I don't feel like talking."

She sighed and went to get it. A moment later she leaned through the open French door.

"It's from the States, Max. You'd best answer this."

He frowned, went inside, and took the receiver.

He recognized Darrell's voice immediately. "Max? Who is this one? I love the accent."

Max felt a surge of impatience; the man never changed, forever sniffing after women. "Darrell…what is it?"

His uncle's voice went flat and serious. "Shamus died in his sleep last night. Congestive heart failure."

Max sat down slowly, his temples throbbing. Shamus, the grandfather who'd raised him from adolescence, was sturdy as a draft horse, indestructible.

Darrell gave him the funeral details as he gathered his equilibrium. A half hour later, he was still sitting there. She brought in his glass of wine and set it beside him.

Later that night she sat in bed, watching him pack his things.

"Sorry about this," he said.

"Maybe it's a good time for me to leave, too."

"I don't see why, but it's up to you, Sylvia."

Her tone turned wistful. "Not quite what I was hoping to hear, my love."

He glanced at her with a look that told her little. He sat down on the bed and kissed her, but it gave no comfort. His mind was miles off.

****

Darrell, his father's younger brother, drove a vintage MG because it suited his rakish style. Even at twelve years old Max could see it was an impractical means of conveyance for all his earthly possessions--three suitcases stuffed full and a bicycle. Darrell somehow managed to strap them on, though, and they set off on the long trip from New Jersey to Michigan. Max had lived for two years with Aunt Ruth, his mother's sister—since shortly after his parents' sailboat had gone down in a storm off the Massachusetts coast. He'd lost both of them at once. Sailing was his father's passion; his mother had endured it for his sake. Max was still deeply grieving, angry with his father and aching for his mother every day, for the sense of himself he saw in her eyes, for her calm, loving nature that disappeared only at rare moments with his difficult father (a figure like a distant star). Philip O'Hara traveled the world, a pianist whose music often overshadowed the people in his life. On occasion he took his son to rehearsals; he'd once or twice attended his Little League games. Max's mother had done the rest, including piano lessons and fishing.

Aunt Ruth was nothing like her. She was unmarried, of a generous enough spirit to step in and make a home for him.

There was money for his support. But she was fussy and critical, often claiming her favored sister had spoiled him. She sent him to public school where he excelled but had few friends. He worked in her gardens for an allowance and mowed her large lawn with a hand mower. There was no special attachment between them, and when she suddenly found someone to marry, she called Max's grandfather, entreating him to take over with the boy.

Max sat silently in the passenger seat of the MG. Uncle Darrell was 24, wore shoulder-length hair and a leather jacket. Though it was late spring and still chilly, Darrell kept the top down and careened though highway traffic like a Grand Prix racer. Max closed his eyes and imagined his life hurtling through switches, a runaway train.

"There's a small room for you. Or you can share the big bedroom with me. I'm hardly ever there." Darrell shouted this over the wind. "They were pretty good parents when they raised your Dad. By the time I came along, I think they were tired." He laughed. "They're a little weird, but you'll be all right."

Max dropped his eyes, unable to hide his desolation.

St. Joseph sat on the shore of Lake Michigan, a town of 8000 with an industrial twin city, Benton Harbor. The St. Joseph River emptied its leisurely waters into Lake Michigan through the funnel of two long, concrete piers. Darrell drove through town into a hilly area bordering the river, turned onto a gravel drive that ran through woods to a crumbling brick carriage house with a sign reading *Not Much News*. Darrell stopped the MG and jumped out without opening the door. Max looked away from the carriage house to the dark structure nearby, looming high above the river, the house in which his father had grown up--a gloomy Italianate sandstone mansion, eaves in dire need of paint and repair, with dark windows shuttered from the inside. He had a memory of being here once at Christmas years before, and once in the summer. He remembered that the mouth of the river and the big lake were not far away.

His grandfather had taken them there in a small boat with a motor, and Max had caught an undersized pike using a red and white daredevil. An uneven brick walkway to the front of the house was moss-covered, leading to weathered flagstone steps and a broad front porch with wicker chairs, a wooden rocker, a hanging Amish swing. Globe lights stood atop tall posts at the base of the steps.

Darrell began detaching the bike and suitcases from his car. "Come on," he said. "They're anxious to see what they're getting into."

Max, carrying two of the three suitcases, entered the house behind Darrell. The doorknob was brass with an embossed bird design. The front hallway was murky with shadows. A stairway with a hand-worn banister wound to the second floor and continued to an attic. They set down the suitcases. Darrell motioned to Max, and they entered the room to the left, a large space of high ceilings, ancient, faded rose-printed wallpaper peeling in corners, brass chandeliers once gas lit, an upright piano, an antique-shop overabundance of furniture predating Max by at least sixty years.

Darrell bent and clicked on a small Tiffany lamp, its illumination barely registering in the expanse of the room. "Your grandmother hates using electricity—so we live in a cave. Stay behind me. There's a path."

Max had already noticed a dampish, faintly moldy smell--like a cave, yes, but even more like a place he'd once been taken to see an ancient, toothless crone who'd held his hand in hers (limp as a boiled cabbage leaf)...his mother's dying grandmother, the oldest person he'd ever seen.

The kitchen was a shade or two brighter thanks to open shutters and some filtered sunlight. Cupboards of a dark wood reached to the ceilings, requiring a stepladder for the higher shelves. The gas stove was an antique—a steel and porcelain Wedgewood with curved legs and porcelain burner handles, and a receptacle for wooden matches to light the burners. The room was jumbled: a sink full of empty jam jars, a table covered with cardboard egg cartons, unwashed coffee mugs, and scattered copies of prominent newspapers: the *New York Times,* the *Chicago Sun-Times,* the *Washington Post.*

Faintly at first, then louder, Max heard a woman humming. In the far corner of the room he saw a shadowy figure move in one door and out another.

"Mother!" Darrell barked.

"What is it, Darrell?"

"He's here, for God's sake."

Mabel O'Hara entered the kitchen with a red kerchief knotted at her forehead. A slight woman with wild white hair and indefinite eyes, she looked and moved like a dust ball blown by a draft. "Who's here?"

"Your grandson. Where do you think I've been for the last three days? Ruth says thank you for taking him off her hands."

Her face clouded. "Oh, dear…here already. I've hardly begun. All I have in the house is some rice pudding. Would you like some rice pudding, son?"

"No, thank you."

"Do you remember me?"

Max nodded.

"Your father was never good at visiting us. He had such a busy, important life, always traveling the world. I've only seen you once or twice, I think—when you were little. My, you're a big boy now."

"Which room is ready?" Darrell asked impatiently.

"Oh, well…take him to Shamus, and I'll see to it right now." She flitted away like a hummingbird.

Darrell watched her go, his expression incredulous. "She was 44 when she had me. It did something to her brain…she's a fruitcake. She forgot you were coming… even forgot we sat with you at the funeral."

Max followed him through a rear door from the kitchen and up a gravel path toward the carriage house. The yard was a wild place large as a city park. Annabelle hydrangeas full of last year's spent blooms ringed the house, growing limp and leggy in untended beds of lilies of the valley. A sea of purple phlox thrived amid wild grasses and scrub, all beneath a canopy of pines, cottonwoods, oaks and dozens of rogues like sumac and mulberry. At the base of the hill the river went winding by. A dock reached a short way into it from the O'Hara property. Through the brush Max caught a glimpse of someone standing on the dock, but he said nothing.

They entered the carriage house by a side door. Shamus O'Hara sat behind a makeshift counter of his small weekly newspaper (with its self-effacing name). A large, red-faced man of 64 with a wild crop of graying red hair, he looked as Irish as anyone could. The place was crowded but orderly…an antique press and linotype machine, stacked rolls of newsprint and boxes of ink, a cast iron wood-burning stove, and an ancient Olivetti typewriter on a desk marked EDITOR. He was banging away with two fingers. They stood for a few moments, waiting. Shamus looked up at last.

"So he's here."

"He's here," Darrell said.

Max felt Shamus looking him over. "Can you type, son?"

Max nodded.

"Your father could type 90 words a minute at your age."

"He could play Chopin, too—Philip, the family prodigy."

"You have your own gifts, Darrell." The exchange had the feel of a well-worn routine. A moment later Shamus seemed distracted by something. He stared through the side window overlooking the back yard and the river, slowly rose from his chair and moved closer.

"What is it?" Darrell moved to look as did Max. The sight was astonishing. A young woman with long red hair was standing naked beside the dock where a small heap of clothing and a towel rested. The dock was in a private place, hidden from view except from the hilltop where they watched; otherwise only a person in a passing boat might see. She was washing herself, bending to cup water from the river, her full breasts lifting as she scrubbed her shoulders and neck. Max saw a flash of red pubic hair, and then she turned away, began toweling off, and pulled on white panties and a loose dress. He was stunned by the vision. It would etch itself into his memory, more enduring than any photograph. She'd appeared at this place, it would turn out, nearly the same moment he had…a nymph rising from the river, with blessings for the earth.

Shamus marched forth and led them down through overgrown lilacs and waist-high weeds to the girl, who was carefully folding her towel. Downriver but still on O'Hara property, they could see a small canvas lean-to secured to two trees, a blanket and backpack beneath it, and remains of a small fire. Their sudden appearance jolted her.

"Young lady," Shamus said, "what in the hell are you doing?"

She recovered herself and smiled--a fresh, freckled face, less beautiful than the long view had promised, but open and pretty. She was around 19 or 20, with green eyes older than her years.

"I was washing up."

Shamus surveyed her little camp. "And before that?"

"I stayed here last night. Is this your property?"

"It is."

She looked at Darrell, whose grin was bending toward a leer, then at Max. Her eyes seemed to lock on his. Her smile warmed, and he looked away, unsteady inside.

"Are you a hippie?" Darrell asked.

"No." She flushed slightly, her pale skin a litmus test of her feelings. "I need somewhere to stay. I'm new in town."

"And broke, I'll bet," Darrell continued.

She nodded, and then offered her hand to Shamus. "I'm Maisie Hope. Who are you?"

Shamus hesitantly took her hand, seeming befuddled. "Uh…Shamus O'Hara. Now listen, young lady…"

"You have a wonderful garden here, Mr. O'Hara. At least it could be. But it needs a lot of loving care. I'm a very good gardener."

"I'm in no position to afford a gardener."

"I'll work for anything you can pay. I'll work for room and board." There was a hint of desperation in her tone. "Please, Mr. O'Hara. I won't disappoint you. I work hard."

Max at last found his voice. "You can stay in my room."

Darrell laughed heartily.

"Who are you to be offering a room?" Shamus growled. "You're as new here as she is, for the love of Mike."

The bedroom he shared with Darrell was as big as a ballroom. Darrell, as he had promised, was not there that first night and very few of the others. He had other places to spend nights, it seemed. Max lay in light pajamas in a huge bed with carved headboard taller than he. On the far wall loomed a black faux marble fireplace with a mounted stag's head above it. A metal single bed, Darrell's, stood near a window with clothes tossed carelessly across it. Like the rest of the house, the room was filled to overflowing with furniture. Through the windows spilled shadowed moonlight. Max leaned over the side of the bed, opened his suitcase, removed a small, framed photograph of his parents and set it on the bedside table. His father was tall and imposing, with the same dark eyes as Max. His mother was a plump, pretty blonde, soft and a bit rumpled, with a smile that warmed a room.

Something swooped past him in the air. Fearfully, he pressed his back against the headboard. The thing passed again, its flight erratic. With a sharp cry, Max leaped out of bed and ran for the door. He scrambled down the dark, winding staircase, upsetting a stack of books piled on the steps. Seeing a light at the bottom of the closed kitchen door, he felt his way through the sitting room. As he was about to push through into the kitchen, his grandmother's voice rose in anger.

"But we're too old to be raising a child!"

"Do you expect him to raise himself?" It was Shamus. "He can help in the shop and the yard. When fall comes, he'll be in school. You won't have that much to do."

"And now a young girl in the back room... What are you *thinking* of, Shamus? I won't have her here another night!"

"We'll talk about it tomorrow."

"This just isn't fair!" Her voice was shrill, emotional.

"Fairness hasn't much to do with it, Mabel."

Max backed away from the door, found an empty chair near a window and crawled into it, his face burning. Through the window he could see the back wing of the house and a light in the small room at the farthest corner of the second floor. He watched a moment, and when the light went out, he got to his feet and retraced his path to the front stairway.

At her room—the one originally designated for him—he touched the knob and the door swung open. The room was very small, a servant's quarters in a previous age, with an unplumbed marble sink in one corner and a three quarter bed in which Maisie lay asleep with moonlight on her face. He slipped in and went to her side, staring at her closed eyes. As he leaned closer, her eyes opened; he nearly leaped out of his skin.

"What are you doing here?" she whispered.

"Nothing."

She gathered herself and rose onto an elbow. She wore a white tee shirt. "Are Shamus and Mabel your grandparents?"

He nodded. "They don't want me here. But there's no one else to take me. My parents died."

She sat up, took his hand, and pulled him to a sitting position beside her. "I'll be your friend. I'm an orphan, too." She squeezed his hand. "Just wait. They'll fall in love with your beautiful eyes and never want you to leave." For the first time in many days, Max felt a brightening. "You'd better get to bed," she said in a half whisper.

"There's a bat in my room."

"Well then--sleep with me."

She raised the sheet, and he hesitantly crawled in beside her. She turned over; they lay back to back. She was asleep in moments, and shortly after, absorbing the warmth of her, he drifted off like a weary, well-fed child.

Maisie Hope had surprising gifts. The following evening she trapped the bat in the big bedroom, whacked it in midflight with a tennis racquet, carefully carried it out to the dock where it regained consciousness and flew off. Shamus was impressed, and she stayed another night. Changes began happening in the yard. Within a week, she'd trimmed most of the bushes, hacked out the weeds and trash trees. She'd discovered and transplanted perennials of stunning variety, trimmed and divided hydrangeas, found a brush pile hiding a rich load of compost near the river and wheeled it up to newly dug gardens.

Shamus and Mabel watched from inside the house while Max ate cornflakes and Shamus sipped coffee. Mabel stood by a window, visibly upset.

"I'd planned on doing those gardens, Shamus."

"Mother, face it, things are getting away from us."

"Can I help her today?" Max asked.

"Go to it, boy. Wish I had the time."

His grandmother scowled at them. "She's mesmerized both of you."

And, of course it was true.

Not Much News was a weekly in tabloid form, with stories of community interest in a community where little happened. Shamus hired a part time pressman and a linotype operator. Local kids made Thursday deliveries. But it was otherwise a family operation. Mabel handled subscriptions—in spite of increasing memory problems; Darrell sold advertising when he thought of it. He also was assisting at Fry's Funeral Home, transporting bodies in the Cadillac hearse, setting up for visitations, mowing the lawn and trimming hedges, and, whenever he got the chance, comforting bereaved women. That last benefit kept him at a job he otherwise despised, especially when Harold Fry pushed him to wear a suit and get a haircut. His number had come up several years before in the draft lottery, but a heart murmur (the great blessing of his life) had kept him out of Vietnam.

Shamus, though he paid occasional stringers by the story, did most of the writing himself. Family news (*the Olsen children from Chicago visited grandmother Bessie and picnicked at Silver Beach*), Garden Club meetings, honor rolls, kids' sports, band concerts, school board meetings, and general small town trivia provided much of the copy, but the heart of the newspaper was Shamus's editorial page where he took local government to task for every shenanigan—and was cheered by many and hated by a few who'd felt the sting of his irony. The town's daily newspaper dared little of the veracity that had gained him a limited statewide fame.

Though near retirement age, Shamus never spoke of retiring. In time, Max would understand that he factored into a master plan. He began a paper route on Thursday afternoons. Before the summer was fully underway, he tried his hand at stories of Little League games, mentioning, as Shamus instructed him, as many names as possible. Darrell had no interest in any of it. Shamus offered a writing assignment to Maisie that she politely refused. When he asked to do a photo feature on her gardening, she grew stone-faced and walked away, as if a shadow had passed over her.

Max's main work, his passion, was helping Maisie in the gardens. Though he didn't sleep in her bed again, he dreamt of lying down beside her in wildflowers, of saving her from the wolfishness of Darrell, of watching her bathe in the river and reach to him with an outstretched hand. He was aware of becoming someone else, a being with strange and feverish longings. And she—this river nymph--was turning Shamus's yard, Max's life, into a fairytale landscape.

She had no past. She gave them almost no sense of who she was or where she'd come from. Though she could drive a car, she had no license, no identification of any kind. She would only reveal that she'd long ago lost her parents at separate times. The pastor of some church had taken her in. She never mentioned names or places, never spoke of her life experiences. Shamus guessed she was on the run.

When Shamus saw Maisie working miracles on his property, he began investing in her work, buying picked-over annuals on sale and paying her a small wage under the counter; she used most of it to buy jeans and flannel shirts from the Goodwill outlet. Shamus and Max were waiting in the Olds one day when Maisie came bursting out of a hardware store carrying a new hoe as if it were a scepter.

"Lord, son, if that doesn't cheer you up, I don't know what will."

Shamus was clearly speaking for himself.

In wanderings through his grandmother's house (for it was surely hers, not Shamus's), Max discovered the O'Hara music room, now mostly closed off, sealed and dark, with walls of books, and a grand piano gathering dust beneath a bank of shuttered windows. A cedar chest near the piano (he knew he had no business getting into it) contained stacks of sheet music and photo albums of his father, many at about Max's age, nearly always at the piano, mugging for the camera or lost in the music he was playing. Max also found a leather-bound copy of Robert Browning's poems, and on the inside cover the elegant flourish of Philip O'Hara's signature. As he dug deeper, he discovered a shoebox full of small, fragile volumes of Poe's stories, and—he laughed aloud--a stack of comic books proving his father had actually been a boy once.

Another day, as he was opening the chest, he was shocked to discover his grandmother standing ghost-like near the piano, holding a cup of tea.

"This room is off limits," she said.

His heart began pounding so violently it took a moment to get words out. "I'm looking at my father's things."

"You shouldn't be sneaking around my house."

"Why are you hiding them?"

"I'm not hiding them. I'm caring for them. I treasure them. No one around here understands. They think I'm a crazy old woman who can't throw a thing away. Well, I don't save just anything. All my things mean something to me. I could tell you stories about every object in this house. I grew up in this house. Shamus and Darrell only live in the here and now. I'm guardian of the past, of things lost and gone." And as if overcome, she collapsed onto the piano bench, still holding her tea in a trembling hand.

Frightened for her, Max said the only thing that came to him. "Do you play the piano, grandma?" For the first time ever he'd called her by that informal, affectionate name--with a surprising result. She set down the tea and grew calmer.

"Oh…well, I was your father's first teacher--at least until he was your age. By then he was beyond me."

He'd never heard this.

"I started him when he was three—probably too young--before he could read. I taught him with a color chart I made. He was so quick to understand."

"He told me he saw colors when he played."

She brightened. "He said that?"

Max nodded and watched her face soften. "My mom taught me piano. Maybe you could teach me now."

She seemed to turn strange again. "Oh…I don't think so…no, no…I'm so old. And it's such a responsibility."

"I want to play Chopin."

"Oh, dear…oh, dear…Chopin is difficult."

"She taught me one little mazurka. But I'd like to play the *Raindrop Prelude*. My father would play it at home--she loved it."

In time, she agreed. Shamus encouraged the connection, paid to have the piano tuned. It was a very old Steinway with a bright, rich tone. Twice a week through the summer, they sat down together. She made him do hours of scales and theory. *Raindrop Prelude* was a long way off.

Shamus interrupted their gardening one June day for an event: a yearly community open house at the mausoleum-like mansion of the Linden family on a high bluff overlooking Lake Michigan. The Linden Foundation gave money to community projects deemed worthy by the board of directors. More than anything, Shamus wanted Maisie to see the widely admired Linden gardens, of a geometric French design--sterile, he thought, compared to her wild English profusion. The O'Hara gardens, despite being a work in progress, had already begun attracting attention.

The big lake was in a record-setting high cycle, and though the Linden family had recently built steel and concrete seawalls, the high bluff was steadily eroding, faster than anyone remembered, coming nearer each month to the house. There was talk of moving it. A long, expensive wooden stairway to the once-broad beach was now battered by waves, near to coming down. Local beaches were washed out and tourism suffering. Lake Shore Drive bisected the Linden property, with most of the Linden gardens, their manicured boxwood hedges, stone benches, geometric pathways, reflecting pools, and perennials in cool lavenders, blues, and purples on the landward side of the road. A temporary fence and two uniformed guards kept the party safely away from the lakeward side and the bluff.

The open house was teeming with children. There were pony rides on a broad expanse of grass, a popcorn wagon, a puppet show, and an ice cream tent. In a large pavilion, Ben Linden himself—the only son of John and Mary Linden, scrap metal magnates—presented a yearly magic show. At one point, Maisie slipped a hand into the crook of Max's arm. A four-piece band began playing some Arabian tune. Ben Linden appeared at the rear of the pavilion, dressed in black satin with a cape and top hat. Pale as a soda cracker, with nervous hands and bulging eyes, he placed his hat onto a table and--after a bit of fumbling--yanked a dove from the depths of it. Maisie smiled at Max as if the man's awkwardness touched her. A long string of colored scarves began flowing from his sleeves and coins poured from his nose into the top hat.

He asked for a volunteer and chose Maisie, who nonchalantly stepped up to the front. He led her to a miniature guillotine, had her place a head of cabbage into the lunette beneath the slanted blade. He moved her aside and, following a theatrical drum roll, slammed the blade down—and the halved cabbage tumbled into a basket.

He called for another volunteer, pointing to a small girl who shook her head and backed into her mother's arms. The finger moved to Max. When he saw Maisie motioning to him, he knew the matter was settled. He allowed Ben to situate him on his knees before the guillotine, his neck beneath the blade.

"Trust me," she whispered.

Max clamped his eyes shut and held his breath. The drum roll sounded. The blade came slamming down. In one motion Ben released the clamps and lifted Max to his feet. The band played, the audience celebrated, and Maisie led Max from the stage, his legs boneless.

"Wait!" Ben called after her. She ignored him, so he called again, "Wait! I know you!"

She stopped and turned with an uneasy look.

"You're a gardener. Would you like a job?"

Her face relaxed. "I have a job," she said.

Across the lawn they saw Shamus carrying ice cream, enough for the three of them.

Max turned 13 in July. Shamus bought him a cake, and they celebrated at a table in the garden. Maisie, wearing her only dress, hugged him and held out her present--a new rose bush tied with a red ribbon. When the party was over, he planted it in an area beneath her window.

That evening, he spent time at the piano. Near dark, he saw Darrell moving up the front walk with an arm around Maisie. They were laughing about something.

Darrell slept at home that night. Max was still awake when he entered late, stumbled across the room, and flopped down on the small bed with all his clothes on.

"Where've you been?" Max asked.

Half drunk, Darrell muttered, "Damn, are you still awake?"

"Were you with Maisie?"

"That's none of your business, kid. Did Shamus say something?"

"No."

Darrell grinned, bending to pull off his shoes. "That's some juicy woman."

When he sat back up, Max stood just inches from him. "Leave her alone, Darrell."

He was amused. "You better mind your own business, shrimp."

More firmly, Max said, "Leave her alone."

Darrell laughed mockingly. "What is this? You have the hots for her, too? You do. Well, I'll be damned…"

Darrell reached and pinched the crotch of Max's pajamas. Furious, Max flew into him, arms pinwheeling. Darrell had to get him in a bear hug and wrestle him down. Half laughing, half cursing, he cried, "Take it easy! I'll share her with you, you little fuck!"

A flyer, folded and stapled, arrived one day in August. Max sat across the pressroom from Shamus, opening mail with a table knife and tossing out junk. The flyer had a handwritten return address: *PASTOR ELIHU HARPER, PO BOX 318, CROWFOOT, INDIANA.* Curious, he tore it open and unfolded a mimeographed sheet.

FOR PUBLICATION AND POSTING

Have you seen this girl? May Harper, age 19, has been missing from her home since March 24. She is five foot six, red haired, with a star-shaped birthmark on her left knee. She is capable of unpredictable, possibly violent behavior. The photograph below was taken four years ago. May God have mercy on her rebellious spirit.

She was last seen in the South Bend area. Please report any news of her whereabouts to the above post office address c/o Pastor Elihu Harper.

The photograph was grainy, a side view of a 15 year old sitting in a straight-backed chair, reading what looked to be a Bible. Her features were blurred.

For a moment, Max thought of tearing the flyer to pieces; instead he walked it over to Shamus. As his grandfather read it, Max saw Maisie through the window, at work in the garden. She stood upright to rest her back, and a ray of sun lit up her hair. He'd seen the birthmark, believed it a sign of a special destiny, and touched it once for luck.

"Call her in here," Shamus said.

Max did what he was told. Shamus motioned her over to the desk and held the flyer out to her. "Does this mean anything to you?"

She stared at it, reading. When she finally handed it back, she was badly shaken. "Have you contacted him?"

"No."

"Please...please don't."

"Do you want to talk about it?"

She lowered her eyes. "No."

"That's okay."

"The things he says aren't true. It's a trick to scare people into turning me in."

He nodded. "I believe you." They both looked at Max.

"I won't tell," he said.

Shamus took the flyer from her, wadded it into a ball, and tossed it in a waste bin. "The police may get this. If they come by, just go on gardening and let me handle things."

But nothing immediately came of it.

Ben Linden would sometimes come by the house, stand and watch them pulling weeds. He was single-minded about hiring Maisie, and yet, loyal to Shamus, she kept refusing him, even when Ben offered an hourly rate double what Shamus paid her. One Thursday, while loading bundles of newspapers into the Olds and MG, Maisie told them about it.

Darrell reacted with surprising vehemence. "Stay away from him. Ben Linden is a nutcase."

She looked puzzled. "What do you mean?"

"He's wacko. The family tries to hide him under a rug. He's been seeing shrinks since the day he was born."

"He also happens to be worth a fortune," Shamus said.

"He's a fruitcake, trust me. Don't ever make the mistake of putting your neck into that magic guillotine of his."

Max went rigid.

Shamus turned to Maisie. "If he's offered you a job, take it. You're worth a lot more than I can pay you."

"I work here," she said.

Yet Shamus persisted, and finally she agreed to gardening for Ben as a second job, mostly evenings—and then only if Max could work as her paid assistant. Ben accepted (though leery of Max) and then went to the trouble of driving them back and forth from the O'Hara's in his Mercedes, nervously attempting conversation with Maisie, ignoring Max. As the growing season slowly wound down, they began planting bulbs by the hundreds for more color in the Linden gardens. Ben would watch from a window, and Max could guess what was in his mind.

Max had started school and found a few friends among the baseball players he'd written about (next summer he intended to play). Through the long school day, he daydreamed of evenings in Ben's gardens. She occupied a warm, protected place in the center of him. At odd moments—tossing a ball in gym class or closing a locker between classes—he would whisper her name aloud. He was beset by joys and fears. Six years separated them. He was hardly more than a child, and grown men--every one who knew her, it seemed--were smitten. But none could come near to the love he felt. He wanted her to know, but had no idea how to tell her.

October came, and Maisie cleared out and pruned back Shamus's gardens; together they did the same at the Linden house. There was a special space Maisie had plans for in the spring—sheltered from the west wind and not visible from the mansion, separated by a line of poplars. She called it the secret garden, and here she would place a stone bench and plantings of less rigid design, a rhapsody of color. Ben approved of all she wanted. Though it was his parents' house, he was most often there alone (they had houses in northern Michigan and Florida) with three domestic workers who kept up the place. One was an older man, a groundskeeper, who resented Maisie's presence, but to no avail.

One chilly evening, Max was digging out sod in preparation for her special space. She sat on the grass, sorting through bulbs, watching him.

"Ben asked me to marry him," she said out of nowhere.

Max stopped digging; she might as well have hit him with a brick. "What did you tell him?"

"No, of course. I hardly know him."

"Does he love you?"

"He says so. But men are full of nonsense about love. They talk about love when it's really something else they mean."

Max averted his eyes. "What do they mean?"

"I forget how young you are."

He stared at the clump of sod at his feet. "Love can be real," he said in little more than a whisper.

She answered gently. "Maybe so, but I haven't seen it. People talk about love all the time, even the love of God, and then turn it into something else, something mean."

He lifted his eyes to hers. "I love you."

She stared at him, her face shadowed and soft. "Oh, Max..."

"Some day our ages won't matter, Maisie."

She sat, considering, and then rolled to her knees, motioning him over. He moved close to her, and she pulled him to his knees. "I love you, too--more than anyone." She took his face in her hands and pulled it to hers. Her lips covered his, his mouth opened to hers; the kiss was the kiss of lovers, the first and most impassioned of any he would ever know. His body responded in powerful, mystifying ways. He wanted more of her, all of her, but had only a vague idea of what that meant. When the kiss ended, she held him quietly and then rolled back into the grass. "You're so sweet," she whispered. "So sweet. Some day there'll be a girl..."

"Not some day," he said.

Within a week she was gone. Max was there to witness it. The last of the daffodil bulbs were going in when a blue Buick rolled into the Linden yard and stopped. Three men emerged, each dressed in dark pants and suspenders with white shirts. One saw Maisie and pointed, and then two set out in her direction. The third stood rigidly beside the car; he was older than the others, maybe 50, black-bearded, a black fedora on his head, intense white face with blood pressure showing in his cheeks.

Max shouted "Maisie!"

She looked up from her planting, saw the men, and a look of panic glazed her eyes. She jumped up and took off running toward the bluff. But the two were on her before she got halfway. She screamed and twisted in their arms like a trapped cat.

Max rushed at them and tossed himself headlong into the fray. One plump young man with a kewpie doll face lifted and held him tight, as the other, big as a bear, carried her to the car.

"This is none of your concern, son," the young man said, breathing heavily.

The one holding Maisie stopped in front of the bearded man. "Well, sister, I wager you didn't expect to see me again." He laughed. "Praise the Lord, boys. Let's take this lost lamb on home." And they stuffed her, still struggling, into the back seat.

The plump one shoved Max to the ground and sprinted to the car. Ben Linden burst from the house, rushing clumsily down the front steps and toward them with a hand raised. "Hold on here!" he cried. "This is private property! You release her this minute or I'll call the police!"

The bearded man rolled down his window. "The police helped us find her, brother--seeing as how she's my lawfully wedded wife, pledged before God and sealed by holy vows."

"No!" Maisie screamed.

"This is a family matter, sir," he said, smiling darkly. The Buick, driven by the bear, spun wheels in the grass and disappeared south on Lake Shore Drive.

Before the day was out, a stricken Ben Linden had hired a detective who set off for Indiana, eventually found a four-corner town named Crowfoot, but no trace of Pastor Elihu Harper. Shamus undertook searches in police and newspaper files, but at last he had to accept that Maisie Hope's bright and blessed presence in their lives had ended. Gloom thick as a March fog settled over the house.

For Max, life moved doggedly forward, yet Maisie would live on in him like a resident angel. She was no old man's wife, he was certain. He began making plans, setting goals for his future—all of them centered on one. His grandparents' home, even without Maisie, was a haven. Shamus taught him to write crisp, efficient prose and read good books. Mabel shakily guided his Chopin. He accompanied them to mass at St. Timothy each week. In his senior year of high school, thanks to his parents' small trust fund and a scholarship, he committed to the journalism school at Northwestern, hoping to carry his quest to a larger world.

During high school Max had taken over a significant portion of the newspaper work, yet Shamus's fragile hope of passing on his publication died quietly. Shortly after Max left for Chicago, Shamus closed up *Not Much News*, confident his grandson was destined for better things. During Max's sophomore year at the university, Mabel died of a stroke--a loss he felt much more deeply than he expected. Darrell, stunned as well, entered night school to work on a degree in mortuary science. In Max's junior year, Ben Linden lopped off the ends of two fingers in his magic show guillotine--was sent for a period to an Eastern psychiatric hospital. The Linden mansion, too dangerous to move, was one of a half dozen grand houses to slide down the bluff a section at a time. The Linden tulips and daffodils in the garden across the road bloomed gloriously for several years, until the land was sold and excavated for a new house.

God returned the O'Hara garden to its natural state.

****

Max landed at Chicago's O'Hare Airport, non-stop from London. The following day he rented a car and drove up to Michigan for the funeral. Shamus's death had made newspapers around the state, celebrating the last of a breed.

If she knew he'd died, she would come. Yet at Fry's Funeral Home, soon to be Darrell's, she didn't appear. At Saint Timothy Catholic Church, three hundred listened to a eulogy and multiple tributes, but she was not among them.

Darrell, now in his forties, wore his hair brushed back and shiny with gel. He'd never married--had a look of success, puffy and entrepreneurial in his dark blue suit. Women still gravitated to him. Max was unexpectedly relieved at seeing him, the elder of the two remaining O'Haras.

But he needed to be alone in his bleak mood, so he opted to stay at the old house instead of Darrell's place near the beach. Darrell seemed fine with it. He told him to be sure to see Shamus's lawyer in the morning—a few things about the will.

Surprised at his celebrity among half-remembered people, but struggling to be sociable, Max extricated himself early from the reception. He drove to the house only to find he had no key. It was late May, and the sun was an hour from setting. Disgruntled, he walked around the outside, checking doorsills, peering in windows where a shutter was open. Things were very different inside. The majority of Mabel's furniture was gone, probably at auction, and rooms now looked like normal, functional spaces. The outside was mowed, cleared of brush, with the scalped look of a bad haircut. The hydrangeas and lilies of the valley, the wild profusion of color, the magic of a master had disappeared as completely as the master had. The rose bush he'd planted beneath her window--now a few brown spikes—still showed some struggling growth at the base.

Instead of returning to stay with Darrell, Max found a small motel out on Lake Shore Drive. He drove around before dark, slowly passing the former site of the Linden mansion. On the east side of the road, an extravagant house stood where the French gardens and so much else had blossomed. How sure he had been she would come. How delusional...how vaporous the mirage. He choked back a burning, bittersweet pain. He was nearly thirty, with experience enough—in his work, especially--to make a cynic of him. Yet here he was, pitiably chasing a rainbow's end.

In the morning a dark bank of clouds shuttered the sky, promising storms. He had breakfast at Beeson's, Shamus's choice of diner in town, then made his way on foot through spitting rain to the legal office of Rex McAllister. A stout old man with a fiery drinker's nose, he had served just behind Max as a pallbearer. Rex shook Max's hand and pointed to the leather chair facing his desk. Max sat down.

"Shamus kept things simple," he started, and commenced clearing out his throat as if revving an engine. "Darrell gets the house and contents…a nightmare as far as

I'm concerned. But he has plans to make it a funeral home, Harold Fry tells me. Darrell's an ambitious one these days… who'd have guessed?" He lit a half-smoked cigar. "The rest of the estate Shamus divided equally between Darrell and you—as the only beneficiary of his deceased son Philip. Any problems so far?"

Max sat in silence for several moments. "Only that I'm shocked. I didn't expect a thing."

"Well, your grandfather had other ideas. Lucky for you, he was a frugal Irishman who didn't drink. His remaining investments amount to slightly more than $280,000."

Max pitched back in the chair. "What?"

"You heard me. There's just one minor hitch--one extra portion earmarked for a third party. I know nothing about this person or the amount designated. Shamus left a letter of explanation for you. He cashed in war bonds to cover this part, so Darrell will never know a damned thing about it." Rex handed a sealed envelope across the desk. Max took it, recognizing Shamus's handwriting on the front: *For Max O'Hara. Private and Personal!*

His grandfather despised the exclamation mark except for the most forceful kind of emphasis. This apparently qualified.

Max left in a daze, not opening the envelope until he was alone at the motel, and then with trembling hands. The letter was handwritten:

To my grandson, Max,

First, let me say how proud I am to call you my grandson. You have turned out excellently in spite of our haphazard parenting. Though still a young man, you have already received journalistic honors that eclipse my entire career. At least I can brag that you started by reporting small town trivia for our little paper.

I think it fair that Darrell get the house and contents. He has made it livable and has plans for it. The two of you will share the rest of the estate—with the exception of a smaller portion designated for another. I think she will meet with your approval. Enclosed is a cashier's check made out to Ariel May Hope, better known to us as Maisie Hope. I want you to hand deliver the check to her. I require it of you. Darrell knows nothing of it. Please keep things that way.

Some years ago, after you left for college, I heard from her. She was in Kentucky, in bondage to a charismatic preacher and his devotees, the ones who stole her away. Pastor Elihu Harper had taken her in as an orphan, raised and educated her to become, at 16, one of his so-called wives—the first and favored one, his second in command. He claimed God had granted him special dispensations when it came to women and directed him to perform his own weddings, several to 16-year-old girls, an age he appreciated. He was a forceful man and few had the courage to question him.

One day Maisie called me; Harper was in jail for sexual assault and bigamy. I drove to Kentucky and whisked her off while the group was in disarray. We travelled to a place I thought he'd never find, to a friend named Henry Gordon, a landscape gardener who works up north on Mackinac Island. In one long day we made the trip, Henry hired her, and there she remains. She asked me to tell no one where she was—including you. After all these years, she still has fears about Elihu Harper. I have no way of knowing how much damage he's done to her spirit, though I've never met a stronger woman. He's out of jail, that much I know, but vanished somewhere. If he's dead, I'll celebrate it. If hell exists, he gets my vote. I spoke to her not long ago--made her promise not to risk traveling to my funeral, whenever that might be.

What I need to say next is an uncomfortable admission. I confess to you and you alone that I've cared for Maisie Hope in a way I have for no other woman. The heart, I've discovered, is never too hard to be touched and softened. Mabel had died. Once Maisie was safely on the Island, I visited her every year. Like the winter cabbage, I was very late in showing up, though she did nothing to make me feel it. She lives on in me, growing like a garden. Her education was narrow, but she is wise in human understanding; she radiates the love of God—a miracle, considering the circumstances in which it grew. You loved her, too, I believe, but as I was too old and too late, you, ironically, were too young and too early. God has the strangest sense of humor.

Mackinac Island is your destination. Henry Gordon will help you find her. Give her this check with my deepest affection. It may provide her some freedom at last. Thank her for brightening all our lives.

What happens after that is your business. God bless you both for having meant so much. What a shame that life is so short.

Your affectionate grandfather,

Shamus O'Hara

Max dropped the letter on the bed and lay down beside it. Later he would take out the check, see her name and the black print declaring the sum of $40,000. How life-giving, how loved was Maisie Hope! How strangely disconcerting to know his beloved grandfather's secret heart.

In the half dozen years he'd lived in Michigan, he'd never been to Mackinac Island. He called and let Darrell know he had some business but would be back. The drive to the top of the peninsula took him until late that evening. The ferries had stopped running, so he found a room in Mackinaw City on the mainland. The May night was cold, the tourist population still blessedly thin, and his spring jacket needed more padding. Morning arrived with a sky full of sun and rising temperatures. At eleven he boarded the ferry, wearing a small backpack, leaving his rental car and suitcase behind, setting out for an island that had functioned without motorized vehicles for more than a century, transporting people and goods by bicycle or horse-drawn carriers.

The Star Line jet boat crossed the Straits just east of the giant suspension bridge joining the Lower and Upper Peninsulas. Within ten minutes he could see the long, white Grand Hotel carved into an island hillside, and above that the West Bluff summer homes of the very rich. From a distance it looked to be another world, a magic land, a fitting place for Maisie Hope. As the ferry rode its own wake into the harbor and docked near the south end of town, his heart began to race. Edgy, oddly light-headed, he held tight to seat backs as he disembarked.

Lilac trees were blooming everywhere. He walked the main street of fudge and souvenir shops, restaurants and bike rental stands, dodging among people, bikes, and teams of draft horses. It was charming enough, but nothing caught him until he found the curved brick walkway to the Iroquois Hotel--its garden fashioned in a narrow corridor leading to the entrance. Spring flowers—tulips of many shapes and shades, daffodils, hyacinths, bluebells, even the last vestiges of winter jasmine—bloomed beside newly planted summer annuals, as if two seasons had become one. The sculptured diversity of plants, colors, and styles had a familiar look.

He went into the small lobby of the Iroquois, asked a young Jamaican woman at the desk if she could direct him to Henry Gordon.

"Up the hill beyond the Grand Hotel, fifteen minutes in all on that road," she said. "His company is there. They do our gardens."

"Do you know a woman named Maisie Hope?"

"Henry sends a lady to us. Very quiet and pretty, but I don't know her name. She has a gift, I'm sure you can see."

"I can see." He smiled to thank her.

The road skirting the elaborate gardens and small golf course of the Grand Hotel was steep. He walked on for nearly twenty minutes before waving over a taxi and being properly redirected. Henry Gordon Landscaping occupied two acres or more of greenhouses, heaps of topsoil, humus and composted manure, landscape stones on skids, horse-drawn wagons, a pole barn for equipment, and a stable with an office attached. A silver-haired man with a deeply tanned, weatherworn face was the only occupant of the office. He looked up without surprise, gave his visitor a silent appraisal.

"Max O'Hara?"

"Henry?" Max went to him. Henry stood and warmly shook his hand.

"Shamus told me I'd see you after his funeral. Sorry I couldn't make it. It's our busiest time of year."

"Shamus wasn't complaining."

Henry laughed easily. They chatted a bit about Shamus getting Henry his first job--trimming trees for the power company--and then writing him up in *Not Much News* when he turned to landscaping.

When Henry paused to pour coffee, Max said, "I have something from Shamus for Maisie Hope. He said she works for you."

He hesitated. "She does. It's her day off. You'll likely find her at her cabin near Turtle Park. You'll need a bike."

"I walked."

"Take one of ours. I'll point you in the direction." He handed Max the coffee. "Hope you don't have plans to lure her away. She's a treasure to me."

Max smiled at Henry's earnestness. "No plans at all," he said, and it wasn't a lie.

Henry nodded, poured himself a cup and settled back in his chair.

The bike was a warhorse with fat tires, three gears, and a huge basket on the rear fender for hauling pots of flowers. The road turned from asphalt to gravel and then became a dirt path through woods of oaks, cottonwoods, ancient apple trees, and cedars arching in a canopy through which gauzy light filtered. At certain high points, he caught glimpses of Lake Huron, sighing in muted rhythms, deep blue against a sapphire sky. Under the trees he saw trilliums, his mother's favorite, and when he spotted the cabin in a clearing, the familiarity of the scene struck him with wonder. It all came back…trails on Cape Cod…hiking when his father was away...small cabins similar to this one, rented by locals to fishermen from the city. His mother sometimes asked if the fish were biting, and the men would chat pleasantly before she'd take his hand and continue on, leaving too soon for them. The memory filled him with inexpressible joy and sadness.

Ahead he saw a figure kneeling in a small flower garden at the front of the cabin. Though he couldn't see her face, he knew it was Maisie. She stood and looked toward his approaching bicycle, a woman in her mid-30s now, dressed in shorts and a blue flannel shirt, red hair tied up on her head. He stopped the bike and got off. She was beautiful still but changed in ways he couldn't yet put a name to. She dropped a trowel and took a step backward.

"Hello?" she asked. "Are you lost?"

"I have been," he said.

She stared at him as if tracking the face backward to the boy. "Max?"

"Hello, Maisie."

She stood as if turned to stone. At last she said, "I didn't recognize you at first. You're a man. What are you doing here?"

"Carrying out a mission for Shamus."

Still a bit dazed, she motioned toward the door, and he followed her. "My gardens are pitiful. I garden for other people all day long. It's hard to find the energy for my own."

"They're lovely. They have your touch."

"Well…at least I enjoy what I do, even if my back aches and my fingernails are never clean."

"I've seen the Iroquois Hotel. The garden is magic."

She smiled. "My secret garden—like the one I never finished for Ben Linden."

"I remember."

They entered the cabin. The log walls were stained a honey color, not quite matching the interior knotty pine. He could see a single bedroom with a double bed neatly made, a simple bathroom, a living room and kitchen separated by a counter with a scarred linoleum top. A couch, end tables, two stuffed chairs, and an old upright piano made up most of the living room décor. Two stools stood at the counter.

"It's not much of a place. Henry gives me a deal on it. Island prices are impossibly high, even for year-rounders like me. Do you recognize the furniture?"

He glanced around again. "I don't."

"Shamus had it hauled up to me, even the piano. They were simplifying the house."

The furniture jogged no memory, but he knew the piano. "The old upright from the sitting room. I've played it."

"Then play it now while I shower, would you? I'm a mess. I'll be quick."

So he did her bidding. He dropped his backpack beside the piano, remembering the ancient three-legged piano stool he'd sometimes spun round and round on. He began playing and winced at the dissonant, barroom sound. He played the *Raindrop Prelude* anyway, and she finished her shower just as he ended.

"Isn't that the one you practiced to death for Mabel? It drove me crazy, but you're better at it now." She spoke through the closed door.

"It's a very romantic piece. Too bad this piano is so out of tune."

"Nobody plays it. Not sure why Shamus had it dragged up here. Turn your head away, would you?"

He swiveled to the wall and heard the bathroom door open. "Why make me turn away? You were naked the first time I saw you."

"I'm not as nice now."

He heard the patter of bare feet and then the bedroom door closing. "You were the first naked woman I'd ever seen," he said more loudly. "A milestone."

"You must've seen your mother."

"Mothers don't count," though he remembered his fascinated and confused embarrassment at her gleaming ripeness in the bath, her round, slightly sagging breasts and the nest of hair between her legs. A mystery, it seemed, as deep as the oceans.

She came out in a sundress and a light shawl, her feet still bare, her hair long and damp, and sat on a stool at the counter. "So—what is your mission?"

He bent to the backpack and removed Shamus's cashier's check, went to the counter and sat down beside her. "Shamus sent this for you—for your well-being—especially if you ever need to avoid Elihu Harper."

She took the check, glanced at it and burst into tears. The storm was brief but intense. "Shamus…how I loved that man. He died and I didn't dare go to his funeral. I should have gone. He was so good to me."

"I know, but I'm here now."

She gathered herself, stared at the check again before putting it in a drawer, and poured two glasses of wine. She sighed and, as if needing to do it, spoke of Elihu Harper, who had been different when she was young, who taught her the Bible and seemed almost fatherly until his ego began corrupting him and things turned strange, and of his housekeeper Brinn, an old woman who taught her a love for gardens and fairy tales.

"Shamus told me you've done well, " she went on.

"God bless him for that. I wanted you to know. You've been important to me, Maisie." He kept his tone as light as he was able--lighter than what he was feeling. "The first love of my life."

She smiled at this admission. "Thank goodness first loves aren't meant to last." She took a sip of wine. "That summer was my happiest time. I was 19. Everyone seemed to be falling for me. I must have been pretty then. Was I?"

He laughed. "Yes. And still are."

"I felt loved. I felt part of a family. And then Elihu showed up, damn him." She stared into her glass, growing solemn. "Elihu and my real life."

He had come here with guarded expectations, so he was not unprepared for her casual dismissal of his confessions. Yet the right word, he hoped, might fan a flame without making a fool of him.

"I'm happy enough now," she continued. "The life is solitary, but I don't mind. There's a man who comes by. He drives a taxi during the season, and then sits around the Pink

Pony all winter with his friends. He's a good enough guy, but it's nothing serious. When the gardening stops, I work as a waitress." She sipped more wine. "How about you?"

"Me? I'm good. My work life is interesting. I live in London right now but travel all over."

"Married?"

"No. Never found the time or the girl."

"That surprises me."

"Well, I have hopes."

Outside, they heard the breeze picking up, saw the hemlocks and tamaracks begin to sway. The wine was making them warm and sleepy. She suggested a walk and then asked him to stay for dinner. She had a fresh whitefish large enough for two. He was pleased. It was not yet mid afternoon, so he would have all day with her, maybe more. They walked a path behind the cabin. She'd bordered it with what she called a blue angel hosta and bright clusters of New Guinea impatiens. They'd planted similar arrangements in Shamus's yard. As they got deeper into the trees, she hoped to show him her resident great horned owl, but her friend did not appear.

Yes, she was no longer the girl he'd known, but from every angle he saw grace. Beneath her sundress, her knees were red and calloused, a sacrifice to her flowers. She fluffed her hair with coarse hands to dry it, and his heart sang. Delicate sun lines showed near her eyes but deepened her presence. Her back was tender, he knew, when she stopped to stretch it out. He offered his arm and she took it. Her emerald eyes, after all the years, still smoldered from within.

They ate together, drank another bottle of wine. She asked him to stay the night—the island hotels were exorbitant prices. The only bed was hers. As always with him, she took the lead. She undressed to her white cotton underclothes and then began undressing him as he stroked the soft curve of her hip. At her coaxing, they made love slowly, savoring it, sleeping only a few hours. In his sleep he dreamt of snow burying houses and fields, bending down the branches of blooming trees. When he awoke at last to a stone gray morning, she had already gone off to work in the gardens, as he knew she must.

In the night she had whispered something about owing him this, about some day, somewhere, a girl.

DRIVING ON ICE

Jimmy had agreed to the weekend marriage enrichment seminar only because he'd had no ideas for a year and was under contract to produce another book. The seminar was Kate's doing--her folks were watching the kids, and Jimmy prayed the three day agony might jog something inside the wasteland of his head. He didn't tell that to Kate, of course. Her motives were pure--she actually hoped to improve their marriage. Kate went to church, and this was a church-sponsored event--they weren't allowed phones or computers, no contact with the outside world. Could he endure it?

It was nearly the end of March; it had rained the night before, but in the pale mid-morning light the roads looked dry. Heaps of dirty snow from highway plows lay in an unending line just beyond the shoulders and wouldn't be gone for several weeks. Jimmy passed the travel mug of coffee to Kate, accelerated up a slight incline on the four-lane road leading toward Lake Michigan, and suddenly found himself in free fall, the car turning in a weird sort of slow motion, utterly out of his control. He stayed off the brakes, turned the wheels against the spin, but nothing would arrest the dream-like ballet. Their car crossed the middle lane into oncoming traffic, slid through both lanes onto the shoulder, and came to an abrupt stop when the tires hit the snow bank, the car facing back toward home. They had miraculously missed a delivery truck and a line of approaching cars; the two sat staring ahead, shaken to the core.

"Are you all right?" Kate asked, exhaling heavily. "What in the world just happened?"

Jimmy shook his head to clear it. "It was black ice. Never saw it. How the hell did we miss cracking up?" Cars passed by now at greatly reduced speeds, drivers shaking their heads—to express relief or some form of reprimand, he wasn't sure which. "We were completely out of control. I've never felt like that before."

"Either have I. I'm trembling. Should we just go home?"

He gave that a moment's thought. "I'll put it in four wheel drive and go slow. I think we'll be okay."

"My heart's in my throat, Jimmy. I feel kind of sick."

"I'll be careful."

And he was. They found the seminar site within thirty minutes--the lodge of a summer camp on the Lake Michigan shore. The beach, visible through the bare trees, was mostly clear of snow but raw-looking, deserted of human beings. Jimmy wondered what kind of genius had planned a beach event for March? The sky was gray as a pot. Massive fields of ice in jagged slabs jammed the first hundred yards into the wintry lake. He'd imagined enriching their marriage with an assignation atop a dune, but it wouldn't occur with frostbite still in the air. Why hadn't he turned back when she suggested it?

Their room in a dormitory wing of the lodge did nothing to raise his spirits. The place was primitive at best, containing two sets of metal bunk beds, two folding chairs, and two battered dressers. An electric heater built into one wall was bright red, but the room was still in the low 60s. Kate dropped her suitcase and sat down on one of the thin, army-issue mattresses. At 33, a mother of two, she was riper than she once was but still inviting, her attraction sharpened by a puzzling complexity he'd lately noticed. Family life had frayed her at the edges, especially because she'd kept her teaching job. But there were depths to her, even after nine years, he knew he hadn't come near to probing. Her marriage to him, he realized all too well, was a trial. She had a temper that sometimes scared him, but in the end her bright eyes and soft, forgiving smile revealed her fundamental good nature. He'd done far better in the deal than she had.

"Jesus…bunk beds," he said. " What the hell kind of marriage enrichment is this supposed to be?"

"You can handle single beds for two nights," she said mildly, standing and shaking out one of the folded sheets. "Sorry this place is so grim, but I know the leaders are good. Anyway, I hope it's worth it. It's costing enough."

He caught himself before he agreed. "Hey, I can handle it. We could be in a dozen pieces on the highway right now. Comparatively speaking, this is a blessing. Give me a sheet and a pillowcase."

After lunch, six couples (Kate knew the couple leading the seminar and another from church) played musical chairs in the great room of the lodge to an ancient recording of Perry Como singing "Love Makes the World Go Round." Whenever the music stopped, there followed the mad scramble for seats—a curiously frenzied icebreaker. Despite some laughs, Jimmy found the game unbearably cheesy. Kate seemed to be getting into it.

Remembering his purpose and trying to keep mental notes about this strange human event, he followed sheep-like as they moved to overstuffed chairs and couches arranged about a large window with a view of the lake. An occasional ray of sun broke through the dense gray clouds, giving Jimmy flashes of hope for a semi-clothed quickie in the dunes. Henry and Ruth DeGraf, family counselors, a relaxed, mid-fortyish couple in designer jeans, were about to get down to the business of the weekend.

"Just to get things started," Henry said with a pleasant lilt, "let's go around the circle. I'd like each of you to introduce yourselves and tell three things you like about your spouses." Henry had a full, graying beard and the remains of a linebacker's body.

"We'll save the interesting stuff for later," Ruth said with a wise smile. She was a gaunt, ruggedly attractive woman—the type who ran ten miles a day. The two were physically intimidating, but with soft edges.

Beside Henry sat a tall, brassy, age-indefinite redhead in a silk shirt and tights showing off very good legs. She'd won hands down at musical chairs. Her nametag read HARRIET BOS. Henry looked at her with a paid counselor's benevolence.

"Me first?" Harriet asked, looking Henry over. "Well, I'm Harriet. Bert, here—Albertus--is my husband, of course. First off, he's a Hollander. God, he's a Hollander." She said this as if there were a world of significance in it. Some titters passed through the group.

Bert, a small, florid, snappily dressed new-car sales type, smiled, unperturbed.

"You can see he has very good taste in clothes. And... well...I'm happy to say he's a Scorpio...very protective."

Eyes moved to Bert, who seemed comfortable enough with her assessment. He sucked several times on his empty pipe. "Harriet is a Pisces, though I don't put any stock in astrology. The two zodiac signs are said to be compatible, good for marrying." His accent was thickly Dutch. He paused in a meditative way. "She's tall. I like tall women. I also think she's always enjoyed being bigger than me. She—"

Harriet interrupted, mimicking his clunky accent. "—she keeps me on my toes." She laughed--an irksome bray--and turned to Henry. "Sorry, but I've heard that line a million times."

Bert kept smiling. Jimmy hunkered down in the lumpy couch, his side pressed to Kate's. He uncrossed his legs, folded his hands, ready to bolt. When he realized Bert was apparently finished (he'd never made it to the third thing he liked about his wife), he barked, "Oh...me?" He scraped out an ear with his little finger and stared at it. "I'm Jimmy Flynn. This is my wife, Kate. Kate's a great mother...terrific with kids...a well-loved school teacher, which I admire about her..." He paused a bit too long, his mind a blank.

Finally Kate blurted, "Good grief, there must be *something* else," She tried to sound light-hearted, but it rang false.

"Easy honey, there's plenty. For instance, I fell in love with her voice the first time I met her," catching her wary look in his peripheral vision. "And there's this odd little thing I find endearing. I'm a writer and she can't spell 'writing.' She spells it 'writting' with two t's."

Laughter lightly rippled.

Blushing, Kate said, "It looks *right* that way. I can't help it. Anyway, that's four things." All eyes moved to her. She crossed her arms, her gaze fixing on some spot at her feet. Smiling, she said, "Well...Jimmy is a dreamer, which is good and bad." She hesitated on that. "He's a good father and also a good writer. Sometimes he doesn't believe this, but I'm his number one fan."

A brief smattering of applause followed this admission.

"Jimmy Flynn...I've heard of you!" Harriet gushed. "What a kick--we have a famous person in our midst!"

Jimmy smiled at the recognition. "Famous in a twelve block area," he muttered as humbly as he could. He could feel Harriet boldly admiring what others had before--his big, loose-jointed boyishness, so opposite of Bert. Women, Jimmy knew, wanted to cuddle and mother him, but Harriet's look wasn't motherly.

The introductions continued around the group: the Packers, a pale couple in their mid-20s, both seminary students, the Fleecers from church, each in second marriages with a twenty year age difference (he sixty, she almost forty), and the Baileys, who held hands constantly and seemed too blissful to need an enrichment weekend.

By late afternoon the group knew each other better and had relaxed. Most were down on the floor now, lying on their sides or leaning against furniture.

Ruth was sitting on her heels in a yoga position. "Keeping in mind the negative effects of the sort of 'you' messages Henry has been talking about, I think we should move to some of the things we consider problems in our relationships."

Henry nodded energetically, making eye contact with Kate.

"Ask yourselves this," Ruth continued, "is there anything that could be improved in your marriage?"

"Communication," Jimmy blurted.

Heads snapped up.

Jimmy backed off a little, self-conscious. "I mean listening," he said less forcefully. He took a deep breath and exhaled. "I know sometimes I have trouble listening. We've been arguing about it for years."

Kate, who was lying back on her elbows, pushed herself into a sitting position. Her face had a look of passionate zeal—here at last were the nuts and bolts she'd come for.

"It's true," an earnestness in her voice. She glanced about, finding support. "I'll be carrying on an important conversation--like things that happened at school--and he'll just wander away—his mind, I mean. Nothing I say seems to be important enough to listen to. His indifference hurts me."

"It's *not* indifference, honey."

She disregarded him. "Sometimes I might as well be talking to the dog…or the wall. I feel like the Invisible Woman." The air suddenly carried a charge. Reclining people rose to sitting positions.

"Excuse me, Jimmy," Ruth asked calmly. "Do you do this only with Kate?"

"Not just with Kate," he said, feeling cornered. "I do it with everybody. It depends on what's going on. It depends on whether I'm in the middle of writing something."

Kate was unrelenting. "It's *me*. Other people think he's marvelous. It's just *me*."

"Come on, Kate. I do it all the time with people. I can't help it if the stuff going on in my head is more interesting than reality. Jesus, I'm a writer."

Harriet came to life. "Hardly unusual for a highly creative person…I mean always fantasizing, right? *I'm* a real fantasizer."

Why had he opened this can of worms? "Yeah," he said to Harriet, "but it isn't always creative. When I'm with Kate's parents, for instance—sometimes I've heard the same stuff a thousand times, you know? I just wander off--start counting flowers on the wallpaper. I can't help it. I'd like to stop it, but I can't."

Harriet smiled approvingly, glanced at her husband. "I guess we all have that problem."

Surprisingly, Ruth added, "Well, just try being a counselor for a day or two." A puzzled silence was followed by a big laugh. The tension dissipated. Jimmy was pretty sure she'd used the line before.

When they returned to their dorm room after a soupy pasta supper, Jimmy felt as if he'd been slogging through a mile of knee-deep mud. The Packers and the Fleecers, it turned out, were here as a last resort before lawyers, and the Baileys, just remarried after being divorced for ten years, were overplaying affection to cover up wounds that hadn't healed. Harriet and Bert had worked out what they called a liberated relationship. It sounded tatty at best. The whole group, with the exception of benevolent leaders Ruth and Henry and maybe themselves, was pretty much a train wreck.

"I need a drink," Kate mumbled, tossing her suitcase on a lower bunk. She opened it and removed a bottle of brandy.

"Thank God--I was afraid we were trapped in this purgatory without alcohol." He went to the bathroom and brought back two small paper cups. He set them on a dresser, and she poured the cups full.

"What a stupid mistake this was," she muttered.

"It's been very enriching—if you don't mind the sight of blood."

His sarcasm didn't amuse her. "Promise me one thing, Jimmy. Say anything you want about me but leave my parents out of it."

"I was using them as an example, Kate, I could as well have been talking about my parents."

"Why didn't you then, you bastard?" Things had obviously been festering all afternoon.

"Do we need the poisonous tone?"

Kate took a deep swallow of brandy, shuddering. "You fell in love with my voice…Jesus."

"I did. Can I help it if it changed?"

"All my voice ever did was put you in some kind of trance."

Wearying, Jimmy slipped an arm around her and pulled her close. "Aw, Kate. Come on. Compared to this bunch we're Hepburn and Tracy. Let's enrich what we can of the weekend."

She jerked away and tossed down the remainder of her brandy. "Great idea. Bang me into submission—that'll fix everything." She grabbed her coat and a knit cap. "I'm going for a walk. Please don't follow me."

He watched her go and felt no desire to follow her. Pouring another brandy, he lay down and stared at the upper bunk, disturbed at her bitter mood. There'd been plenty of fights, but this was odd--a strange flavor. Some moments later he heard a rap on the door. Who else but one of the train wreck crew? He had no desire to continue with enrichment games, but the knock was so persistent he got up and opened to find Harriet, holding what looked like a glass of Scotch.

"We thought you might need a stiff one after this afternoon."

He took it, finishing off his brandy and crushing the cup. "You hit the nail on the head. Thanks."

"Come on down. We're in room 15. It's a dump just like this, but it's warmer."

"My wife is out for a walk."

"Leave her a note. Tell her where we are. Ruth might stop by."

He shrugged, scribbled a note on a kleenex, and followed Harriet down the hall.

She took his arm. "We had no idea there'd be a celebrity along this weekend. You'll probably use all of our secrets in a book, right?"

"Who'd believe it?" Actually, Kate had more than once accused him of that very thing.

Her laughter rattled in the bare hallway. "Maybe you'll give me your autograph some time."

"Sure."

When he found that Bert was away in town (breaking weekend rules) to buy more Scotch, he wasn't surprised. Ruth wasn't there, either, of course. He disengaged himself from her arm and also the soft press of her breast. But she didn't give up easily.

"Stay a while, Mr. Celebrity. You just got here."

"Let me go find Kate," he said. "She'd hate to miss this. Be back in a minute or two."

"Do you really have to?" Her disappointment was tinged with a touch of irritation.

Jimmy winked at her. "I think I better." She flashed a wry smile and sighed theatrically. And though Jimmy felt pleased with himself, he wandered out of the room trying to imagine what that big body would be like…what kind of ride it would be. The price of it, of course, would be much too steep. But the thought provided him several minutes of welcome diversion.

He went back for his coat, then out of a steel exit door at the end of the hallway. He crossed a cracked tennis court lighted by a spotlight on a post, and skirted the edge of the bare woods still trimmed with traceries of snow. The night was cloud covered and densely black. Hesitating, doubting that Kate would try the beach in this kind of dark, he spotted a stairway down to the water, the top landing lighted by a single dim bulb. He hesitated again because she'd told him not to come after her. But something was making him uneasy. Within half a dozen steps he saw two people, a man and woman, seated on a bench of a landing halfway down to the beach. They appeared, in the muted glow of the bulb of the upper landing, to be engaged in an animated conversation. Jimmy stepped behind the branches of a small spruce. He could hear the low buzz of conversation but not the words. For a moment he saw her put her face in her hands; she apparently was crying. The man wrapped her in his arms, and she pressed her face into his coat. The last thing Jimmy saw before he escaped back to the lodge was the kiss, passionate and lingering. He had no doubt that the man was Henry. Though he hadn't clearly seen her face, the woman was Kate, he knew. For the second time in a day, he felt black ice beneath him.

He had to go to the front doors to get in. Ruth was in the great room, setting up materials for tomorrow's session. She saw him and immediately grew concerned.

"Jimmy, you look like you've lost your best friend. What's going on?"

"Who the hell can say?"

"Tell me."

"I don't think you want to know."

She took his arm and led him away. Her room was off a hallway in the opposite end of the compound from the dormitory. The place was opulent compared to those of her clients—a large queen bed, upholstered chairs, a small kitchen.

"Wow," he said, "how'd you manage this?"

"The perks of leadership. I know how dismal the dorm rooms are. Sorry."

"At least you and Henry get to sleep together."

"No, Henry has his own room. Do you happen to know where he is?"

"I'm afraid so."

"Hmmm. You apparently don't know we're divorced."

"You gotta be kidding me. You're a marital counseling couple, and you're divorced? How the hell do you make that work?"

"Oh, we still do well together on these retreats—maybe even better now. Our practices are entirely separate, of course. Did you know your wife is seeing Henry?"

"Jesus…you know, too?"

"As a counselor, I mean."

"What? She never told me. I haven't seen any indication of it...things like bills. Never a frickin' word."

"Maybe he's doing it as a friend."

"I suspect it's friendship," he said bitterly, "since I just stumbled on them getting very friendly on the stairs down to the beach."

She took a moment to absorb this. "You might be mistaking what was going on. He's ordinarily quite professional."

Jimmy sat down on her bed, leaned on his knees and dropped his head between them. "Yeah, he seems to be a pro at what he's doing. The phony bastard…I feel like I've been run over by a truck."

Ruth sat down beside him and put an arm around his shoulders. "I know the feeling. I'm sorry."

"Honestly, are there any good marriages on earth?"

"A few. Not many are made in heaven these days." She sighed and shook her head. "Tomorrow's session is about restoration and healing—mostly bullshit and band aids."

"I'm not sure I'll be up to it." He leaned limply against her.

She touched her forehead to his temple.

"I'm glad I ran into you," he half-whispered.

"So am I." She brushed his cheek with her lips.

"Is Henry a snake?"

"No more than any of us. His intentions are usually good."

Jimmy left Ruth nearly two hours later, each assuring the other that none of it ever happened. He found Kate asleep and breathing evenly in one of the lower bunks. He sat down in the dark and stared at her. In sleep she looked vulnerable, young, lovely. A steel band about his chest tightened until he could barely breathe. He had come to this place hoping for something to jump-start his creative life. But now his heart's barrenness reduced the importance of that to nothing.

Were separation and divorce next on the agenda? Already he was feeling a panicked sickness about his children, whom he loved. It would all be Kate's doing (even though now he was culpable, too), so he damn well intended to keep the house, and the kids in their rooms. *His* stories were the ones they loved to hear. They could visit her instead of vice versa.

Upheaval would rule their days for an indefinite period of time. But the more he thought about it, about the dark adventure of it—impending disaster, chaos and change, the emotional parley of love and hate—the more he knew it was the stuff books were made of.

ABISHAG

Abby O'Shea's life was falling apart, but at least it was a warm spring day. She'd stumbled on a small classified ad while searching for jobs in the *Examiner*. The ad read simply: *Seeking young woman. Live-in assistance and home help for an older man. Good opportunity for the right person. See 1 Kings 1:1-4.*

A local phone number followed.

Naturally, she didn't have a Bible. She didn't have much of anything, having sold her last possession of value, a fairly new laptop, in payment for a month in this tiny studio apartment with Shelly, Shelly's boyfriend Nick, and their baby, whom she'd agreed to babysit. Abby's son Jack was there, too, of course. She couldn't look up 1 Kings 1:1-4 or hunt for better job offerings online because Shelly had the laptop with her at school. Only a few employers advertised in newspapers any more. Abby couldn't afford a cell phone, so she might as well have been living on a desert island. Her bed and a few battered pieces of furniture were locked in a storage room at the roach apartment house from which she'd recently been evicted. Jack was supposed to begin kindergarten in the fall, and the two of them were down to their final two days on the sofa bed, one step from the streets. What a model mother she'd turned out to be.

Pushing aside gloom and doom, she used Shelly's kitchen phone to call the number in the ad, half expecting an unpleasant run-in with a religious fanatic. The phone rang only once.

"Gabriel Miles." The male voice was deep and decidedly curt.

It startled her. "Oh, hello. I'm calling about the job you have advertised." She tried to sound cheerful and interested.

There was a long pause. "Excuse me for asking," he went on brusquely. "But are you a prostitute?"

Her chirpy voice flattened. "I think I've called the wrong number."

"No, no, please--I'm the one who advertised for assistance and home help. But the first two women got the wrong idea entirely. I think it was the Bible passage." His voice softened with each syllable.

"I'm not a prostitute. Sorry."

"I don't want one. That's my point."

"Oh...well..."

"I live downtown near the university. Why don't you come over and we'll talk. I'm a retired professor."

"Oh. Well, that's different. Does a bus go by there?"

"Take a taxi."

"I can't afford it."

"I'll pay, of course. When can you be here?"

"When? Let me see. I'm watching my girlfriend's baby right now. She'll be home at four. I could be there by about five."

"That's fine. What's your name?"

"Abigail," she told him. "Abby O'Shea."

"Excellent," he said, his voice gaining some slight enthusiasm. "That may be a sign. You may be the one I'm looking for." He gave her the address—she recognized it as an area of once grand homes slowly mutating into shabby student apartment houses.

Shelly, who'd had to meet with her hair design instructor, returned from classes twenty minutes late. The baby was screeching her lungs out, and Jack lay curled up under the table, pressing his palms to his ears. He hated Shelly's place as much as she did (five of them slept in the same room; the kitchen was slightly larger than a sailboat galley), yet her son had no idea how much worse things could soon become. Shelly had honestly needed the laptop, but it took a hugely generous heart to put up with such chaos and loss of privacy. Shelly was a saint.

Her boyfriend, on the other hand, stayed away until well after the kids were in bed. He installed cable tv for a living and was waiting out Abby and Jack in local bars. Shelly was far too good for him. He was one of a legion of defective men Abby had known in her life, including Jack's long departed father (a lapse in judgment whom she'd never considered marrying), her weasel of a stepfather, and a former restaurant boss whom she'd slapped for grabbing her ass. Her blood father, a moody truck driver rarely at home, had died twenty years ago. She was seven then and had never much noticed his absence except for her mother complaining about money. With the encouragement of her grandfather, Abby had worked hard at school, hoping some day to escape the thin, colorless life she led. What a laugh.

The cabbie was Syrian, spoke only a few words of English, and made his way so carefully through rush hour traffic that she arrived 25 minutes late. He didn't understand why she wouldn't pay him, so she took his arm and led him to the door of the large, somber sandstone house. A giant pine tree in front was full of noisy grackles—apparently nesting there and dropping excrement everywhere on the mossy slate roof. She knocked on the door and a middle-aged, red-faced woman appeared, dressed in a plaid apron, gripping a twenty-dollar bill.

"How much is it?" she asked in a crisp Scottish burr.

"Seexteen and eighty-fife," he said. If nothing else, he knew the language of money.

She handed him the twenty and shooed him away. "Robbery," she muttered, and ushered Abby inside. "You're late, young lady."

"Sorry."

"Off on the wrong foot, I'd say."

Abby didn't reply. The place was dim and overburdened with furniture—deep green walls wrapped in dark oak, with high ceilings and heavy brass chandeliers. The foyer was nearly the size of Shelly's entire apartment. The sweet, stale odor of cigar smoke permeated the place—once the aroma of her grandparents' home (until her mother and the weasel had inherited it).

"I'm Mrs. Reid," the woman said. "Dr. Miles is upstairs. Sit and I'll tell him you're here."

Abby sat down in the sagging embrace of a wing-backed chair, its soft leather faintly smothering. While Mrs. Reid went to find him, Abby looked around. On either side of a large fireplace she saw stone, melon-breasted female figures—ugly and misshapen, and suited, she thought, to a museum, not a home. In a nearby room--his library, obviously—wall to ceiling bookcases held haphazard stacks of heavy volumes, more books than she'd ever seen anywhere but a public library. The books made her feel inconsequential and out of her element. It didn't help that she was dressed in worn black slacks and a white blouse frayed at the cuffs, the best she owned--her former waitress uniform. She caught a glimpse of herself in the glass door of a cabinet. Her heavy dark hair shrouding her thin face made her look slightly deranged. Taken aback, she rummaged in her purse for a hair tie and quickly roped the mess into a lopsided ponytail.

It was then she heard footsteps descending briskly on the wide central stairway. She'd been anticipating a slow, step-at-a-time rhythm with perhaps the click of a cane. Instead she rose to greet a tall, erect, somewhat wild-looking man with a mass of white hair swept back and an unkempt beard curling down his neck. He looked uncared for, in need of major restoration. He wore sagging khaki cargo pants and a baggy knit turtleneck sweater with crumbs on the front of it. As he approached, he looked at her uneasily.

"Abigail?" he asked. His voice seemed only slightly more assured than his eyes.

"Hello," she said, reaching out a hand. He hesitated, and then shook it. His handshake was firm but freezing cold. "You must be Dr. Miles."

"Yes, well…why don't we go into my library?"

She followed him. A large, mahogany desk occupied a back corner of the warmly wooded room; nearby, in the curve of a bay window, a grand piano reflected the golden light of a late afternoon sun. He situated her in a small chair beside the desk, and, once he sat down behind it, he seemed more in charge of things. His brown eyes were set deep in nests of wrinkles, yet there was something youthful about his face—a face that seemed to have weathered mostly in the eyes and deeply grooved forehead.

"I'll begin by asking if you've read 1 Kings 1:1-4?"

"To be honest, I haven't. I sold my computer, and well…I don't have a Bible."

He seemed crestfallen. "I very much hoped you had."

"I'll be glad to read it right now if you'd like. Do you have a Bible?"

"Of course. Dozens of them. I think the NIV is the clearest rendering of this passage. Let me get it." He swiveled in his chair and, still sitting, pulled down a thick volume. He opened it, found the passage quickly, and handed it over. "Read it aloud please."

She apprehensively took the Bible from him. "Aloud?"

"Please."

Abby cleared her throat. *"When King David was old and well advanced in years, he could not keep warm even when they put covers over him. So his servants said to him, 'Let us look for a young virgin to attend the king and take care of him. She can lie beside him so that our lord the king may keep warm.'*

"Then they searched throughout Israel for a beautiful girl and found Abishag, a Shunammite, and brought her to the king. The girl was very beautiful; she took care of the king and waited on him, but the king had no intimate relations with her."

"You can stop there," he said.

Abby stared at him in disbelief. "I'm not **that** desperate for a job."

"But wait…"

"Sorry," she bristled. "Not interested--or qualified. I'm not beautiful. I'm not a human hot water bottle. I'm not a virgin. In fact, I'm a single mother with a five year old son."

"You are? Oh, dear. I hadn't figured on anything like that."

She stood, clutching her purse. "That makes two of us. The whole idea is very creepy, if you want my opinion."

His face filled with dismay. "I was afraid of this. The last thing I want to do is offend you. This isn't about sex at all!"

"Really. You could fool me."

"But I mean it! Please try to understand. It's been eight years since my wife passed away. I'm 72 years old and no danger to any female. I miss her physical presence every day. I miss her body next to mine at night. The worst thing about old age is the loss of that…that blessed contact and the comfort of body heat. I can't get warm. I wear socks to bed and pull on two comforters, but it doesn't help. That's what I need, not sex!" He took a deep, emotional breath. "And then, well…I also need help around here. Mrs. Reid might be leaving me. As it is, she goes home to her husband at night. I'd want you to live here, of course, but factoring in a child…it's not quite what I had in mind."

"No. It's not quite what I had in mind either."

He stood and offered his hand, looking ruffled and unhappy. "Thank you for your interest."

"Will you call a cab for me?"

"Mrs. Reid has offered to drop you on her way home."

"Oh. Well, that's okay, I guess."

As if by magic, Mrs. Reid appeared at the door with her purse under her arm.

She drove an aging but well kept Honda sedan, spotless on the inside as if she vacuumed it daily.

"So you're a single mom, are you?" She'd obviously been listening in. "Who's babysitting?"

"A girlfriend."

She turned onto an expressway, staying silent until secure in a middle lane. "He's brilliant, you know." Her voice had lost most of the sharp edge of their initial meeting.

"Who? Dr. Miles?"

"His field is anthropology of religion. He's retired but still quite well known. He writes books on religions of the world." She glanced over at Abby. "It wouldn't be a bad job, in spite of that Abishag business."

"It's very weird."

"He isn't that way, dear. He doesn't know much about women, even though he's had two wives. The first wife left him for one of his colleagues after two or three years of marriage—a student fifteen years younger than him, a silly girl who had a thing for archeologists. He didn't marry again for years. It was about the time I started working for him that he met Mary Peele. She was his nurse through a bad bout with yellow fever he'd caught in South America. She was such a sweet, simple soul—they were an odd couple, right enough, but good for each other. She died after just six years of marriage, and he hasn't recovered from it." She sighed heavily. "He's the smartest man you'll ever meet, but he's not at all worldly about women. A bit of a babe in the woods, I'd say. I know he'd get used to having a child around. My husband and I want to move back to Scotland, but I first have to see the poor man in good hands. I know for a fact you'd be safe with him, if that's your worry."

Abby glanced at her with curiosity. She couldn't recall many men (her long-dead grandfather was one) she'd ever felt safe with. "It's nice that you care about him."

"I feel a responsibility. Would you think about the job?" It was an earnest plea.

"It doesn't interest me."

"Give it a day or two, at least? I heard the things you said to him. You spoke clearly and honestly. I liked you for it."

Abby sat silent a moment as Mrs. Reid turned into Shelly's apartment complex. "Well…I guess I can think about it."

"Thank you," she said, smiling hopefully. "You seem intelligent. Have you been to school?"

"Two years of community college—but that was a few years ago."

"Before your son came along, I'm thinking."

"You got that right," Abby said, jumping from the car and ending the conversation.

Late Friday morning she stood in the lobby of Shelly's apartment building with Jack in one hand and a battered cloth suitcase in the other. Shelly held her baby, looking guilty and close to tears.

"I'd let you stay longer, you know I would," Shelly told her. "But Nick says if you don't leave, he will."

Abby hugged her. "You've been great. A deal is a deal. We'll be fine."

"What are your plans?"

Abby shrugged. "Don't worry. I have some possibilities."

"I do worry. Here--" pressing a twenty into Abby's hand.

There was a time Abby would have pressed it back, but this was not such a time. "You're a good friend, Shelly."

"God bless you. Good luck."

And with that, her last option vanished. Her mother, the only family left, had meekly supported her alcoholic second husband when he'd banished Abby from their home for beating off his advances with a bowling trophy. She'd hurt the bastard, actually fractured his nose and broken his trophy, and the memory evoked a dark smile.

They walked a couple of miles into downtown.

"Mama, are we going back to our blue room?"

"No, honey." They'd been evicted from the blue room. "I'm trying to think of what to do."

"I'm hungry."

"We just ate breakfast at Aunt Shelly's."

"But I'm hungry."

So she pulled him into a Greyhound Bus Station with a small snack counter. She paid for a banana and an orange juice, and they sat down in the waiting room to eat. At five o'clock they were still there, nibbling on power bars. Jack had taken a long nap with his head on her lap. The two of them used the ladies' room several times. At six, when the outside temperature began to drop, she heard a furnace kick on. There were worse places, she reasoned, to spend a night.

On Monday morning, after an anxious night in the station and two more in their first homeless shelter where she'd held her son and her purse tight to her breast and prayed, she'd grown desperate. She phoned Dr. Gabriel Miles from the shelter and said she'd take the job--if her son were part of the deal. To her surprise, he hesitated only a moment: he was willing to give the arrangement a try.

****

In many ways, she would write some years later (as an author of note…still living with a daughter in the old Miles house), her real life began with that phone call. By nightfall of the first day, Jack was tucked in his own bed in a room they shared, full of ponderously heavy tiger maple furniture—but spacious and high-ceilinged and clean, thanks to Mrs. Reid. Jack was exhausted, weepy, and asleep before she finished the ongoing story of a brave, clever girl named Natasha and her adventures in strange places like the land of giant, man-eating chipmunks. She'd read him a book or two of Shelly's (they owned none of their own), but he preferred her Natasha stories.

With a queasy sense of dread, she left him there sleeping to join Dr. Miles in his library. Jack seemed safe for the moment—it was her single concern--yet she also knew she had nothing left to barter with but her self. She heard the piano before she reached the bottom of the stairs. Dr. Miles was playing with the soft pedal engaged, muffling the chords of some classical piece she'd heard before but couldn't identify. She entered the room and sat down. He didn't notice her until he'd finished, and then he turned on the bench with a sheepish look.

"That was nice," she said, trying to start on a positive note.

"I just dabble. It relieves stress."

"I took lessons, but I never sounded like that."

He seemed nervous and embarrassed. "I apologize for my misleading job description," he said suddenly. "I guess I didn't think it out."

She hesitated. "We'll see how things go. Thanks for taking my son."

"I'm a bit uneasy. I've been married but never had a child. He doesn't seem obstreperous like some of them."

The word eluded her but she guessed its meaning. "Well…now and again he can be… a bit obstreperous."

"I'll need it quiet for my work, of course. I write from 9 to 11, and then again from 1 to 3. I have a fairly strict schedule arranged for each day, even weekends. I find it helps me."

She felt a small surge of irritation. "I understand."

"I've done some checking. There's an elementary school close by."

Her irritation evaporated. "Thank you."

"This is a big house. I'm sure we can stay out of each other's way."

"I'm sure we can."

"It's also very old. I worry any day the place will come crashing down around me."

She smiled. "It's certainly clean."

"That's Mrs. Reid. She vacuums like a dervish. Wears out a Kirby every three years." He smiled faintly. "Do you cook?"

"Um…I can learn. I'm better at fixing things--like plugged up sinks."

He nodded, and they sat in silence.

"When do you want me to begin this Abishag business?" she asked at last.

"Oh…well, **that**." His face reddened, especially his ears. "I apologize for that. We'll begin only when and if you're ready. It's entirely your decision."

"My decision?"

He nodded.

"But I thought…" she said.

"It's your decision," he said again, meaning it. "It's not a requirement of the job."

The tension began to loosen in her neck and shoulders. She nodded, sighed through an exhausted smile, and went back to check on Jack. An hour or so later, showering in a claw-footed tub in the small bathroom designated as Jack's and hers, she felt the stains of the homeless shelter swirl away and the burden of her fears diminish by a small but discernible weight.

Mrs. Reid, reluctant to leave, stayed on for several months to see to her training. Within that space of time, Abby was surprised to find herself taking responsibility for all household bills, balancing the checkbook, and freeing Dr. Miles from every financial concern but the larger investments. Electronically deposited each month were his university pension, his social security check, the required minimum distribution on his IRAs, and his income for teaching (on Tuesday evenings) a class in Religions of the Ancient Near East. Royalty checks, sometimes for stunning amounts, would arrive in the mail. She would give them to him to sign and deposit in the checking account. And then she found herself empowered to sign, make deposits, and write checks herself. Though Dr. Miles lived like a monk, he was a comfortably wealthy man.

The summer passed. More and more was entrusted to her, though she openly expressed her self-doubts. What blind confidence they showed, as if they knew something she didn't. By the end of August, Mrs. Reid gave over all responsibilities to Abby and tearfully departed the household. In those initial months on the job, Abby had never once assumed the role of Abishag. Dr. Miles said nothing about it. She called him Dr. Miles as Mrs. Reid had done, but Jack, who'd quickly settled into the large museum of a house, preferred shortening it to Da. The man and boy went about sharing space without apparent friction, even when Jack knocked over one of the ugly female figures by the fireplace. Da dismissed the statues as mediocre copies of a smaller original, a fertility goddess from the Upper Paleolithic period. With a faint smile he cautioned Abby not to touch them, just in case. The three of them ate together and talked, usually about what was happening to Jack in kindergarten. When Abby called him Da once without thinking, he laughed, so she kept doing it, at least when outsiders weren't present. The smell of cigars began to disappear, and she asked if he'd quit smoking. He explained that the cigars had been Mrs. Reid's...thin ones she'd enjoyed late afternoons with a sip or two of brandy. "Good for Mrs. Reid," she said with a laugh.

Abby observed her employer with puzzlement, a man at once brilliant and yet sometimes naïve and even bumbling. He'd traveled the world but seemed to have little that was worldly about him. She saw no meanness in him, yet he was demanding about his daily routines--rigid, especially about his writing and class preparation. He rode a stationary bicycle at eight each morning. He needed food at set times. He gave no thought to what he wore, so she (at Mrs. Reid's urging) set out clothing for him. He showered immediately after riding the bicycle and let his wild hair dry by degrees. She could not convince him to go out to a barber so pushed to have one come to the house. It was a hectic, demanding, and not altogether fulfilling life, yet he paid her well and provided room and board, and her son was secure for the first time in his five years. She was expected to cook (which she was laboring to learn), to clean (but without Mrs. Reid's fanaticism), to fix parts of the house that were indeed falling apart (she learned electrical and plumbing repair from YouTube), to handle finances in a trustworthy manner, to buy groceries and all household supplies, to do washing, and to drive his Buick on errands (especially to seek out a brandy carried by one French specialty store downtown). In many ways, the house was now more hers than his, and she felt increasingly responsible for it. That fact weighed on her at times and left her bemused.

One day in September, he handed her handwritten legal pads--his new book just underway--and asked if she would mind typing his manuscript into the computer. The keyboard of his iMac was too sensitive for his touch. He'd pounded for years on an ancient Smith Corona until he'd worn the typeface away. He appreciated computers, of course, but his touch was as heavy-handed as his piano playing. Uncertain of her own capabilities (as always), and irritated at being given more to do, Abby flatly told him there was just so much of her to go around.

"Of course," he said calmly. "Forgive me. You have my permission to let some things go. Cut back on cleaning the house for a while. I won't mind. Order takeout food. I need your help--this book is far more important than cleaning and cooking."

Thus did her job undergo a curious evolution. Dr. Miles seemed unaware or unconcerned that she was a meagerly educated college washout, so she blundered ahead with whatever he asked. When the occasional colleague dropped by, he'd introduce her as his personal assistant. If this was an elevation in status, her pay didn't reflect it.

In late September, with Jack away at his morning kindergarten, Abby answered the front doorbell to find Shelly holding her baby, now as sweet and pudgy as a cinnamon bun.

"You said this time of day would work. I hope you don't mind me bringing Jennifer. Nick disappeared two weeks ago, and I can't afford a sitter."

"Oh, Shelly…that bastard!"

"I don't get my styling license till early November, so this is all under the table, understand?"

"Sure."

"Nick knew I couldn't afford the apartment by myself. Anyway, that's my problem, not yours."

Abby took Jennifer in her arms and led Shelly to the kitchen near the back of the house. "There's a room just behind the kitchen with good light. I found a tall stool for you."

At exactly 11 a.m., the time his writing came to an end for the morning, she went into the library to remind him of the appointment. He began to get testy about it, so she told him firmly that the stylist had already arrived, that she was a dear friend who needed the work, and that he looked like Rip van Winkle or some banjo-whacking hillbilly. Her words seemed to amuse him. He shrugged and sighed and followed her across the house into the makeshift salon. A baby squirming on the floor with a pacifier and a plastic ball didn't seem to faze him. "Shelly, this is Dr. Miles."

His appearance momentarily overwhelmed her. "Haven't seen anything like this in beauty school," she said. She asked his advice about what to do.

"Just trim a little," he said.

"He's a professor," Abby said. "The look we're going for is distinguished."

Shelly nodded skeptically but set to work with electric clippers, razors, scissors, combs, and a hair dryer. Hair began to fly. When the baby fussed a bit, Abby lifted her and went into the kitchen. She fed her some strained carrots from a jar.

When Dr. Miles emerged from the back room forty minutes later, the transformation was dramatic. Places like his neck were too white and slack, a shorn sheep look, but the spiraling growth on his neck (it had made her itchy) was gone. His white hair was swept back, shaped, and cut above his collar. His beard was full but short, symmetrical, and...yes, distinguished. He looked almost new.

"Well, what do you think?" he asked.

"It's a miracle."

"Good. Now it's your turn."

"No way."

Shelly nodded agreement. "You could use some work, Abby."

"Or a banjo," he said under his breath. It was the first wisecrack she'd ever heard him make.

Shelly came again that fall with Jennifer in a rickety stroller to do their hair (Abby felt as transformed as he did). Shelly was by this time struggling with day-to-day survival.

Abby explained this to Da, and he nodded and nodded as she made a case for the majority of men being no-good bastards. She told him Shelly had her stylist's license but needed a place to cut hair and get on her feet. She could no longer afford her apartment.

He stood silent, chewing his lower lip, wrestling with the situation. At last he said, "I see your point. I'll leave the arrangements to you. Those rooms at the back were servants' quarters years ago. There's a bathroom. She and the baby could manage there, I'd think. I believe a house needs people in it or it starts to die. That part hasn't been used since I've been here. She might put up a sign and cut hair if she wants. Plenty of students around. You'll let her know the rules, of course."

"Of course," she said. "What would you expect for rent?

He scratched his beard. "Does she cook?"

As he returned to his library, she watched him with a dazed sense of gratitude. The man surprised her on a daily basis.

To everyone's good fortune, Shelly loved cooking and was thankful and willing to take over that part of the household duties. Shelly put up a small sign for her business, though she was nervous about zoning restrictions. In this neighborhood, Dr. Miles assured her, no one would notice. Customers soon began trickling in.

Abby typed his manuscript, deciphering one handwritten legal sheet at a time, but that wasn't the end of it. He expected her to sit with him and talk about the writing itself, the clarity of the content, the emerging structure of the whole. The book was entitled *The Scientist's Faith* and involved his own struggle to come to a faith in God.

"I'm not smart enough," she protested. "You're expecting too much."

"That may be the case. But you've always shown competence in everything I've asked of you. You seem to be intelligent and could gain from further education. Consider this the start of it."

She sighed and sat in the small chair beside his desk with her hands folded on her lap.

"I get a sense you believe in God. I hear you praying with Jack at night."

"Of course I pray with him. What parent doesn't? I want Jack to believe someone besides me is looking out for him. I haven't been to church much—never felt at home in one."

"But why do you believe?"

She shrugged. "I just do. It seems natural. I figure somebody wiser than me had to create everything. It had to start somewhere."

"Yes, the First Cause argument. But who made God?"

"Nobody. He was always there."

He nodded and thought and turned a few pages of his manuscript. "Maybe it's that simple. I'm a scientist and historian. I've studied religions—the most primitive to the most modern—all of my adult life. I've proceeded on the premise that religion is entirely the invention of man—that the ritual and magic of religion are designed to influence imagined deities, and that fear of the unknown--of nature, of death and whatever else--causes men to conjure up divine protectors. I believe religious and political leaders have always used those fears as a means of social control. I believe, even though life is apparently purposeless and the universe chaotic, humans can't live without a sense of intentionality, so they invent a purpose, surround it with ritual, and call it religion. Fear is the basis of it, and fear, of course, is the source of a great deal of cruelty. Religion and cruelty have always gone hand in hand."

Abby crossed and uncrossed her legs. "That's pretty depressing. What about all the good things about religion--like the Salvation Army? They help poor people all the time. I know—I've been one of them."

"I agree. I know it's true. There's good in the world that isn't the least bit logical or self-seeking. That's why I'm questioning my foundations. It seems I'm going through some sort of life adjustment that I don't yet understand."

"Well, as far as Shelly and I are concerned, you're a one man Salvation Army."

He laughed sharply. "Hardly." He took a moment to gather his thoughts. "I think having children in the house is part of it. The rooms feel like they're waking up, getting younger. Do you feel it? It's something I'm trying to grasp but it keeps eluding me. I still don't sleep well at night, but I'm actually hopeful when I get up in the morning. What do you make of it?"

"I'd say you've been lonely, and now you have people around."

He laughed with a kind of glee she'd never heard from him before. "You have a way of keeping things basic, Abby O'Shea."

"You think too much, Da. It's not that complicated."

He laughed even harder, placed his cold hand on top of hers. "Let's drink to that. I have a good French brandy. Yes...yes, indeed. I think too much!"

Late that night, as she lay fitfully sleeping, unsettled by too much alcohol, she heard Da get up and go into the master bathroom at the far end of the hall. Jack was curled in a tight bundle, breathing softly. A cold November wind, the first to feel wintry, rattled a window she had on her list to fix. A few moments before, Shelly's baby had fussed far away on the first floor--then she'd gone quiet again. Da's sounds were the ones she was most attuned to. He read until late each night, coughing sporadically. He sometimes put on a classical radio station and listened at very low volume. She found it pleasant enough.

His bladder usually got him up around three. It was only 2:30--no doubt the brandy's doing.

She heard the toilet flush, the splash of a faucet. The bathroom door creaked open, and he returned to his room. The whining sound of the wind chilled her. She needed another blanket but lacked the ambition to get up to find it. She wondered why his hands were so cold. Maybe it was a side effect of yellow fever. How had he managed so long alone at night in a huge, empty house without even the comfort of prayer?

She thought about how much his rigid routines had aggravated her until she'd begun to realize they were his way of keeping hopelessness at bay. Lately, the sharp edges of his rigidity had begun to soften. Somehow, in unlikely ways, they were making a difference in each other.

The hardwood floor was cold on her bare feet. Floating like a ghost in her white flannel nightgown, she entered the dark chill of his room and padded to the large four-poster bed. He lay on his back on the right side of it, his eyes open.

"Abby?" he asked in a half whisper.

She slid under a thick down comforter on the left side. She touched his right arm and pressed close against his side.

His body was warm, and in the dark, it felt ageless, a man's body. "It's Abishag," she said.

His arm encircled her shoulders and drew her close. "No, it's not," he said. He wore what felt like boxer shorts and a tee shirt. Wool socks covered his feet. She could feel the cold beneath the socks. His hands were chilly, but warming on her nightgown. His breath smelled of brandy and toothpaste. He touched her gently, not at all sexually. "It's Abby O'Shea," he said and tucked her head into the hollow of his neck.

Neither of them woke until late. Light poured in through the windows, and Jack stood beside the bed, tugging at her hand. She sat up with a start. Da opened his eyes, momentarily confused.

"Mama," Jack asked, "Why are you sleeping with Da?"

"He was cold," she said. "I needed to keep him warm."

"Okay," Jack said, understanding. "Can I come in?"

She slid away from Da's arm to make room. Jack climbed up and nestled between them.

" Nice?" Da asked with a smile.

"Yes, very nice," Jack said.

SACRIFICE

Pastor Ben Brown recalled reading somewhere that Aeschylus, the Greek dramatist, had died when an eagle dropped a turtle on his head. The eagle had mistaken his bald skull for a rock. Trudy's death, to his thinking, was no less bizarre. In his eight years of dealing with death and dying, presiding at perhaps three dozen funerals, Pastor Ben had never encountered anything like it. He rose from his desk and his laptop notes for her eulogy, puzzled as to the spiritual light in which one might bathe such an event.

Trudy, whose full name was Gertrude Odriana Ten Hoopen, seemed as awkward as her cumbersome Dutch name. Yet over his eight years of serving as senior pastor at First Reformed, he'd seen unexpected glimmers of grace in this quiet woman who came for Sunday services and nothing else. She'd intrigued him. She was a mystery he'd never entirely fathomed—one who had reason to be needy and complaining but wasn't, unlike the woman waiting outside his office door.

Maybelle Richter had thin hair dyed inky black; she was edging 70 and had phoned him at least three times every day since he'd taken the job as senior pastor. Thanks to Caller ID, he answered few of her calls and returned no more than one a day. The look of suffering in her eyes—a pathetic puppy expression she had developed to perfection—warned him she needed to tell the story of some new ailment…twenty minutes of his time at least.

"Hello, Maybelle," he said. "Good to see you." He knew better than to ask her how she was.

"Hello, pastor. Is your throat feeling better?" It was an old trick he was too smart to fall for. If he told her he was still a bit under the weather, she would use it as a platform from which to launch her litany of bowel obstructions, bladder infections, and hiatal hernias—in more detail than anyone, even a pastor who was paid to listen, needed to know.

"I'm sorry, Maybelle. Love to stand and talk, but I'm due at the Ten Hoopen house in fifteen minutes."

Her look was slightly stricken...she was a bundle of endless needs. "Oh…of course. It's just a tragedy…a tragedy. Did you know my Russell was Trudy Ten Hoopen's boyfriend years ago…at least until he met me?" He caught a touch of coyness in the curve of her lips.

Russell was Maybelle's long-suffering husband who took out his hearing aids whenever he was home alone with her.

"Yes, I've heard that story. We'll talk soon. I have to run."

And he burst through the back door of the church where his battered Dodge Caravan awaited his escape. Before seminary, before he had felt any sort of call to this life, one of his college teachers (his Bible as Literature prof) had suggested Ben consider the ministry. Surprised, Ben had laughed and told him that any church of his would be called the Church of the Healthy and Wealthy. If a member got sick or had other needs, he was out. If family income fell below a certain level, excommunication followed. The prof had taken it with good humor. At times, though, Ben wondered if the joke hadn't touched some truth. How often had Jesus tried to escape the relentless crowds needing his ear, his words, his healing touch, his compassionate presence? Even the Son of God grew weary of it.

The Ten Hoopen house was in the inner city, an area of large, once fashionable homes that were now mostly ramshackle apartment buildings. Adrian Ten Hoopen had been long-time pastor of a formerly Dutch-speaking Netherlands Reformed Church that stood two blocks from the house. The building was empty and deteriorating. When the church had changed pastors 27 years ago (Adrian had retired at last) and moved to a suburb, the old structure became a Pentecostal Church with a largely black membership, then a food pantry, and now it served as an illegal shelter for vagrants and neighborhood drug dealers.

Trudy had lost both her parents—new Dutch immigrants—in an accident involving a faulty space heater. Adrian and his wife had taken in the infant survivor and later adopted her. When Trudy was ten (the youngest Ten Hoopen child), her adoptive mother died giving birth to a stillborn son. As soon as they were able, a brother and two sisters spirited away, leaving Trudy, just out of high school, to care for her demanding father. She continued that service into his retirement and protracted old age, even after his disabling stroke at 89. All of the siblings by then had moved out of state. The focus of her life slowly narrowed to his 24-hour care. She quit her job doing housekeeping for a downtown hotel. Ladies from the church managed her shopping. One of them watched him an hour and a half a week so she could attend First Reformed, a moderate RCA congregation that ordained female elders--her single rebellion against a father's iron will. The stroke had affected his speech, but he had not stopped preaching to her, his rigid Calvinism undiminished by the passage of time. At long last, three years ago at the age of 94, he had died, leaving most of his estate to Trudy, less a tithe, of course. Her siblings grumbled among themselves but did not contest it. She was free at last, and Pastor Ben had gotten to know her in that short three-year space when he'd begun visiting her every week or two, concerned about her loneliness and safety. Her unsentimental tale of sacrifice had touched him deeply.

As he was pulling into the driveway of the carefully kept yet visibly declining Ten Hoopen house, the jangle of his cell phone startled him. A local police cruiser stood in the driveway just ahead of him, the May sun glaring off the rear window.

A call was unusual--he gave his cell number to as few people as possible. "This is Ben Brown," he said warily.

The shock of Shelly's voice momentarily took his breath away. Shelly was his former fiancé, telling him cheerfully that she was back in town for a few days and could he meet her for a drink tonight?

"I have a Consistory meeting tonight," he said reluctantly.

She laughed. "Of course you do."

"Sorry. But I could slip out and meet you at 9:30. Hugo's Pub all right?"

"Fine." She remained cheerful. "Is there any night you don't have a meeting?"

"A few. It's not that bad." But it was that bad. As solo pastor, he was expected at every gathering--three or four evenings a week, sometimes five if you counted socializing with church members. It was one of multiple reasons Shelly had decided she couldn't be a pastor's wife. She'd intentionally attended another church while she dated him; First Reformed people knew little about her, a help to both of them. She was bright and creative, very pretty, worked as editor for a publishing house, and had recently taken a transfer to Chicago as a way of cutting ties with him. She'd become a bright presence in his life, and his heart was barely beginning to heal. Why in the world was she here?

A young police officer he'd met on the day they'd found Trudy's body stepped through the front door and waved to him. Ben hurried her off the phone with an apology but no explanation. She said goodbye crisply.

The young officer, his face seemingly stuck in an expression of earnest authority, shook Ben's hand and led him inside and up an open stairway to the second floor library where a pear-shaped man in a wrinkled white shirt and red tie balanced on a ten foot stepladder, examining something near the ceiling. A massive bookcase lay sprawled flat, with several hundred heavy volumes and notebooks scattered through the room, some tossed open with pages spread like fans.

"Pastor Brown, this is Lieutenant Evans, one of our detectives."

Evans nodded from atop the ladder and climbed down. He shook Ben's hand. "You're the one who found her?"

"No, that was Molly DeWitt. She'd come over to drive Trudy to church. Called me in a panic. I was the second to arrive."

"And she was dead when you found her?"

"Yes. Molly and I confirmed it before the ambulance arrived. It wasn't hard to tell she'd been dead a few days. I managed to lift up the bookcase just enough for Molly to pull her partway out. Molly's a nurse, thank God. I was very weak in the knees."

"Understandable. I've never seen anyone crushed by a ton of books before."

"Either had I."

Evans went to a chair, lifted his jacket, and put it on. "I've ruled out foul play, though in this neighborhood you never know. As I see it, she was on the bookcase ladder, dusting books on the top shelf, lost her footing somehow...then made a grab for the top of the case and tore the stabilizing bracket out of the wall. The whole shebang came down on her. A real mess."

"Yes...it is. May I start cleaning things up, Lieutenant? The books are quite valuable."

He shrugged. "I'm done here. I think it's all right. Come on, Duffy. Let's help him get the bookcase upright again."

This was a library piece--ten feet tall, five wide and solid mahogany. It took the three of them all they had to get it back in place. Catching his breath, Ben thanked the officers and saw them out. As he began lifting books, he noticed a potted azalea exploding in pink flowers on a table in a south window. He had given Trudy that plant as a birthday gift nearly three years ago. How amazingly she had nurtured it! Though he'd visited her occasionally before the birthday, their friendship had clearly begun with this gift. He knew she kept a small garden in back of the house. She enjoyed caring for flowers.

He remembered that evening's conversation very well. He hoped to hear the story she'd carefully avoided up to then, so he took a direct approach--asked about her father and their life together. Nervous, looking cornered, she began by saying what a strong man of God he was—a church leader respected by all—and a man unafraid of rebuking sin, as so many pastors are today.

"He put the fear of God in us," she said.

"You, too?"

"Oh, yes, I needed it. I was a lost sheep. They took me in when my parents died. It was more than I deserved...I mean, adopting me. Then one day she died and father was left with his own three children and the extra burden of me." She grew more agitated. "You need to understand that when my father spoke, it was like God himself. Father and God were close—father said they talked together."

"Honestly?"

"That's what he told me."

"Does God talk to you?"

"Why would He talk to me?"

"Why wouldn't He? You're just the kind of person He wants in His world."

"That's not so. I'm a lost sheep." She sat silent, staring at her hands. By degrees, though, some sort of knot seemed to loosen a little in her. She looked up, a faint gleam in her eyes. "I heard about First Reformed Church from a friend at the hotel where I worked. She said people were very welcoming, especially you. To be honest, I went because my father objected, and he was too old and weak to stop me." A small smile appeared on her lips, the first Ben ever recalled seeing. "It was *not* because of Russell Richter, who used to be interested in me. The silly woman he married spread rumors about me wanting him back." She laughed suddenly…a small miracle. "The truth is, for the first time in my life I was doing something against my father's will, and it made him furious. Then one Sunday, in the middle of an awful tantrum, he had his stroke." She inhaled deeply as if needing oxygen. The energy drained from her voice. "I'm to blame for it."

"You aren't to blame at all!" he half shouted.

Startled, she glanced at him, and then slumped in her chair. The gleam drained from her eyes. Having pushed her harder than he meant to, he jumped up, grasping her hand and pressing it with both of his. "Forgive me. I didn't mean to upset you," he said. "I've asked too many questions. I've stayed too long. Happy birthday, my dear Trudy. God bless you." Wishing to say more but not knowing what, he hesitantly left, more mystified by this peculiar woman than ever.

The pulsating boom of rap music from a passing car jarred Ben back to the task at hand. He glanced down at the books he held, wondering at the logic of Adrian Ten Hoopen's organizing. Dozens of loose leaf notebooks, still in a semblance of order and containing, he discovered, years and years of Ten Hoopen sermons (the oldest, most faded ones in Dutch), had no doubt fallen from the bottom shelf. From the other end of the room he gathered a dozen heavy Bibles and commentaries along with a thick volume of Calvin's *Institutes of the Christian Religion* in German. These had fallen from high up, a place he would reach only when the case was firmly secured. Atop the *Institutes* he placed Jonathan Edwards' *The Nature of True Virtue*, then *The Reformed Confessions of Faith, The Genevan Psalter,*

Augustine's *The City of God,* Aquinas's *Summa Theologic,* and on and on. Trudy, Ben thought with faint irony, was hardly the first to be crushed under the weight of such stuff. He found random stains but no trace of blood anywhere on the hardwood floor.

Ben excused himself before the end of the Consistory meeting and was settled into a secluded booth at Hugo's Pub by 9:15. He had a glass of white wine waiting for Shelly. She arrived promptly at 9:30, spotted him and came over smiling. She seemed genuinely pleased to see him. He noticed that her hair was shorter—he liked the cut. In a wispy spring dress and a pink scarf tied loosely at the neck, she looked ten years younger than he, though in truth only five years separated them. He'd often wondered what someone so vivacious saw in him.

"Mine?" She indicated the wine. "Pinot Grigio?"

"Of course."

"I'm impressed. Such a gentleman." She settled into the booth, lifting the glass in a toast, to which he raised his beer glass. "To old friends," she said.

At his urging, she caught him up on her new life in Chicago, summing it up with precisely the right amount of detail (one of the qualities he admired most in her), then turning the conversation to his agenda. Good conversation required a skillful give and take, and Shelly was both skillful and caring. Ben spent so much of every day listening that it was a great blessing to find an interested listener. Skipping the usual church news, he told a brief version of Trudy's story…of her strange life and even stranger death; Shelly listened with wide-eyed attention.

At one point she interrupted. "This is a story you should write, Ben. It's fascinating. The poor woman's life was pure sacrifice."

"Yes…I agree. But it was also *uncomplaining* sacrifice. I find something… heroic about it."

"Maybe. I find it heartbreaking." She laid one hand on his out of habit, but after a moment moved it away. "How is your writing coming?"

"My writing?" He smiled. "I write sermons."

She laughed. "Too bad. I know you have plans for other things."

"I'll get to them some day soon."

"Right."

"Honestly, I will. There's been some talk about an associate pastor to free me up a little."

"Just what you need--another staff member."

They both went silent. He took a long swallow of beer, glanced around the room, finally coming back to her eyes. "I'm curious…why are you here, Shelly? I thought things were over and done."

She looked down at her hands. "I'm here because I have something to tell you that I couldn't do by phone."

His mouth went dry. She seemed to catch an instant of something like alarm in his eyes.

"I'm not pregnant," she laughed.

He felt a bit childish. "I almost wish you were."

She stared at him. "What are you saying?"

Shaking his head, he muttered. "I'm not really sure. What do you need to tell me?"

She lifted her glass and finished the wine in a gulp. "I've met someone else."

The momentary silence was heavy. "Not another pastor, I hope."

"No. Not another pastor. He's a normal human being."

They both laughed, but it didn't last.

"Congratulations," he said.

"I'd hoped you'd come up with something more than that…something forceful...or at least interesting."

"Oh? Like what?"

She shrugged. "Like, 'Shelly, I need you more than I realized…'"

"Yes?"

"Or…maybe something like…'Shelly, I know we can't live our lives in a glass house and be at the beck and call of 200 bosses. I want to serve God but not in a job that takes every minute of my day and night. And I certainly won't ask you to become the dutiful dimwit they expect a pastor's wife to be. I love you too much for that.'"

He sat silent, gripping his beer glass, and then sighed and said "Haven't we been through all of this before? A dutiful dimwit? Good grief, Shelly, it's not like that. You can be whatever you want to be."

"No, I can't, Ben." She took a deep breath. "I should never have dredged up this stuff."

"Why did you?"

With feigned lightness, she said "Thought I'd give it one more shot."

"But why?"

They sat silent. She looked down at her hands, and tears popped from her eyes. "My God, you're such a dope. He's a college teacher, Ben. He writes textbooks and takes all his summers off. He has just loads and loads of time for me. Don't you get it?"

"Do you love him?"

"He's very nice. Very smart." She took a deep, trembling breath. "But the hell of it is, he isn't you." She buried her face in her hands and wept quietly. He looked at the top of her head, the auburn color of her hair, aching to reach out and touch the velvet of it, to comfort and hold her again. He yearned so deeply for the physical joy of her, joy they'd somehow resisted until after their engagement, that he sometimes feared his desire for her was clouding his love of God. And now, just when he'd begun to make headway praying away the pain, it was back with a vengeance.

"The church is full of good people, not just difficult ones," he told her.

"Yes--there are good people who deserve a pastor to walk alongside them. But you spend most of your time with the others—the squeaky wheels—enabling the hopelessly needy ones. What a waste of your time and talent."

"It's not that bad."

"It isn't? How many times has Maybelle called today? How many times did she call while we were having dinner or making love? She owns you, Ben, and so do a dozen others like her. You're their personal compassion slave." She got to her feet and tightened the scarf encircling her neck. "This was a mistake. I don't know what I was thinking. You'll go on doing what you have to do. You're a caring and sensitive man, Ben, and a good pastor, too. I shouldn't try to change you. It was a mistake to come." A silken wisp of her skirt brushed his arm as she went out.

Two of the three Ten Hoopen siblings had flown in for the funeral. A tall awkward brother with a cane and a seriously overweight sister, both (Ben estimated) in their early 70's, listened as he told the story of his frequent meetings with Trudy, their growing friendship, and then her shocking death. The three sat at a rickety formica and stainless steel table in the kitchen of the Ten Hoopen house. Ben asked them for memories of Trudy that he might use in his eulogy.

The brother spoke up. "She got the short end of the stick—that's what I remember. I feel like we all ditched her. The old man chased away the only suitor she ever had."

The sister bristled at this. "Our father provided her a home for her whole life. She appreciated it. Don't use what he says, Pastor Brown. He and father always had problems."

"That's why I joined the Navy and got out when I could. Old Trudy got stuck here."

"Honestly, Bert. She was kind and loving to father all those years. She chose her path. She was adopted and very grateful. Taking care of him gave her life purpose. We all appreciate the sacrifice, but she did it willingly because she loved him."

"Thanks for that, Bess," Ben said to her. "Now are there any specific stories about her you'd like me to tell?"

Further conversation made clear they didn't know much of anything about their youngest sister. They offered a few more inaccurate generalities. Once he'd left them, Ben could only conclude he knew Trudy far better than they. The thought saddened him.

A day before the funeral, Jacob Vanderlaan caught Ben in the church parking lot. Jacob wrapped a heavy arm around Ben's shoulders and squeezed. He was huge and bearded, a grizzly bear of a man for whom Ben felt real affection. Jacob was a lawyer always ready to help, a true friend, a constant source of support and quiet generosity. Ben wished there were twenty more of him in the church.

"Hey, pastor—good news. The Ten Hoopen brother and sister found three key rings in Trudy's kitchen drawers. They're hoping one of the keys fits a lock box somewhere. They stopped by church and asked for help finding the will. No telling what if anything Trudy arranged, but First Reformed might have something to gain if she did."

"Wow…a will…of course. I'm glad you're around, Jacob. It never occurred to me."

"Leave it to a lawyer. We'll see to the paperwork, you see to the souls."

"More money in the paperwork, I'm sure."

Jacob barked a hearty laugh, got into his pickup truck, and roared off.

Ben went into his office and opened his laptop to incorporate into the eulogy whatever small bits of the siblings' comments might shed some honest light on Trudy. He knew he was duty bound to stick to the sister's message, though he intended to add some telling concrete detail where he could. But her real story? He shook his head in discontent.

Before he faced the task, he checked his emails and found 38 messages. Shelly's words drifted through his mind, and a stone settled in the pit of his stomach.

Jacob was at the door of Ben's small condo early the morning of the funeral. Ben heard his rapid knocking and fought off irritation. He was still struggling over the notes about Trudy. It was 8 AM. The funeral was scheduled for 11.

"Let me in, Ben. It's important."

Ben rose and opened the door. "What's going on? I have a million things to do."

"I know that. Pour me a cup of coffee. There's something you need to see. It'll take ten minutes."

Jacob flopped down at the counter, hefted a briefcase onto it and unzipped it. Ben set a coffee in front of him as Jacob handed him a single sheet of paper. "Read it. Blow your mind."

Ben warily glanced at the paper. "'Last Will and Testament of Gertrude Odriana Ten Hoopen…'" he read.

"Skip to the last paragraph."

Ben followed his direction. "'I, being of sound mind and body, leave my entire estate consisting of property, bank accounts and investments, to Pastor Benjamin Brown, First Reformed Church of Grand Rapids, Michigan.'" He silently skimmed the rest of it. "This is it? What about the siblings? The church?"

"Nothing. You're the sole beneficiary."

"Good Lord. That's ridiculous. What am I going to do with a huge old house?"

"Hold on. More surprises to come. Bank accounts and investments amount to almost…would you believe $300,000? Looks like they never spent a penny they didn't need to. You're not a poor man any more, my friend."

Ben slumped into a chair. "I'm stunned—I feel like I've been whacked on the head. Is this one of your jokes?"

"I never joke about wills."

"But it isn't right. The siblings and church should be--"

"--but they aren't. They just don't know it yet. The siblings will likely toss a fit. The church? I can't really predict that one. The will is legitimate, by the way—drafted by a local lawyer, some young guy, just three months ago.

It's the only one Trudy ever made. Oh, and one other thing--stop by my office some time this week. Your benefactor left a personal sealed envelope for you and only you. Maybe it'll clarify things."

"This is absolutely bizarre, Jacob."

"Unusual, for sure. Let me get my thinking together. We'll talk soon, if you don't mind me running interference for you."

"Be my guest. I'd appreciate it."

Trudy lay in a closed casket at the front of the sanctuary. Neither Bert nor Bess, the siblings, offered to participate in the service, even to read Scripture passages, nor did any one of the two dozen mourners volunteer to tell personal stories about her. Perhaps no one was able to. Ben handled everything but the organ music. In his short eulogy, he repeated essentially what Bess had said, added his own stories about the azalea she had nurtured, the selflessness of her life, the quiet sacrifice of her days. The true story, he suspected, was too bleak to tell in church. He was acutely aware of how little truth there was in his words. The truth would no doubt die with her. How sanitized and inadequate his message had turned out. Silently, he asked forgiveness of Trudy.

Jacob's office was in the penthouse of a high-rise building. The furnishings shone with chrome and brass and crystal, gleamed with leather couches and massive meeting tables. All of it looked out over a wide river and the city of Grand Rapids. An attractive secretary in a business suit led Ben in to see Jacob, who rose from his swivel chair to greet him.

"I can't get over how this office doesn't fit you, Jacob—you're like a lumberjack in a five star hotel."

"It's a fact…I'm incongruous."

"And thank God for it." He laughed lightly. "Well, here I am. What's up?"

"Here's your secret message from Gertrude Odriana Ten Hoopen." Jacob tossed him a large manila envelope, which Ben caught with two hands. It was sealed and heavily taped. He recognized Trudy's careful handwriting: "PERSONAL! To be opened by Pastor Benjamin Brown." He could not begin to guess what it contained.

Jacob sat back down and pressed his index fingers to his mouth. "Ben--did you tell Bert and Bess—the siblings—about how often you went to see Trudy?"

"Of course."

"Well, they're running with that--talking seriously about contesting the will. They feel you may have intentionally ingratiated yourself to a vulnerable person of unsound mind for personal gain."

Ben flushed with sudden embarrassment and anger. "Trudy was of no more unsound mind than I am. *Personal gain*? This is absurd, Jacob!"

"The Consistory knows about the will. The news of your windfall has not, I'm afraid, inspired many warm feelings toward you."

"I had nothing to do with it."

"I know, I know…but you need to understand what you're dealing with. There seems to be resentment from some quarters. Even some agreement with the siblings."

"Good Lord. That makes me sick to my stomach."

"I understand. I feel the same way."

"What do I do?"

Jacob drew in a deep breath and exhaled heavily. "Here's my advice as a friend. Don't take the inheritance. Give it all to the church. That will pretty much pull the plug on the sibling's case—lay the groundwork for an easy settlement--and save you a ton of grief."

Ben put both hands on top of his head and pressed down hard. "This is amazing. All I did was befriend a lonely woman. Let me think about what the hell is going on and get back to you. I'm too furious and too confused right now."

"Whatever you do, Ben, do it quickly, okay?"

Ben shook his head as if trying to clear it, stood shakily, and wandered out.

Not until late that night as he sat in bed did he open the manila envelope. He needed scissors to get through the tape. Inside, he found a smaller envelope with his name on it. He opened it with care, using one blade of the scissors like a letter knife. He found a folded, handwritten paper, which he spread out with reverence and dread:

My friend,

Thank you for your kindness to me. If you are reading this letter, it will be because I have passed on. I have done what I have done with my last will and testament because of your kindness.

My life was not what I would have chosen, but that is true for many others, too. Long ago a young man showed interest in me, but my father did not allow it. My father told me that I was a special gift of God to him—a helpmeet to replace his wife who died. He made me swear never to tell anyone about what he did to me. He said God understood everything, but others would not. I was afraid, so I kept the secret, but now I tell you because you are my friend and perhaps will believe me. I am certain no one else would. We all have our crosses to bear.

Thank you again for your kindness. Several ladies at your church have been good to me. But every Sunday I see people who expect so much of you. My gift to you could be your deliverance, if you should ever need it.

God has given you a caring heart, but you must not sacrifice everything as I did.

With blessings and love,
Trudy

He read the letter a dozen times before he finally folded it and turned off the light. He closed his eyes, hoping for sleep, but could not rid his mind of the dark and terrible truth.

Ben's cell phone rang just as he entered the expressway bound for Chicago. He was lost in thought about the church—about how sometimes through him the Spirit had touched lives so deeply…and touched his own as well.

The phone rang on. Glancing down at the number of the caller, he saw with dismay that Maybelle Richter had somehow located his cell number. With a mild curse, he punched his phone to shut it off. He reached and rebalanced the pink azalea on the passenger floor beside him. A faint grin broke through his scowl, and he laughed quietly at the thought that the call might actually be a sign from God.

An hour earlier he had told Shelly simply that he needed to talk, that things had changed. She was hesitant but curious enough to say yes. There were many ways, he'd already decided, of serving God. As far as he was concerned, the church could have the Ten Hoopen estate, or share it with the undeserving siblings--except for a small tithe, a deliverance he would be unbending about.

ONE DEATH

Harry Merrill lifted the thick edition of the *Toronto Star* from his front porch and looked up with gloomy relief as the bulldozer across the way finally ceased its frantic roar and methodical destruction. He had watched it that morning gouging away the remains of a huge, wooded vacant lot serving as makeshift soccer field and play space for the neighborhood. A new medical building with massive asphalt parking lot would replace it.

A box at the top margin of the *Star* said the weather would continue in the mid 90s through tomorrow. Sighing, looking to a sky heavy with a week-long, unmoving pall of fumes, Harry went to his leather chair in the living room, collapsed into it, and adjusted a small fan to blow directly on his face. The air conditioner had died the previous weekend, and no one could get out to repair it for three more days--sparing Harry the guilt of running it through these ever-more-frequent heat waves.

Less than ten years ago they'd bought this place and already the city had swallowed them up. A modest bungalow in a woodsy suburb, the home they'd sunk every cent into was now overshadowed by upscale high-rise apartment buildings blocking the sunset and half the sky. In the bowels of each he could imagine machinery sucking up the earth's resources, heating and cooling human bodies—pampered, self absorbed creatures expecting more than the earth could safely provide. He liked to imagine he was not one of them, but the thought, he knew, was delusional.

"I'm dying of the heat!" he wailed, snapping the paper open.

"What, Dad?" His eight-year-old son Chris hopped into the room on one foot, dragging his stuffed kangaroo. He wore only a thin pair of white cotton shorts. His fragile shoulders and broad, freckled face were crisp with sunburn.

"I said it's hot."

"It is, kind of."

"Did you see the field?"

The boy nodded, unperturbed. "It's going to be a parking lot, so we'll have a place to ride bikes."

"Oh, trust me, you'll miss the field. We need trees and grass—not more asphalt." He pulled the sports section before he dared navigate the tsunami of the front page. He heard his wife come up from the basement and begin putting together something for dinner. The rattling of dishes and pans irritated him no end, but instead of speaking to his wife, he yelled at his son to stop his hopping about.

"Harry," she called from the kitchen. "Did you hear about Haiti? It's simply horrible."

"I'm getting to it," he barked, thinking: if they'd only leave me alone for a minute before clobbering me with the daily calamity of human life! Against his better judgment, he took up the front page and read the headline. He was staggered. "My God…"

His wife's auburn head popped through the doorway. She was chewing a celery stalk. "Isn't it horrible, Harry? What sort of earthquake could kill a hundred thousand people?"

"Very large," he mumbled, hoping she would vanish into the kitchen again.

"What's wrong with you?"

"I'm sorry. It's the heat. What's for supper?"

"Cold cuts and fruit. I'm not up to cooking."

"Good."

She waited a moment, saw he had said all he wished to, and returned to her preparations.

He pondered the catastrophe. So it was a hundred thousand, and probably twice that number once final counts came in and disease had run its course. Utterly staggering. Hideous. And he sat staring at a bloody splash of fly on the wall.

But after the initial shock of the story, a curious kind of numbness overtook him and the edge went off his irritable mood. He read about 85 civilians killed by a suicide bomber in Baghdad, and a Detroit gangland slaying that claimed eight narcotics pushers and one innocent bystander. Another American high school had been shot up, 21 killed. So engrossed was he that he barely noticed his son setting up dominoes in a long line on the floor beside him.

"How many people is a hundred thousand, Dad?"

"What, Chris? How many? It's a great many."

The boy tipped the last domino, bringing the others down in a clap. "They all died?" A sad, puzzled look appeared on his face.

"Yes, they did."

"Even the kids?"

"It's terrible, I know."

"Why did it happen to them?"

Ordinarily he would have put the boy off, but he was feeling, in spite of the heat, mildly philosophical. "I don't know, Chris. No one can say. Maybe it's one of God's ways of solving earth's problems. There are so many people now…too many. It's getting hard to find room enough for them—or enough water and food."

Chris grew quiet. Where he sat, the late afternoon sunlight revealed the soft down on one cheek and along his neck. For an instant Harry thought of him as grown and wondered what sort of world, if any, awaited him. But the face quickly became young again, drawn now into a worried, oblique squint.

"Dad, would God do that to us?"

"Of course not. You don't have to worry about us. We don't have earthquakes here."

But the look remained. The answer was feeble, and he knew the boy knew it. Harry returned to his newspaper. He tried the business section, relieved to find dull, neutral reading…a slight uptick in the stock market, refugees starting a cell phone repair business. Hearing Chris fiddling with the piano keys, making small, dissonant chords as he did so often in his distant moods, Harry said, "Son, stop a minute, would you? I'm trying to read the paper."

Chris swung abruptly around on the piano bench. His eyes were wild, glimmering, unhappy. Sunlight poured through windows, streaking his face, turning it stark and pale.

"Jerome's mother told him you want to kill babies."

"WHAT?"

"Dad, I'm just telling you." Tears popped into his eyes, filling the corners.

"That stupid, fanatical woman. I would never want to kill babies. My God, Edie, did you hear that?" But his wife was out of earshot. "Son, I'm part of a group called Canadians for Choice. We believe that ladies who don't want to have babies should have a choice about it. That's all! We're trying to do some good."

Chris nodded and rubbed his eyes.

"I'll have a talk with Jerome's mother. You know your father would never want babies killed. Good Lord."

"I know."

"Hey, come on, cheer up. Let's go for a walk—see what progress the human race has made today." Harry rose from the chair, trying to contain his outrage for the sake of his son. "Edie!" he shouted. "Chris and I are going out. Be back in half an hour."

Above the clash of silverware he heard, "Good. Come back in a better mood. I'll pour some wine."

The sun still pounded down, in spite of the haze and the hour. Harry took his son's hand, and the two crossed the street. The soccer field was now gone, replaced by a barren, gouged out expanse of sand and gravel. A small marshland at the end of the field was being filled with whatever the bulldozers scraped away. Two blocks down, they passed the new Heath Funeral Home, resplendent in red brick and white canopies. In the front yard on top of a post perched a large copper digital clock. It read six twenty. Odd that Heath would place a clock right out in front for everyone to see. Was the idea to remind us of time running out…as if we needed to be reminded?

The boy suddenly pulled at Harry's hand and pointed to the nearest of the new high rise apartment buildings. "Look, Dad. Someone threw a blanket off a balcony."

"Where?"

"Partway up that building."

"Are you sure it was a blanket?"

"See?"

A number of people, mostly women, had gathered on the lower balconies. A man in an undershirt leapt a privet hedge and ran to a small white heap in the grass.

"Lord, Chris. I think someone's fallen."

Harry crossed a street and began to run; the boy kept pace at his side. Three Italian-looking matrons had gathered about the crumpled, bleeding body of a young woman. Harry approached her warily, a strange tingle in the back of his head as when a limb has gone to sleep. Her eyes were large, open, her face extremely plain. Acne had scarred it badly, had made it hard and discolored even about her ears and throat. Her neck was turned at an odd angle, as if broken, and a thin curve of blood flowed from the corner of her mouth. One thin white leg was uncovered to the thigh.

"Where is the man?" He choked on his words.

"What man?" A stout, large-breasted woman spoke to him.

"In the undershirt."

"Mr. Simon? He went for his cell phone to call the cops."

"Is she—"

"I think she's dead. She fell seven floors. Look at those eyes. She's on drugs for sure, Rose."

Rose, a dark, withered woman who despite the heat was shawled in wool, nodded to her but said nothing.

Harry gave them a fierce look. "For God's sake, get something to cover her with."

"I'll get something," the stout woman said, "but it won't do her no good now."

Harry bent to the pale, homely face. On his ear he felt a faint chill of breath. She blinked once and then blinked again. "She's alive! Where in hell are the police? We've got to get some help."

He looked up. A crowd was beginning to gather. Then he noticed Chris watching in stunned silence, eyes large, freckles bold against his pallid skin.

"Chris! Go home right now! Go away! I mean it!"

Chris backed up a few steps, bumping a fat, bearded man whose fingers played about his moustache. Harry again bent to her and opened her mouth, horrified at disturbing the grotesque angle of her neck. Was artificial respiration the proper procedure? Why didn't one of these idiots step forward and help him? He glanced around the crowd, grown large now, silent and helpless. With his lips he covered the hard, bleeding mouth, the acne scars rough upon his inner lip, the blood smell vaguely sweet. He blew breath into her, one hand pinching off her nostrils, the other holding up her chin. Within him, voices shouted, demanded that she sit up and breathe.

And he whispered. "Live. Please, girl. You're a lovely girl. Now you've got to live."

And as if in response to his plea, her breathing grew suddenly stronger.

In the crowd someone shouted, "She's okay!" and a collective sigh went round.

But the spurt of life was momentary. Panicked, Harry again lowered his face. For an instant her lips trembled. A brief gasp leapt from her mouth to his and was caught and muffled there; he tasted it, smelled it sweet and faint like cut grass. He lifted his head, reached and touched her cheek; it was cool, plastic. "No," he mumbled. "Now it's gone."

And a curious thought occurred to him: it was the one death, the only death, he had ever witnessed.

His head was a millstone; his neck ached to lift it. He remained kneeling beside her until a rescue squad arrived with equipment bags and a gurney. He stood and watched them bundle her body, cover even her pale, pocked face and finally haul her away, sirens screaming.

He turned and found Chris still standing there--in the midst of someone's flowerbed near the privet hedge. Ruffled white and pink petunias covered his naked feet. The color had not returned to his face; a shock of yellow hair hung over one eye. Harry shook his head, sighed deeply, and held out his hand for his son to take.

They walked toward home in silence. The boy's hand was hot, pressed in his. There was dirt under the small, transparent shells of fingernails. Harry looked; the boy had begun crying softly. He tightened his grip.

"I'm sorry, Chris. I wanted her to live."

In a half strangled voice the boy said, "I know, Dad," then swung about and gripped Harry's legs, great convulsive sobs bursting from him.

Harry cried out, lifting the boy, grasping him fiercely into his neck as much to smother his own erupting emotions as to quell his son's. And Harry held the boy tightly until he grew quiet. It was true: he had wanted her to live…more than anything he ever remembered wanting in his life.

COCKTAIL PIANO PLAYER

A noisy crowd of alumni blew in late from the football game, and the piano player did what he knew they would expect—played "The Victors" and was obliged to repeat it twice before Charles, the bartender, called for the last round. A broad, basset-faced woman, her chains and jewels clanking on his ebony Yamaha, asked him to play "Alley Cat."

"I played it twenty minutes ago, honey," he said with a twist of smile.

"Well, I like it," she said, and so once more, once more, he forced his tense white hands to produce the inane music that was part of his business. The woman, staring glassily as if into a jukebox, nodded at the tune, slipped a dollar bill into his brandy glass of tips, and turned to chatter with her companion.

At home, the piano player dismissed his mother's nurse for the night. He knew he would not sleep, though his body prickled with exhaustion. Spread across the Steinway baby grand—he'd had it lifted into the large loft apartment by crane—was music he'd composed the day before. He'd played with the idea of a jazz concerto for a dozen years, but it wasn't until Cherry, his long-term girlfriend, moved out that he'd actually begun.

The relationship had been strained by a promise he'd made to his mother: she'd never, under any circumstances, have to live in a nursing home. He knew the decision to move a sick woman into his place was presuming too much, but Cherry's sudden, almost cheerful departure had left him feeling forsaken. With all her things gone, the living room resembled an empty stage, for there was nothing in it but the piano and bench, a few stiff chairs, and a lamp. Cherry had been good for him, a good distraction, but if he was honest, she had begun to seem a bit like the music he played at the cocktail lounge. After a few days, her absence was no longer as painful. He knew he was intended for better things.

"Dear God," he'd muttered, "spare me any new loves."

Yet after some weeks without her, he found himself wishing for another presence besides his mother to occupy his time. The barely begun composition sought him out like an accusing finger. Cherry, at least, had given him reason and excuse to go on devoting his time to making a living as a cocktail piano player.

From the bedroom came the sound of his mother's bell, a weak, tinkling little child's bell he'd tied with a ribbon to the side of her bed so she could be heard. He went to her, not really wanting to but knowing it was the most positive thing he had done in years. For a time before she had arrived from the hospital, he'd found himself disabled by an odd inertia—uncertain of his talent, incapable of reaching out beyond the feeble and unappreciated service he rendered his cocktail lounge audience. Now at least he was doing something for his mother in her final days; he was involved in her dying. Distasteful as it could become, it had meaning to him.

"Tea, Carlyle. Tea, Carlyle. Tea…." Her voice was a tinny, distorted monotone, a gramophone voice running down. The stroke had taken her speech, and only a portion had been recovered. A plastic umbilical of catheter tubing linked her to a bag at the base of the bed. Her nose was red, chafed, and brittle as a saltine. A small pot of cold tea stood on her night table.

"Evening, mother," he said. "How do you feel tonight?" Without waiting for an answer, he set a wet teabag on her lips. She commenced sucking it noisily. Her lips were thin and parched, her gums toothless, too shrunken now to accommodate her dentures. The nurse had put a fresh pad under her before leaving, and placed a baby blanket along the useless arm and leg, both swollen with fluid. Though not yet 75, she had become shockingly frail, her hipbones poking up like the wings of plucked chickens. Her throat and lungs were full of fluid that gurgled like water in a drain.

"Carlyle," gripping his hand, "I dreamed I went to California on a bedpan—in a big flowered hat."

The lucidity of her speech surprised him, and something in the image struck him as dryly funny. He laughed and smoothed back her oily hair. He could smell her hair, sweet and rancid, along with camphor and her catheter bag. It was her humor that made this ordeal nearly tolerable, and for a moment he loved her as deeply as he thought he ever had—this dear woman who had lived so vitally, who had raised a large family and taught school and been more interested in life than he'd ever learned to be. She had been the first to recognize his musical gifts; it was she who had taught him notes by means of colors, before he'd ever begun to read. Even now he saw his music in colors, chords in purple tones, or bright yellows, or the rainbows of Bach.

"I hope you weren't self-conscious," he joked.

"Oh, I was. I didn't like the hat." When he laughed again, she smiled. "Dip this for me, Carlyle."

But the teabag had split in a corner, and tea leaves began clotting on her lips and gums.

"Mother, you've broken it," and he wiped out the soggy leaves with a wet washcloth.

A thin tear drooled from the corner of her eye and ran to the pillow.

"There, mother, there," he said, attempting a breezy manner. "No problem, we'll brew up another pot."

"Let me die," she mumbled. "I want to die."

"Mom, please. Don't say that. Your speaking is clear today. And we've got those toes working again, haven't we?" He looked expectantly toward the little sheeted hills that were her feet. He tried to suppress the thought that the lower half of her was already a corpse.

"Have we?" Her voice was a small rusty hinge.

"Of course! Please don't be negative." He felt a senseless rush of anger, turned and hurried off to the kitchen for more tea, understanding such feelings all too well. In her hopeless moments, he saw his utter impotence. There was nothing he could do for this woman who had done so much for him. His ineffectiveness sickened him.

She began to cough and metal balls rolled in her throat. She was drowning, and he could do nothing. He felt a need to grab hold of some antagonist and struggle, but there was nothing to grab. The night before he had dreamed of strange new music; his fingers, though, had floundered on the keys like stunned birds, unable to express it.

She would not recover, ever. She was the next thing to dead. There was nothing he could do but provide inadequate comfort and be there to see her pass.

When his mother had at last tired of the tea, he had to check her catheter, an unpleasant chore that embarrassed them both—he had not yet learned to look at her nakedness. Then he rolled her on her side for sleep and pulled the blanket up under her ears as he might for an infant. It was 4 AM before she finally slept. Her breathing was shallow and rattled ominously; he thought he'd never heard it quite so bad.

As he was getting into his pajamas, the phone rang.

"Now who in the name of goodness--" He rushed into the living room before the noise woke her. He'd left his landline phone on the piano and each ring caused an eerie humming in the strings. It would be Cherry, he was certain, probably missing him. Only Cherry would be impulsive enough to call at this hour.

"Carlyle? Is that you, you old dog?" The voice was male, faintly mechanical as if at a great distance, but assertive as a sledgehammer.

"Who is it? Keller?"

"Hey, how's everything, pal? How's Cherry?"

"Keller, do you know what time it is?"

"I'm at a tremendous party, Carlyle. I'm in Beverly Hills. You should see this house. They use it as a movie set."

"It's four in the morning, for Pete's sake." Keller was the last person on earth he wanted to hear from. During the dark ages they'd been fraternity brothers at University of Michigan. Keller had played a fair trombone but had given it up for the appliance business, which had treated him well. He was now head of national sales for a major company, though the piano player didn't remember which one. Keller was loud, aggressive, alcoholic, and generally a pain in the ass. His only endearing quality was his love of good jazz. Half a dozen times he'd paid the piano player and a combo to jam at his house for weekend guests. Carlyle had expected something bigger to come of the sessions, considering the wealth of the partiers, but nothing had developed.

Keller was a man who generally got what he wanted, regardless of the cost, regardless of the hour.

"Listen, Carlyle, you won't believe who I have here. Are you anywhere near a piano?"

"I'm sitting at one."

Keller's voice became muffled as he covered the phone to speak to someone else. "Sitting at one..." Carlyle heard him repeat. "Tone—tell him who you are—take my phone—" then noisily, "Carlyle? You still there? Here's someone to talk with you. Tone, Tony, come here. He plays the best piano you ever heard...." There were blunt rumbling sounds as if the phone were being passed from hand to hand. Keller laughed uproariously at something Carlyle couldn't hear.

"Keller, for God's sake, my mother is sick—"

There was more rumbling, and then Keller's laughter stabbed into his ear. "Well, old dog, Tony's too shy to talk. Alec—how about you? Come on, just a word. Aw, hell, Carlyle, you know who's standing here beside me? Ever heard of Alec Baldwin? How about a guy named Tony Bennett?"

"*He's* there?"

"In the flesh. And Alec Baldwin. You, know, the hilarious Donald Trump guy on tv?"

The piano player laughed now. "Keller, you're crazy. How come you're calling me? Is it really Tony Bennett?"

"Tone, say something. Sing a few notes."

"The man is skeptical, is he?" The voice was distant, but there was no mistaking it. What, he wondered, were the conditions that produced someone with Keller's mindless self-confidence? He could envision Bennett struggling to escape while Keller held him by a bicep.

"Hello there."

"Mr. Bennett?" He tried but could not keep the obsequious tone from his voice.

"Mr. Keller informs me that you play a fine piano." The cool, raspy ease of his delivery was the essence of Tony Bennett.

"Why, yes I do," he said, and then laughed too loudly, to make clear he was kidding, even though he wasn't. In the background, with the tail end of his senses, he caught the weak tinkling of his mother's bell.

Then Keller was back on the phone, more brash and determined now that he had proven himself. "Carlyle, here's our plot. Listening? You believe me now?"

"Every word."

"Tony and Alec and I want to sing a song, but we need a fourth voice and some good accompaniment. You're the best there is. I *told* them that."

"Come on, Keller."

"No joke, buddy. Alec, what'll we sing?"

Carlyle heard some muted protestation, the sound of someone laughing, then Keller laughing, and the sound of ice cubes clinking in a glass. He had begun to be amused himself, though Keller was no doubt thoroughly soused. It was a neat trick, something to laugh about years from now; they were making a memory, and he was aware that the story would thereafter be the major bond between them. "Remember the time, you old dog, when I called from Beverly Hills?"

The amusement passed when it became clear Keller was making an ass of himself. It was obvious neither celebrity wanted to sing, but Keller wasn't giving up. Carlyle felt embarrassed for the poor, boorish sot and then felt like a fool for not hanging up the phone. "Keller, this is getting ridiculous—"

"Agreed, Tony? Terrific. Carlyle—hey, buddy, you still there? You know a golden oldie called 'Dear Old Girl'?"

"You're kidding." He knew the song. It was a favorite of his mother—one she'd tried in the last month to get him to play, but he'd refused, pretending to have forgotten it. It was painfully sentimental, though a pro like Bennett might somehow resuscitate it. "I don't think I know it, Keller."

"Sure you do. *'Dear old girl, the robin sings above you—'* Remember? Tony knows it. I thought you knew every song in the book. Come on, Carlyle, get with it."

"I guess I can fake it," he said grudgingly.

"Key of C, Tone? Give us a C, buddy." Carlyle set the receiver on his piano and hit a chord. He heard them struggle for harmony; their voices were distant and Munchkin-like. "Hit it, Carlyle," he heard Keller command.

Carlyle began the song. Though their voices were reedy, nearly indistinct, he harmonized as best he could:

"Dear old girl, the robin sings above you.
Dear old girl, he speaks of how he loves you.
The blinding tears are falling
As I think of my lost pearl,
And my broken heart is calling,
Calling to you, dear old girl...."

Carlyle sang three choruses, hoping his mother hadn't heard, and realized at the start of the fourth that the others were silent. He waited on the phone for at least a minute. He said "Hello" at intervals, but Keller had apparently wandered off. He grew furious wondering how long he'd been singing by himself. "You dumb bastard, Keller," he said. "You big shot jerk."

As he was about to hang up, Keller returned to the phone. "Carlyle, hey listen, Tony thought you were great. He said if you're ever out in California, look him up. You've gotta move out of the Midwest, buddy. This is where it's at. You'd really make it out here. I'm not kidding. You're one of a kind."

"Thanks, Keller."

"Any time, Carlyle. It was a gas."

Carlyle hung up the phone and entered the kitchen for a brandy. Afterwards he went to look at his mother. Her pale nose glowed like a radium dial in the semi-darkened bedroom. He shook his head and smiled when he thought of having spoken to Tony Bennett. The offer to look him up was no doubt showbiz bullshit. The difference between Keller and Carlyle was that Keller *would* look Bennett up, and make him listen as well.

He felt a strong desire to tell his mother about these celebrities who had sought him out. To her it would amount to more than the drunken manipulations of Keller—which is all the jaundiced eye of Cherry would have seen. No, his mother understood his value; she had been his mentor, the cheerleader through his college triumphs, his encouragement all the years. The Steinway had been her gift to him. She, more than anyone in the world, believed in his talent—even more, perhaps, than he did himself.

It occurred to him that the secret of whatever artistic success he had known was this woman. His mother was the one to whom he had played from the start and to whom he played now. His head was very clear, and the thought loomed before him in an aura, so true did it seem.

Then things began to cloud, and he could only see himself as an accompanist—adjunct to an unending procession of human experience, secondary always to what was being celebrated, eaten, drunk, or said.

And in the gloom of that thought, California--a fresh start--seemed not such a bad idea...though not while his mother needed him...not while there was a nurse and other medical expenses to see to. His mother had some money, possibly enough, but for now he would need to continue his steady job. The composition could certainly wait. It had waited this long.

But when the piano player touched his mother's face, he discovered with a shudder that ran the entire length of him, that nothing would have to wait at all.

GET A LIFE

Preston teed up his drive on the first hole, took a deep breath, waggled twice, wound too fast into his backswing, came up and out of his downswing and topped the ball 75 yards on the ground. "Shit," he muttered.

Allen, his old friend and former plant manager, laughed and said, "Take a mulligan."

Golf had been a pleasant diversion when Preston had no time for it; now that he could play any day of the week, he found the game frustrating, even tedious. He wondered why all the years of watching the pros on television, practicing on the range, upgrading equipment, developing muscle memory had resulted in so little. His drives were shorter, his short game erratic, his patience inconsistent.

Most of his friends played, so he was on a course at least three days out of seven. For some reason, things went best with Allen, a man several steps into dementia who chose his clubs randomly and forgot strokes on every hole. Allen simply enjoyed getting out, and his wife Joy appreciated Preston giving her some time off. When they played again next week, Allen would have forgotten they'd played today—each experience somehow blessedly new to him. The man was an avid reader, a history buff, a brilliant engineer, but some sort of plug had been pulled and things were leaking away.

Preston hammered his mulligan but watched it wander into the trees to the right. Allen, who couldn't keep his head still, dribbled the ball to the ladies' tee. It satisfied him. Thank God there was almost no one else on the course at this hour of the day.

Preston's wife Sylvia, like Joy, seemed relieved to see him disappear for a half day or more to some distant course—the oftener the better. In his pre-retirement years, when he spent long days heading up a tool and die company, she had resented his playing even though she knew he did business on the course. She had small children to care for, and piano students coming and going from their home--plenty of reasons for complaint. But now their three daughters were grown and married; they saw their grandchildren less than they wanted, usually at their sports events.

His wife, as it happened, was ten years younger than he and still working, her student roster full and accompanist jobs multiplying. He wanted to travel—they had the money--but she didn't have much time for it. The house had been her space for years, and now he was underfoot. He tried to help her out. He fixed faucets and puttered in the garden (their landscape service did most of that), yet she didn't want him butting into what she'd always done… especially the cooking, the shopping, the laundry, the bills, the holiday preparations and gift buying, even the furniture arranging.

Shortly after he'd retired, he'd overheard Lisa, their youngest and least tactful daughter, say to her mother, "What is he going to do with himself? I pity you."

His wife had replied, dismayed, "The man needs to get a life. He has no hobbies except golf, and even that seems half-hearted. He putzes around on the computer—I swear he's addicted to it. He'll spend hours and hours on YouTube learning how to change a taillight or sharpen a chain saw. Honest to goodness…"

"Maybe he could volunteer at church."

"Great idea. You talk to him about it. He's driving me crazy."

And so the man with the high-powered job, a captain of industry who issued orders and had them obeyed, suddenly found himself an irrelevancy, like the extra buttons on the tail of his shirt. Though their attitudes didn't help, he knew in his gut they were right. His days were full of space he didn't know how to fill.

He punched the ball out of the trees with a four iron, wondering whether there was anything meaningful this game provided him besides a little exercise. On rare occasions, usually a wet and dazzling morning, he'd try to focus on the natural beauty around him, but the game kept getting in the way. He took a six on the first hole, one of the easiest. After eight or nine strokes, Allen called it a five. His delight at winning the hole was more endearing than bothersome. Someone, at least, was enjoying this.

Whenever they played, usually once a week, Preston drove Allen to and from the course. Allen's doctor no longer allowed him to drive, though Allen didn't seem to be aware of it. With a full 18 hole round behind them today, creeping through rush hour traffic toward his friend's suburban home, Preston felt bone weary and lacked the reserves to steer the conversation in productive directions. His friend's mind dulled quickly. This time he would let the recorder in Allen's head run whatever worn, wearisome tape he chose.

"The road wasn't always this busy," Allen said. Preston could recite the rest. "When we first moved out here it was two lane." He pointed at a strip mall they were passing. "That used to be a horse pasture."

"I remember you telling me that."

"What a difference from when we first moved out here. There weren't near as many cars. I think there was a horse pasture around here. I can't believe how many cars there are now. I think this road was two lane." He paused, searching for something outside. "I kind of remember a horse pasture somewhere."

"Yeah, there was a horse pasture."

"I wonder where it was?"

When they arrived at the house Allen had once planned and built, his wife, a spry, stringy woman who seemed younger than her mid-70s, was waiting for them in the driveway. "How did he do?" she asked Preston, as he lifted Allen's clubs from the trunk.

"He did well," Preston replied cheerfully. "Our scores were close."

"Does he still know the right clubs to use?" Allen was standing beside her, although she spoke as if he wasn't there.

"No problem," he said, rankled. Allen didn't seem to register the disrespect.

"Well, that's good news. Did you get your shoes out, Allen?"

"Did I get my shoes?" he asked Preston.

"All set. Shoes are beside your bag. See you next week, my friend."

"Thanks for taking him," she said. "It's a nice break for both of us." Aside to Preston she said, "The other day I caught him trying to put oil in the gas tank of the lawn mower. It's getting hard. I don't know how long I can do it. I may need to find a place for him."

"I'm sorry, Joy," he told her sincerely. Did she mean a nursing home? He couldn't imagine she was serious—just speaking out of weary frustration.

"Did I get my shoes?" Allen asked. Preston's old friend stood in the driveway and waved until the car was out of sight.

Tuesday marked a monthly, all-male gathering of retired colleagues in tool and die--for breakfast and coffee at Lucy's Home Made Restaurant. It was always good to see them, at least for the first half hour or so. They talked politics and the ups and downs of business, but the conversation inevitably trailed off into medical problems: hip and knee replacements, by-pass and back surgeries, prostate troubles…the list was endless. Preston had been blessed with a body that didn't often fail him. He'd never in his 69 years stayed overnight in a hospital. And it wasn't that he lacked compassion, but the recital of maladies was mind-numbing. Travelogues were worse. Cell phones (to Preston the most disruptive technological advance of the age) were inevitably close at hand with hundreds of random photos--Mayan temples, pristine beaches, cruise ship dining rooms with obscene quantities of food—vacation memories that would never be edited or arranged into albums. That was a lost art, and only a few, his wife among them, still maintained it.

Jerry Blunt, a former sales rep for Preston's company, sat directly across from him. He was heavy, his face sagging into his neck and piling up. "Do you see much of Allen?" he asked.

"I play golf with him most weeks."

"That's damn nice of you."

"No great sacrifice. He still plays pretty well."

"I hear he's slipping, though."

Preston shrugged. "He takes a little patience. I don't think he's as bad as his wife believes."

"Well, she's with him 24-7. Except for golf, I mean."

"Funny, you get him out on the course, and his mind seems to clear up a bit. He needs to be doing something with his time."

"Yeah…I know. So what are *you* doing with your time?"

The question stopped him for a moment. "Trying to reinvent myself, I guess. I'm just not sure how to do it."

Preston's honesty touched a button in Jerry. "Amen to that! I never dreamed my identity was so tied up in my job. I'm taking piano lessons—it's that desperate. Always wanted to play, though. It's a big step out of my comfort zone."

Preston was impressed. "Great idea. I should try it—I mean, I took piano right up into high school. My wife might like another student."

"Pay somebody, Preston. She doesn't need to see more of you."

Preston grinned. "Yeah, you may have a point."

Jerry gulped coffee and shoveled in home fries while he talked. His eating habits were unnerving. "I go to a lot of grandkids' sports stuff. That passes the time."

"I'm sick of tee ball games, if you want to know the truth," Preston lamented.

Jerry grinned. "It's only May, pal."

"I guess if you want life to slow down, that's the way to do it. I love my grandkids dearly, but, damn, it's like watching paint dry."

The two exploded in laughter, momentarily stopping conversation around them. Preston was curious about the notion of taking up piano again. He'd always wanted to play in a band, although at his age, he knew the odds were heavily against it. Still, it was an idea. He remembered reading that Jack Lemon had taken up the piano in his 60s and was playing in a jazz group within a couple of years. For once, Preston was glad he had showed up at Lucy's.

He had noticed for some time that whenever they watched movies, the names of actors he'd known for years escaped him. Sylvia rattled them off so effortlessly that Preston began to wonder if this slippage was normal. How could he not come up with Lauren Bacall? Yet friends his age complained of the same thing, so his memory lapses concerned him only now and then. He tried to imagine what it would be like to be Allen, to lose touch not just with names but with a whole life? He couldn't begin to get inside the thought. All that Allen had been, all the earned respect and admiration had dissipated like smoke on a stage, leaving a pathetic figure, a living cartoon. Respect, he knew, was a key. It had somehow become the center of his own problems. He'd had no issue with self worth his entire life. But in retirement he quickly found there was to be no resting on laurels. He had assumed, albeit uneasily, that this would be a time of kicking back and savoring life. What a myth. If he'd known he was expected to prove himself all over again, he'd never have quit working.

The piano idea started well. Feeling he couldn't go to an outsider for lessons without mentioning it to Sylvia, he was surprised to find her not only willing to teach him but mildly excited about it. Though she didn't say it, he could tell she felt it was a first step out of an inertia he was mired in.

They sat down at the piano to see what he remembered. He could still read fairly well. He knew the keyboard. He could count.

"You're way ahead of the average beginner," she said.

"I should be. I took lessons for six years."

"I know. But you've forgotten five of them. I have an adult beginner's book that should be just right."

"How long will it take me to play something?"

"Are you in a hurry? Is there a concert coming up?"

Just that quickly he could sense trouble ahead. Within a couple of months, even though he was playing a simple version of "Für Elise," (something her ten year olds did for recitals), he realized his chances of playing in a band were as remote as his golf skills launching him onto the senior tour. Jack Lemon may have had the knack, but Preston knew it wasn't in the cards for him. And in the long run what difference did it make, since Lemon was dead anyway?

So he took his daughter's advice and reluctantly tried volunteering at church. Church had always been more his wife's business than his. Sylvia made meals for the sick, visited shut-ins, played services at homeless missions and nursing homes. Do-gooding had never been a natural part of his make up, but he could at least make an effort.

He started simply enough, driving members to and from doctors' appointments, mostly ancient widows whom the pastor referred to as saints of the church. When one after another tried to work him for many more rides than scheduled, their saintliness dimmed. Within a month, he quietly gave up the job.

A local food pantry was part of the church's mission. The idea of feeding hungry people was so basic that it had some degree of appeal to him. He could choose pickup and delivery of donated food, or clerking in the pantry store. Since his mid-sized sedan barely accommodated two golf bags, he signed onto a two-day-a-week shift in the store. People who qualified (most of them poor, some unexpectedly out of work and without resources) could visit each month for free groceries. Preston wondered what they did for the rest of the month, especially the ones with kids.

Some came to shop in surprisingly nice cars, puzzling him. Others walked in with pull carts and shopping bags and had to haul the groceries home on foot. He thought about offering rides, but most of them were women, and he figured it wasn't wise. He tried his best to be welcoming to them and respectful, even the ones (it took every ounce of his patience) who felt they were owed more than they received. Why were certain poor people so irksome and demanding? Why had he worked hard his whole life only to be helping people who hadn't?

He stayed at the job through the remainder of summer and into the fall, but the hard luck stories began to weigh on him. He often had to drag himself to work. He mentioned his discontent one night to Sylvia, who stood beside him on their large deck sipping wine, watching him grill marinated chicken breasts.

"If you don't have a heart for it, don't do it."

"It's just the way I'm wired. Maybe I expect too much of people. I get impatient when I see them making no effort to climb out of the holes they're in."

"It's not that simple, Preston. Some dig the holes—lots of others have them dug for them."

"I don't know, Syl...sometimes I feel like an uncaring bastard."

"Honey, you aren't an uncaring bastard. Open your eyes. Everywhere you turn there's a need. Just find a way to make the world a little better."

At the moment, the only need he could see was his own hollow life.

By late September, rain fell nearly every day. Golf courses turned into swamps. Allen and he had not played a round for three straight weeks, and the season was nearing an end. Preston wondered whether his friend would still be playing the game once next May rolled around. When he'd called to cancel that morning, Joy was understanding but discouraged. He'd felt vaguely guilty for not suggesting an alternate activity, but he could not imagine what it would be.

Around noon the same day he was at work in the pantry store, packing a bag for a weary-looking young mother with a crying toddler and a baby. As he offered the toddler a lollipop, hoping to quell the caterwauling, he happened to glance out a window at traffic passing on the busy street in front. In that brief instant, he spotted Allen driving by in his red Ford pickup. He was certain it was his friend. He knew the truck well, had borrowed it numerous times. He also knew Joy had hidden the keys from him. Anxious, half sick to his stomach, he went to the store manager's office to borrow the phone because his cell was in the car. He let it ring a dozen times, was close to hanging up when Joy answered. She sounded groggy.

"Preston? Sorry, I was sleeping. I'm not feeling well."

"Is Allen there?"

"I think he's out in the yard."

"Is the truck there? I thought I just saw him drive by."

"Ohmigod, let me go check." She was not gone more than ten seconds. "He took the truck. What am I going to do?"

"Does he remember how to drive?"

"He can drive. But he doesn't know where he's going."

"Shall I call the police?"

"Oh, Preston. That'll make so much trouble for us. I want to look for him first."

"He was traveling south on State Street. Any ideas?"

"No. He knows the north end best, not the south. He drove off like this one other time...made it to the Ford dealership for a tune up. Thank goodness they called me. They had nothing scheduled for him, and I'd taken it in for a tune up a month earlier. I'll go there first. You go south and see if you can find him. You're a good friend, Preston."

"I'll keep you posted."

In a city of 180,000, where was he supposed to look? He drove slowly south on State, looking down side streets, into parking lots. A misty fog didn't help matters. Red Ford pickups seemed to be fairly rare. Allen's had a Michigan Tech license plate. State Street followed the river all the way through town and beyond it for several miles until the river turned west and State continued south. The river worried him; it was swollen to flood stage, blackish brown and moving like an avalanche. It was dangerous to get anywhere near it.

He drove for twenty minutes, called Joy who hadn't found him at the dealership. He kept driving. The fog grew thicker. When he spotted the gravel road into Riverbend Park, he remembered something, braked nearly to a stop, and turned in. He passed an open green building with roof and picnic tables. He passed a playground and ragged softball field. It was then he saw the red truck parked near the water. Frightened for his friend, he slowly rolled to the spot. Allen sat on a large rock just a few feet from the rampaging water. Fog obliterated the opposite shore. Preston stopped the car, got out quietly and went over to him. Allen looked up.

"Hello, Preston. What are you doing here?"

"Looking for you."

"I'm glad. I don't know where I am."

"It's Riverbend Park. We used to have our work picnics here."

"Did we?"

"Joy is worried about you."

"I'm sure she is. I don't know where I am. It bothers me. I don't even know where the hell I am, Preston." He stood up and took a step toward the water.

"Careful, Allen. Slip into that river and you'll be gone."

"That occurred to me."

"Please sit down on the rock."

Allen hesitated, and then obeyed. Preston sat at his side and put an arm around him. Staring into the dark, violent water, he could for the first time dimly envision Allen's world. He could feel it there in the water and fog--the terrifying darkness, the bottomless hole to nowhere. Alone. Blind. Mindless. No past or future. No memory or hope. Buried in a nursing home with a television set.

The horror hit him like a wave, swept him up, deposited him gasping, half-drowned on a beach. Moments later, when he managed to struggle to his feet, he took Allen's hand tightly in his own and guided him to the truck.

As he drove his friend home, Preston's mind raced like a rat in a wheel. The fog began to clear once they came into town. They passed the food pantry; he glanced in the windows and saw his manager stocking shelves. "Allen," he said suddenly. "I need you and your truck."

"What for?"

"To make the world a better place."

Allen seemed amused. "I don't have that much going on. I could probably do it."

And just that quickly, for a brief, blessed space, they had a life.

THE LION

Halstead was thinking about the lion before the third hour literature class even began, and by the time his students had filled the furthest reaches of 201C, he knew he would beg off lunchroom duty and spend noon hour at the zoo.

It was a new zoo, completed in early August, three weeks before school resumed. Because it was just a block from City Central High School, there had developed among the faculty a running joke about the analogous qualities of the two places. Halstead had enjoyed it for a while, but once the lion had arrived, the joke had begun to wear thin on him. He was not an animal lover, but the animals—particularly the lion—did not deserve comparison to the yahoos he had to teach.

When the bell rang, he stood and opened the anthology to Browning's "My Last Duchess," and instantly he could sense that something was the matter. Lance Kegman, the All-State hockey player, leaned so close to Amy Shroeder's ear that he appeared to be gnawing on it. Laura Lathrop and Florence Cole, the weird sisters of City Central High, were purple with bitten–off lunacy.

"All right, what's up?" he asked, glancing down at himself. It wasn't his fly. It had to be the large coffee stain, a nearly perfect circle, on the lower front of his baggy fisherman-knit sweater. His wife had taken six months to knit the sweater, and now that she was his ex-wife, he was diligently trying to ruin it.

With a weary sigh, he looked again to Browning, and the lion came loping into his mind, as it had so often in the last month. It was a great male lion, pacing the too small, temporary cage (a larger habitat with painted concrete cliffs and caves was being prepared), a thick-maned lion with a ferocity he'd never seen in a zoo lion before. The stunned, faraway look of its eyes spoke of jungles and newly killed antelope.

"Page 743. Lance Kegman, read the poem, would you?"

Kegman grinned. Owl's head pivoting on the massive neck, his eyes travelled from face to face, as if confirming some private joke. "Aw, come on, Mr. Halstead, do I have to?"

"Poetry is good for you."

"That's what you say."

"Good for you, Lance, it's good for you. Pretend the words are hockey pucks."

"I hate it."

Halstead steeled himself for what he knew was coming. Student frustration, even outrage, at poetry had once challenged him—maybe four years ago—before his dreams, hell, his life, had begun caving in. Not caving in either—just sagging like his fisherman-knit sweater. Now it was mostly repetition, the daily monotony of inane gesture and rehearsed response, signifying nothing.

"Why, Lance?" There was no spirit in his voice.

"They never say what they mean. It's not worth the bother."

"Hmmm…interesting observation. You've apparently heard of the bother-worth theory of literary criticism. You can apply it to anything, especially poetry. Take Eliot's 'The Waste Land,' for example." Halstead knew that no one in the class (with the possible exception of Mary Little whose face occasionally glowed at his reading of a poem, whose clunky writing at times showed surprising sensitivity) would recognize the title.

"Suppose you went to all the trouble of analyzing and explicating that bloody poem—got out your encyclopedias, your Bibles, your mythologies and so forth—"

He was losing them, even Mary today, he could see; she appeared to be cleaning out her notebook. Martin Engles, who worked a late shift in a Marathon station, was sound asleep. Kegman yawned gigantically.

So Halstead shifted easily into a kind of interior monologue, something he had developed in self defense, strictly for the entertainment of himself.

"—and so forth," he repeated. "What was I saying? Yes, and you went to the trouble, and then you discovered finally that whatever spiritual or esthetic edification you had gained was really not worth all that bother—you see? You would have judged the poem unworthy according to the bother-worth theory of literary criticism. Mene, Mene, Tekel, Upharsin…the handwriting on the wall. It has been weighed in the balance and found wanting."

"Jesus—" Kegman muttered to Amy Schroeder.

"Read the poem, Lance."

"Sure, Mr. Halstead," a hint of contempt in the tone.

Kegman set about murdering Browning. Halstead's mouth began to taste of sour milk.

"No, Lance. Don't end-stop your lines. Read through them. Watch the way the sentences are built and read the sentences, not the lines. Try it again."

Kegman's voice sounded to Halstead like the sputter and drone of a snowmobile engine: "'For never read strangers like you that pitchered continent—'" he read for "pictured countenance," and a few lines later "dust" for "durst." It was nothing unusual. This cell phone generation had an electronic, perpetually short-circuiting language. The magic of words meant nothing to them unless translated into some form of cyberspeak.

Kegman lumbered on, butting up against unfamiliar terms every other line. In eight years of teaching, Halstead had encountered hundreds of these witless children. And though he had once been a poet, he had begun to hate poetry. He had taught "My Last Duchess" three times a semester, six times a year for eight years. Forty-eight times he had made the same comments about Italian Renaissance royalty. Later in the hour he would do Emily Dickinson's "The Chariot"; he would tell the story of his former professor who, studying in Amhearst, Massachusetts, had inadvertently followed the path to the grave that Dickinson had traced in her poem. It was a wonderful story. He recalled the tremendous lift of spirit he had felt upon hearing it. It was much too good to waste on them forty-eight times over.

Kegman dragged his tongue through the final lines, sighed heavily, and clapped his book shut.

"Well, Lance, what did that do for you?"

"Nothing."

"What's the story, at least?"

"I couldn't follow it while I was reading."

For Kegman, it was a good answer. Halstead charitably allowed him to pass.

"Mary? How about it? Iron things out for us, will you?" It sounded as much a plea as a request.

Mary stopped shuffling her papers and looked up. She appeared embarrassed, and it bewildered him. She was a fairly confident, outspoken girl not given to the hummingbird antics of most seventeen-year-old females.

"Mr. Halstead, did you know—"

Kegman jerked about in his seat and glowered at her.

"Mary?"

"Oh, nothing. The poem is a dramatic monologue. A duke describes the qualities he didn't like in his last duchess…I think he's had her killed. He does it to clue in this envoy from the count. The duke wants to marry the count's daughter…"

Halstead's fingers combed through his massive, grizzled beard. His face and head over the last year had sprouted like an untended garden. He nodded and nodded as Mary spoke. He was very tired and thinking of the lion.

He bought a hotdog at the zoo and ate it in front of the lion's cage with a bottle of Orange Crush. Mustard dribbled through his beard, and he wiped it away with the only thing handy, an assignment sheet from his sixth hour comp class.

In the zoo he often thought about how teaching had once been for him, of those few students he had actually touched in small, significant ways. There weren't many, but George Bishop had to be numbered among them. Halstead had raised him from the mire of developmental comp—bonehead English—helped make of him a poet who just two springs before had won a Hopwood Award at the University of Michigan. George Bishop… Halstead very much desired to see him, sit down with him over a beer. It had been three years, at least, since George had last stopped. Years went quickly when one taught, even if hours didn't.

Halstead's adult life could be measured out in old grade books. And a million dismal student papers. The stack would reach halfway to the moon. His wife had hated his always diddling with those papers—Sundays, evenings, holidays. Always. They, he'd determined, were as much responsible for his divorce as anything.

God, where were the George Bishops when you needed them? Why did none come along any more?

The lion, sleeping now, was startled by a passing city bus. Halstead watched the jaws spread, heard the rumble from the throat like a castle door closing. The lion stood and stretched, the superb musculature flexing, gleaming in the warm October sunlight. Then it began to pace, loping back and forth on leather paws, measuring its confines, gauging the strength of the bars with those enormous, distant eyes. Halstead loved the pacing, loved the feel of power nearing the point of explosion, the latent ferocity and violence of a great caged spirit.

"God, lion, I know," he muttered. "I know, I know."

"Mr. Halstead?"

The voice struck like a gunshot in the forehead. His neck snapped. Mary Little, her thick glasses two pools of sun, hovered beside his bench.

"Were you talking to someone?" she asked.

"No one, Mary."

"May I sit down?"

Halstead closed his eyes and pressed thumbs to his temples. "If you'd like."

She sat primly, her skirt pulled down over tight-pressed knees. Halstead noticed, as she clutched her cell phone, that her fingernails were bitten to the quick.

"Mr. Halstead, are you feeling all right?"

"Of course, Mary. Why do you ask?"

She hesitated. "What you did in class today was the same thing you did Friday."

Halstead looked at her oddly, and then glanced away. The lion continued to lope, to measure, to gauge.

"It was?"

"Yes."

"Why didn't someone tell me?"

"I—no one dared, I guess."

"Wow, I wonder what that means. Senility, you think?"

Mary was silent.

"I mean I wish you'd told me, Mary. That's pretty embarrassing."

"Lance Kegman—he didn't want anybody…"

"Of course. Kegman."

"He heard you'd done it in first hour." Embarrassed, Mary stood, gripping her books beneath her small bosom. "I've got to be back for a meeting, Mr. Halstead."

"All right, Mary. Thanks." She began to walk away; he called out "Mary!" in a voice much too loud. For a moment a wave of hatred and disgust swept through him. Had he the strength to stand, he could have cheerfully torn open her throat. But it passed, the violence dissolved, and he felt next as if he were going to weep. "Mary," he said quietly. "How's your writing coming, Mary? You have something, young lady. If I haven't said it before, I consider you a real diamond in the rough. I'd like to see you go on with it in college."

She looked at him, eyes flat and magnified on the dense lenses. "I don't know. I don't think I'm very good at it. I'm thinking of a business major."

"Business," he said. "Well, you ought to give it some thought at least."

"Bye, Mr. Halstead. I will."

The sour milk taste was in his mouth again, and he was filled with a frightening sense of powerlessness, of loss. The lion's loping grew more frantic; it actually broke into a run now—as much of a run, that is, as its steel confines allowed. Then, suddenly, it stopped. Its monster jaws opened as if to utter some gigantic anguish. Halstead peered into the terrible mouth, awed by the huge ivory teeth and orange curling eel of a tongue.

But a long, withdrawing hiss was what emerged.

THE PRODIGY

When she was not yet four years old, Alice suddenly found herself living in a large house with a man and woman, strangers to her, who said they were her true parents. She wept inconsolably for a number of days. As time passed, though, she became accustomed to this new life and the stately old house, but at moments she was sure she remembered a dark, tiny house where she'd slept under a staircase with a cat. She also seemed to remember a brown, bearded man and a pale woman with a baby, and a sock doll with hair made of yarn.

Alice played the violin; the man and woman who said they were her true parents were also her teachers—her father, Mr. Adler, a mild, patient, but determined man, taught her violin, and her mother, Mrs. Adler, far more solemn and exacting, taught her to read, work with numbers, and write down her thoughts. Once she wrote a paragraph about the half-remembered man and woman, the baby and the sock doll, and the dark, tiny house. She drew a picture of them and the cat as well. Her true mother frowned at the drawing and asked, "What is this?"

"Things I remember," Alice said.

"No, my dear, things you've dreamed," she said, walking away.

By the time she was twelve, Alice was sometimes playing solo violin with the famous symphony orchestra of her city. Her true father was a gracious but demanding teacher, and Alice practiced hours and hours for him every day. At times she felt that Mr. Adler--his pinched face and tortoise shell glasses, drooping moustache, small white hands measuring out tempo with outstretched fingers—was the only human being she ever saw. Though she loved Mozart passionately, sometimes she felt a prisoner of *Concerto No. 3 in G Major*. When she had overworked at it, the music occupied her dreams, repeating and repeating—and she would waken exhausted. She sometimes labored for Mr. Adler until her arms and fingers ached, until her fair, freckled skin turned ghostly pale, her head throbbed and noiseless tears filled her eyes. If he saw the tears, he would stop the lesson and in a kind voice say, "Go out to the gardens and play now, Alice." A single swing, hung from a high limb, served that purpose. Several times she heard Mrs. Adler admonish him for being too soft.

Adults called her a musical prodigy, an extraordinary child from her earliest years. She had little to compare herself to, though audiences seemed to be pleased by her playing. The newspapers featured her in stories now and then. She began attending a special school for gifted students and made a few friends who were also musicians. Her life was small and protected, given almost entirely to music. And though she was happy enough, she always felt that something…something she couldn't name…was missing.

For a short period of time, in her fourteenth year, that feeling went away. Mr. Adler had other students coming daily to the house for lessons. His fame as a teacher was widespread. One student, a tall, quiet boy of sixteen named Jonathan, began talking to her about music. The bus dropped him twenty minutes early for his lesson, so he waited in a library where Alice studied. She knew he did not play the violin as well as she, but he spoke of his music with such passion—with the sort of intensity she experienced herself--that she began to believe their minds and hearts were alike. Her feelings for him grew, and she found herself thinking of him even during the times she practiced. Mr. Adler (she called him father now), listening in another room, would call out her name sharply to reproach her for lack of focus. He would ask her if something was wrong, and she said that, no, she was quite happy. Jonathan sometimes held her hand as he spoke with enthusiasm of violinists like Heifetz and Perlman.

"I'll never be like them," he said one day, as if in pain. "But you…for you it's possible, Alice."

"I don't know that…" she answered, squeezing his hand. "I know I'd like to play duets with you."

Mr. Adler entered the room just then, stood silently a moment before calling Jonathan to his lesson. It was the last time Alice saw him. Her mother and father never spoke of him except to say he'd found another teacher, and never acknowledged the pain she was so obviously feeling.

Mr. Adler, who was careful and caring to the extreme about her well being, did not show up one day to drive her home from school. It puzzled her, but since the school wasn't a great distance from her house and the route was etched in her mind, she decided to walk. She set off, carrying her violin case, wearing a backpack for books and feeling blissfully free. She passed a familiar Greek restaurant called Zorba's and caught the fragrance of spiced lamb. She noticed that someone was living above the restaurant, something she had never seen from the car. Walking revealed so much she hadn't known before…narrow side streets with laundry drying on railings of balconies, people leaning out of windows, talking to others on the sidewalks, smells of fish frying and cigarette smoke. She saw black girls playing hopscotch and a large cluster of motorcycles parked in front of a place called The Dark Alley.

She walked on, recognizing every street and every turn, every sign on every business they'd passed on their daily auto trips. Her mind was a latticework of organized memories. Learning music was so simple for her that she wondered why others agonized over it.

There was so much else, she realized, to discover by foot, and when she reached a narrow, alley-like street called Auburn Lane, she stopped because the name touched a memory of something like music from a distant time and place. She hesitated, glancing around to identify the spot where she stood. She knew all the landmarks of this main street, but Auburn Lane was not on her mental map. On an impulse she turned to explore a block or two of it—a street so narrow it was one way only, almost more driveway than street. Many of the small shops on Auburn Lane were empty, their windows boarded and FOR LEASE signs posted on the sheets of plywood. At a tattoo parlor called Pay for Pain, a pony-tailed man sat on a folding chair in front, smoking a dark cigarette. A tattooed chain encircled his neck. He greeted her as she passed, and she smiled at him, knowing no reason to feel fear.

By the third block of Auburn Lane, the majority of people she saw were black. Some of them, mostly men, stood in the shadows of doorways and watched her as she passed. She began to think about turning back, but something compelled her one more block, and then one more. Ahead she saw something that seemed familiar—a small, shabby park in the middle of which stood the statue of a soldier holding a rifle at his side. Two old men sat on the concrete pedestal of the statue, drinking beer. One of them with a wreath of white, nappy hair looked at her and said, "Hey, girl, you looking pretty lost."

When she said, "No, I'm not lost--but thank you," they both smiled and went back to drinking. "What is the name of this park?" she asked them.

"We call it the Brass Man Park, on account of this brass man," said the same one, pointing to the statue. "Nobody knows what he's doin' here. Nameplate been stole."

"He's a Civil War soldier. That's a Union uniform," she said.

"That so? You been here before, child?"

"I think so."

"Maybe on Sunday?"

"What's on Sunday?"

"Drums. A hundred funky people with all kinda drums. They come here and start to play, and folks take to dancing. Sounds like Africa right here in Cleveland."

At that moment, to her amazement, her father's car pulled up at a nearby curb. He opened the window. "Alice…thank goodness I've found you. I had a flat tire. You should have waited for me."

"It's all right, father. I knew the way home."

"This isn't the way."

As she moved toward the car, the white-haired man said, "Come on back Sunday if you want a good time."

"Thank you," she said, and got into the car.

Her father turned at the next corner and made his way back toward the main street to home. She'd rarely seen him so upset, except at her playing. "Why did you go down here, Alice? This is not a safe neighborhood."

"It isn't? I wasn't afraid. I thought I remembered something about that street. It was the little park, I think. Did you ever take me there?"

He seemed unhappy about her question. "I don't know. Maybe I did."

"How did you know to come down that street to find me?"

"A lucky guess. Thank goodness I was right."

"I enjoy seeing new places, father. You should show me more of the city."

"You have a performance to prepare for. After that we'll talk about it."

But he never got around to talking about it. On summer days, as they passed Auburn Lane, she would open the window to listen for drums. But they passed the spot only on weekdays, never on Sunday, so she didn't hear the drumming until two years later, the weekend before her graduation from the school for gifted students. Mrs. Adler, her mother, was taken ill suddenly. Mr. Adler rushed her off to the hospital, leaving Alice in charge of the house. Alice owned a cell phone now that kept her parents closely in touch. This day, she put her cell phone in her purse and set off for Auburn Lane.

Before she even reached the head of the street, she heard the drums and their wild and shifting rhythms—it seemed like hundreds of them. She walked swiftly toward the sound and soon was standing on the outer edge of the Brass Man Park, amazed at the dancing crowd surrounding a motley assortment of drummers and drums—bongos and congas, trash cans and beer kegs, snare drums and tom-toms, kettledrums and djembes, slapsticks and wood blocks, maracas and castanets, tambourines and triangles, cymbals and cowbells. The players were of all colors and costumes, some with shaved heads, some with Afros or dreadlocks. And the rhythm surged and repeated and changed, a cacophony that somehow stayed together. She became aware that one man with freckled, caramel skin and a lion's mane of thick hair encircling his face was clearly the lead drummer. He played two large kettledrums, each of different pitch, with heavy, padded mallets—a rhythm so sure and a sound so overpowering that all else harkened to him. Like those onlookers around her, she began to move to the rhythms, feeling a rush of some luminescent chemical in her veins. This was music of the body—not of the mind and heart as when she played Mozart. It was rough, sensual and primitive, even a bit frightening. She closed her eyes and let the rhythms pulse through her. When she opened them again, a thin, long-haired boy danced inches from her, moving in sync with her rhythms. She lurched away from him, and he pitched into the dancers and quickly found someone else.

Several policemen strolled the outskirts of the crowd, carrying sticks, their presence reassuring, at least until she felt herself being swept deeper into a pulsating mass of dancers, jostled by bodies and barely able to breathe. For a moment, she felt fear, lost in a churning sea of legs and hips and sinuous arms. But then--in a stunning instant--the drumming stopped; a strange hush rushed into a vacuum and immobilized the park. A moment later applause erupted, the dance area began to clear, and Alice could move and breathe again. She was drained, trembling, intoxicated. The life had gone out of her legs; she melted into an unoccupied bench. To her dismay, the drummers had already begun packing up, the crowd dispersing. She'd just arrived, and it was over!

She looked about for the lead drummer and spotted him covering his kettledrums, loading them into a large, two-wheeled pushcart. She watched as he moved off down Auburn Lane. She stood and began following him, half a block distant, for several blocks. At one point he stopped, set down the handles of the cart, and turned around.

"Do you want something?" he asked her. There was a faint British/Jamaican lilt to his voice; his freckled, cinnamon skin glowed in the late afternoon sunlight.

"I'm Alice," she said.

"Hello." Turning back to the cart, he made his way up the front walk of a small, dingy house where a boy, a few years younger than Alice, sat on the porch, quietly strumming a guitar. She felt, as with the Brass Man Park, that the place was like half-remembered music. She followed the drummer several steps up the walk. He swung around to face her, puzzled.

"I loved your playing," she told him sincerely.

"Thank you. But it's over now. Time to go home."

"I'm sorry to bother you. You really don't know me?"

The boy stopped strumming the guitar and stared at her.

"No...should I?" the man asked.

"Did I live here once?"

He snorted slightly; she thought it was a laugh. "We've been here 20 years. I don't think so."

"I'm Alice Adler. I play the violin."

He nodded, looking at her more closely. "Sure, I've heard of you," the man said. "The violin prodigy. Nice to meet you."

"I had a sock doll with yarn hair. At least I think I did. I think I remember playing with it in the Brass Man Park."

The boy looked at her oddly, then at the man.

"I'm afraid you've made a mistake," the man said. "Sorry I can't help you. If you'll excuse me, I need to put these drums away."

"But who are you?" she asked hurriedly.

"Nobody."

"I mean your name."

"My name is Joe Jones. This is my son Joe, Jr. Nice meeting you, Alice. Maybe I'll see you another Sunday some time."

She saw that Joe, Jr. resembled his father, though with skin just a shade lighter, more butterscotch than cinnamon.

"Yes..." she said, reluctantly turning away. "I guess I've made a mistake. I'm sorry..." and she turned up Auburn Lane for the walk home.

As she passed the park, her cell phone rang. It was her father, asking where she'd been. He'd been trying to call for the last hour. Her mother was now in intensive care. He wouldn't be home until late that night. Could she manage dinner? She said she would pray for her mother, and *of course* she could manage dinner. As she turned off the phone, she also prayed he'd heard none of the street sounds swirling around her.

Toward the end of her first year at the Eastman School, Alice was invited to play Mendelssohn"s *Violin Concerto in E Minor* with the New York Philharmonic Orchestra. Though

Sarah Chang had done it as a 15-year-old some eight years before, the invitation was still a great triumph for a girl of 17. And even more of a triumph, it seemed, for her father. Her mother had died the previous summer just before Alice had gone away to college, and poor Mr. Adler, mourning her, now rattled around in his large house with only a dozen students to occupy him. Alice was sorry for him but found it disconcerting that she felt so little about her mother's death. She took solace in knowing that her father, her long-time teacher, shared in this dazzling period of her life.

Two months before the concert, he visited her at school and brought an astonishing gift—a 300-year-old Stradivarius from an admiring, anonymous patron. A brief note accompanied it: *My sincere congratulations, dear Alice. My investment in you and your family seems to be paying rich dividends. I would be honored if you would play the Mendelssohn on this magnificent instrument—and consider it on indefinite loan from a long-time admirer.*

She was puzzled by the note but justifiably staggered by such a lavish gift. Who was this mysterious patron? Her father didn't know. How had this person invested in her and her family? Why were there whole areas of her life that seemed lost in shadow?

She discovered that the sound of the Stradivarius, its sweetness and depth, was the richest she'd ever caressed from a violin. The concert came…she felt over-prepared and manic with nervous energy, but that was when she did her best. Her dress excited her--a stunningly simple black evening gown, borrowed from an older classmate. Her father had begged for something younger-looking, but he hadn't prevailed. At last onstage before the largest audience she had yet experienced, she played as brilliantly as she ever had or perhaps ever would—reaching a new pinnacle of her powers. A lengthy standing ovation followed, a dressing room half full of flowers. Her father joined her in receiving the accolades. If anything, he was more self-satisfied, more full of glory than she. When the dressing room finally emptied out but for the two of them, her father held her hands and said, "So much effort and expense, Alice, but now all worth it. So much sacrifice of time and people and energy. Yet now we have the world at our feet."

"Do we father?" she asked innocently, uncertain of the extravagance of his remark.

In response, he squeezed her hands tightly in his.

The *Times* review the next day spoke of brilliant technique, but also of a shortage of mature feeling that would no doubt develop in time. Her father, still aglow, told her, "Ignore it. New York critics are forever nitpicking. It was a glorious triumph. The audience knew it. Everyone knew it!"

Alice's lack of concern about the critic's comments surprised her. Yet she was troubled by something else, something she'd experienced at a curtain call—a person she'd noticed as she took her bows…a dark, bearded man standing in the aisle near the back row—a man who seemed to be watching with great intensity, applauding but not smiling. Though it hardly seemed possible, she was convinced she had been looking at the lead drummer from the Brass Man Park.

Shortly after Alice's 28th birthday, her father, Mr. Adler, died of cancer. He was in his early 60s but seemed much older. Alice had continued to perform, but never with the success she'd known at 17. That fact seemed to disable Mr. Adler. In Alice's mid-20s, the mysterious patron had asked that the Stradivarius be returned. Her father had reluctantly carried out that mission. Alice was gifted without a doubt, but she knew very well she had fallen short of world-class performer ranks. Technical brilliance…shortage of mature feeling: the reviewer's words had stuck. No longer did anyone use the word "prodigy" when they spoke of her. Something vital was missing. She'd always known it but could never define it.

She now taught at DePaul School of Music in Chicago, played in the Chicago Symphony and two string quartets. She went out with men, mainly musicians, but had not found anyone interesting enough to consider a life with.

Her father's death gave her no choice but to take a leave from teaching and return home to Cleveland to settle her parents' estate. She learned they had left her a modest amount of money, yet the house, she was surprised to discover, belonged to someone else, someone who had arranged for them to stay indefinitely to help develop musical talent, primarily Alice's own. She had expected a windfall from the sale of the house, but now she would simply be organizing and selling the contents. The fact did not bother her much—only the drudgery of it. So she hired an estate auction firm to handle the lion's share of the work, fully expecting them to cheat her at every turn.

She spent her time in her father's library, boxing up the books and music she wanted for herself, not allowing the auction people to touch the room until she was finished. In her father's desk she found the combination to a wall safe she already knew about, set behind a shelf of books. The family papers were there in a metal box. Among them she found nothing in the least unusual: her father's Doctor of Musical Arts diploma from Oberlin, a copy of the will, which she had already seen. Their lawyer held all papers having to do with the house, including the identity of its owner, whom he was not at liberty to reveal. Her birth certificate was near the bottom of the pile. She took it out of its worn envelope and looked it over. She had a copy of this very document at home. She'd needed it often for passports, for school and employment, and a half dozen other legal matters. Born in Memorial Hospital of Fremont, Ohio, on May 20, 1989, daughter of Jacob and Marie Adler. It was all there in official form. They were her parents, in spite of her strange early memories, in spite of their odd, business-like relationship to her. She found their marriage license, dated September 3, 1983, six years before she was born.

Discovering no insights into the mysterious corners of her life, she returned the papers to the metal box and packed the box among the few things she was taking with her.

Just before she began the drive back to Chicago, she did something she had half-planned and now felt compelled to carry out. As she nosed the car into the narrow beginnings of Auburn Lane, she noticed changes—a renaissance seemed to be underway in the neighborhood. The boarded buildings had been transformed into restaurants and coffee shops, small bookstores, a French bakery, a high-end used furniture store. Young people were sitting at sidewalk tables drinking lattes, strolling in and out of shops. To her dismay, the Brass Man Park was gone, replaced by trendy-looking townhouses. She held her breath as she came near to the house she sought and exhaled when she saw it was still there, though newly painted--with a small garden of bright zinnias planted in front. She parked and got out. The lead drummer's son, now in his mid-20s, wearing Bob Marley dreads and a bright island shirt, sat on the porch—just as she'd met him years before—quietly strumming an acoustic guitar.

"You're still here," she said.

His look was puzzled. "I live here." His voice had none of his father's Jamaican lilt.

"I don't think you remember. I met you once. I'm Alice."

"Alice…oh, yeah, yeah. Alice the violin prodigy. Wow, that was a long time ago."

"Is your father here?"

"Uh-uh. I live here now. He's back in Jamaica. My grandpa died, and he went home for the funeral. Don't know if he's coming back."

A young white woman carrying a honey-skinned baby came through the front screen door. She looked at Alice and then at him.

"My wife Tessa and our daughter Alicia. We named her after my mother." He hesitated. "Sorry, Alice. I don't know your last name."

"Adler," she said. "I was hoping to see your father."

"Sorry."

"Is your mother here?"

He shook his head. "Died a long time ago--I was still a baby. I can't even remember her except for a few old pictures."

"I'm sorry," Alice said with feeling. "What happened?"

"She was just sick for quite a while. My father went through some hard times then—paying her medical bills and everything else. Nearly lost this house, I guess—but he somehow figured it out. I'm not even sure how. My mother died, and he raised me by himself. I think I turned out halfway decent."

"Halfway," Tessa said in a flat but affectionate voice.

"I make a living with this..." lifting the guitar, "but I'm second class compared to him. He has the gift, like you."

"No...I don't think I have the gift."

Surprise showed in his eyes. "That's not what I heard."

She leaned against the porch railing. What had he heard? "Do you have a picture of your mother?"

Something began closing up in him now, as if he'd already said too much. "She was white, if that's what you're wondering."

"No, I wasn't. I guess I knew."

"What are you doing here again?" he asked warily.

She hesitated. "I'm not sure. My life has missing parts."

"Don't ask me about missing parts. I don't know any more than you do."

"I know almost nothing."

"That's just what I'm saying." He stood suddenly. "I know even less than that. Hell...wait here a minute." He went inside, leaving her with Tessa and the baby. In less than a minute, he was back on the porch, holding out something to Alice. It was a soiled, ratty sock doll with a few nubs of yarn hair. Something like an electric shock arced through her. She wavered, gripping a porch rail.

"They must've taken care of you for awhile when you were little. You can have this mangy thing. He kept it for some reason. Glad to be rid of it."

It took a moment to begin to move her mouth. "Of course. You're right. They probably looked after me. What else could it be?" She took the sock doll from him and turned toward the car. "I'd better go." She was desperate to be gone. "You two have a beautiful baby. I hope she grows up happy," she said, holding the sock doll tightly to her pounding breast.

The 350 mile drive to Chicago allowed her time to pull herself together and construct the bare framework of a story...a bizarre, disturbing story with large pieces still missing—fiction likely, though would she ever know? The memory picture she'd drawn as a child had been a *real* memory after all and not a dream as her mother had said. And the lead drummer...could it really be he had drummed all these years in silence? She could imagine an imperious patron subsidizing a struggling family in a devil's pact...a deeply gifted child taken away for careful development, a high-risk, potentially high-yield investment. The scenario sickened her, darkened her mind; she gripped the steering wheel as if clinging to a lifeline.

And as she neared the outskirts of Chicago, she began to see there might be only one way she would ever understand her life. She would need to marry and bear a child of her own and let the truth of it set her free.

THE HEART SPECIALIST

The small, secluded piece of Lake Michigan beach drew him almost daily as he neared the end of his seminary classes. Arthur was older than most of his fellow seminarians by five to ten years; on the whole they seemed to him naïve undergrads rather than pastors-to-be: bright-eyed, overzealous, snugly conservative (well…not all, not Arthur) even though a fair number of their professors were left of center. This cove had given him a place to hide out and work on a long paper explaining his personal beliefs—pecking away at a laptop on his gritty yellow blanket--a project that had progressed steadily until two days ago when a woman had begun quietly intruding on his space. Other beach-goers came and went, of course—he didn't own this stretch of sand. But they were few and rarely distractions.

The woman had first shown up in the afternoon on Sunday, descending a weather blackened wooden stairway from an imposing, lodge-like cottage with many windows on top of the bluff. She'd struggled down the sixty some steps with a beach bag slung over a shoulder and a wriggling little boy in her arms. Arthur had watched her uneasily, nearly jumping up to help but then sensing the presumptuousness of it, seeing nothing very specific about her beyond a short white robe and a floppy straw hat. Not until she made her way into a circle of chairs surrounding a fire pit, clearly the property of the cottage, where she set down the child and beach bag and slipped out of the robe, did her tanned, athletic body begin to concern him. She wore a single piece black bathing suit, cut high on her hips and low between her breasts. She bent over and pulled a red shovel and pail from her bag, and the boy plopped in the sand to play. Arthur glanced away the moment she caught his eye. He'd been staring and was embarrassed at his thoughts.

On Tuesday, arriving mid morning, he found her already there, in a bathing suit nearly the color of her skin, accompanied by the same small boy. Arthur said hello to her. She returned his hello and a friendly smile. It was the first they'd spoken.

"Do you have a cottage nearby?" she asked.

"No, I'm a squatter—a student at the seminary in town. Trying to write my final paper. My apartment is hot. The library is crowded..."

"And I'm invading your privacy."

"Not at all. If that's your place on the bluff, you have more right to this beach than I do."

"Not really. You're on a tiny piece of public access property."

"I know. I'm trying to keep it a secret."

The little boy leaned over and poured a bucket of sand on her feet. She pretended to be angry, delighting him.

"Your son?" he asked.

"No...my sister's. I'm taking care of him while she's recuperating. She's up in the cottage resting."

"Anything serious?" There was honest concern in his voice.

"She's had a congenital heart defect repaired. My husband performed the surgery. He's a heart specialist."

"What a blessing for your sister."

"Yes. He's very good at what he does. He'll be here on the weekend. If you're still around, maybe you'll meet him."

"Maybe. I'm Arthur Brown, by the way." He set down his blanket, towel, and laptop, offered his hand, which she took. Her face was open and rather plain—her nose a touch too small and dotted with freckles—but a face he found pleasant to look at.

"I'm Hannah Marsh. Good luck with your paper. Just ignore me."

He nodded, amused, spread out his blanket a reasonable distance from her, pulled off his shirt, exposing his heavy keg of a chest, and opened the laptop, ready to pursue a line of thought (not original to him but one he strongly believed in) that God's revelation was progressive, that an understanding of Biblical truths was ongoing, neverending. The moment we claimed a corner on the truth, he intended to write, it slipped through our fingers.

As he sat poised to work, he felt the thread of his ideas slipping through his fingers. Ignore her? He focused on his opening word "Genesis." Against his will, he glanced up as she applied lotion to those already golden legs, the bare triangles of her hips, her shoulders and chest and the soft crescents of her breasts. In the bluff's shadow, her suit looked like naked skin. He deleted "Genesis." A moment later his eyes wandered away from the screen as she removed her hat and roped the cascading auburn hair into a ponytail. He saw her slide to her knees, stand the child up, and rub all his squirming bare spots with sunscreen. He imagined her hands slippery, silken, moving like the easy wash of waves up the beach and back again.

A surge of dismay churned in his stomach and turned sour in his mouth. The woman was innocently enjoying the beach with her small nephew, doing nothing to turn him on. He knew himself too well—knew that a fair number of the major problems in his life were the result of his perpetually nagging sex drive. His one near go at marriage—to Lisa, his talented videographer (with her and others at the McLean

Agency, he had directed infomercials for seven lucrative but soul-killing years)—had self-destructed when she rightly accused him of infidelity. Why was the world so full of women who attracted him? And why were they equally drawn to him? He was built like a bear. His hair was an untrimmed bush of heavy curls. He was shorter than he'd like to be. His nose had a permanent bend from a cycling accident. But women, single or married, gravitated to him. It was a mystery he accepted with misgivings.

Ah, Lisa. There were days when he missed the comfort of her physical presence so deeply that his heart felt raw, empty. Yet in this new life of seeking peace, pursuing truth, he tried hard to use the pain as a means of growth. He'd managed to avoid any serious entanglements throughout his stay at seminary. Now he was nearing the end of the task. He'd been feeling good about himself, and yet God's refining fire apparently had not yet burned all the dross away.

He retyped "Genesis" and went on. "Genesis, read as a Hebrew narrative rather than Greek, tells a story not of a fall from perfect innocence, but of human kind living their early adolescence in a good (not perfect) place close to God, then one day disobeying Him, being punished, and embarking on a long journey of slow but measureable maturing. Had Adam and Eve stayed in Eden forever, there would be no story to tell, no central conflict driving events. "

He breathed a sigh. His brain was still working, albeit slowly and in short bursts. The paragraph had taken him an hour and a half. The sun was directly above him; the shadow of the bluff was gone. He looked up and found to his relief that the woman and little boy were resting on a bench near the top of the stairs, preparing to enter the cottage.

Hannah Marsh had not gotten past feeling lost in the six-bedroom cottage her husband Jason had bought a year and a half ago. Though he hadn't shared details with her, she had overheard a figure beyond a million dollars.

She worked as head librarian at a Catholic College in Grand Rapids and taught creative writing to interested older adults. She wrote poetry that she showed to only a few, never to her husband. The money she made was laughable compared to the heart specialist's kingly wages. At the same time, she found it puzzling that he had no idea what to do with leaking faucets in their custom-built, five-bathroom East Grand Rapids home. Her father, the plumber, had taken time to teach her the rudiments of his work. Could a leaking heart valve be that much different?

Hannah found it strange and not at all comforting to be married to a man who made more money than she'd ever be able to spend, who saw no reason why she shouldn't quit her work and live like a queen on the fruits of his labors. Her sanity, however, depended on never succumbing to that temptation. She looked back with fondness on their modest beginnings; a downtown apartment, cheap wine, and a mountain of med school debt to pay off.

It was noon Friday; Jason was due to arrive mid afternoon. Her younger sister Jenny, recently divorced and struggling to support her small son Noah, nestled in a soft recliner, still weak from her surgery but looking serene as she gazed out at the gleaming lake. Jenny was in the midst of a worshipful period focused on Hannah's husband—he was her savior, her comforter and keeper who had repaired her heart and made his cottage indefinitely available to her.

Noah sat at a small table, nibbling at a sandwich Hannah had made. A smear of peanut butter marked each of his cheeks. Now and then he picked a green grape from a bowl and popped it into the little o of his mouth. Hannah enjoyed caring for him. He was easy and undemanding, the kind of child she hoped for herself. Jason seemed to adore him. They were ready for a family, but she hadn't become pregnant in the two years they'd been trying. The seven childless years before had been mutual career choices. She wondered if they'd waited too long. With Jason's impossible hours, sex (when it happened) was often a weary, late-night affair.

"Who is the man always down there on the beach?" Jenny asked, turning toward her. "I see you talking to him sometimes."

"Arthur? The one on the yellow blanket? He's a seminary student trying to get his thesis done. I do my best to leave him alone, but he talks to me now and again…mostly about literature. We seem to have similar tastes—like Victorian novelists and Anne Tyler. He's oddly attractive."

"Is he married?" Hannah saw in her sister, always the prettier of the two, an amusing spark of an old competitiveness.

"I haven't asked."

"I wish I could handle those stairs to the beach."

Hannah laughed. "Well, you can't. I'll ask him up for a glass of wine, if you'd like. I've been thinking about it anyway. While Noah is napping, I'll go see what his plans are."

"Aren't you a good sister." Jenny smiled. "Jason insists I need all this rest and recuperation, but I'm going a little stir crazy. I know he's right, of course."

"He generally is."

"Yes, I like that in a man." She was perfectly serious. "How in the world did you ever come away with a prize like him?"

Hannah smiled wryly. "I got to him before you did."

Arthur said yes without hesitation; she'd expected some resistance. He insisted on diving in the lake first to wash off the sand and sweat, so she waited on the shore as he plunged into the waves like a small whale. When he came back, he shook out his hair like a dog and dried off vigorously in front of her with a sandy towel.

The moment took her entirely by surprise and left her shaken. So vital, so passionate was the close presence of this man that she found herself mentally tearing off her things and making fierce love to him there on the yellow blanket. The tidal wave of arousal swept through her and away. She swayed dizzily, her heart pounding. Nothing like it had ever happened before.

"Hannah? Are you all right?" he asked. "Your face is flushed."

She was trembling inside. "I don't know…I feel light-headed. I…I really haven't eaten since breakfast."

"Can you manage the stairs?"

"I'm sure I can. I'll sit down on the steps while you get your things together. I'll be fine."

"Sorry about visiting your place in a damp suit. I'll sit on a towel till it dries."

"It's no problem. We all do it." A part of her suit was damp, too, and she hoped the robe covered it up. She sat for several minutes, gathering herself, but her legs were rubbery on the way up the stairs. He laid a hand on her back twice to steady her.

The first glass of white wine seemed to restore her. Arthur sat on one of their folded beach towels in a wicker chair next to Jenny. His shirt of bright, bold tropical flowers was splotchy where it touched his bathing suit. Hannah slipped into a beach wrap to cover her suit and sat down on his other side. The sun was still high up, dazzling the water below. He was charming and solicitous to Jenny, who enjoyed it and yet seemed less taken with him than Hannah had expected. He listened to the story of her heart problems and surgery, the words now as well worn as the path in a pony ring. He quickly discovered Jenny's passion for French cooking and drew her out on it with knowledgeable ease. Hannah watched how he offered his devoted attention…a pastor's skill. When he turned at last to Hannah, he smiled with his eyes, and they seemed to tell her "you are now the center of my universe." It was an enticing illusion. "Hannah, do you write?" he asked. "I'm guessing you do. Your insights into books amaze me."

"Oh, she's a poet," Jenny chirped. "But she never shows her poems to us. She's actually head librarian at St. Anthony's College."

"I'd love to see your poems."

Hannah blushed. "Honestly, Jenny…you'll all see them someday when they're ready."

"I'll be patient," he said, implying further connection between them.

Just after three, she heard the muted, muscular roar of Jason's Jaguar. He inevitably revved the engine two or three times before shutting it off, as if the sound boosted his testosterone. She found the habit curiously annoying.

Jenny looked toward the door with an expectant smile. "Is that Jason?"

"Yes…announcing his presence." Hannah glanced over at Arthur. His eyes were on her. She began fussing with her skirt and took a large swallow of wine.

Jason entered with an "I'm not on call this weekend" look of haggard relief, hefting a grocery bag in one arm. When he became aware of a stranger in the room, a guest not expected, his face fell, but he quickly recovered himself.

He disliked surprises, Hannah knew, so she went cheerfully to greet him, and took the grocery bag away. Her husband was a tall, gaunt, good-looking man--in his college days a marathon runner who still managed five miles a day.

"Jason, this is Arthur…Brown, is it? I'm sorry. You told me once."

Arthur got to his feet, smiled at her and nodded.

"He's been on the beach all week finishing his final seminary paper. We took pity on him."

Jason went to Arthur with extended hand. "Good for you, Arthur."

"Sorry to intrude on your Friday. I'm only staying for a glass of wine."

"So you two don't really know each other?" Jason asked, pouring himself a glass of chardonnay.

"We met on Tuesday, I think." Arthur sat back down. "A few more years on the beach and we'll be old and dear friends."

They laughed, and Jason visibly relaxed. He took a chair beside Jenny and set his right hand on her left. "How's my little patient?"

Basking in the attention, she said with a sigh, "I'm trying to be good, but it's so hard just sitting. Thank goodness the view is heavenly. I love this place."

"Enjoy it. You're in good hands."

"I know I am. I'd love a glass of wine, though."

He hesitated. "One glass and no more?"

Jenny's brief display of girlish glee, one of her oldest and least endearing routines, caused a tightening in Hannah's jaw.

"How incredible it is that you repair hearts," Arthur said with sincerity. "Especially the heart of someone so close to you—it's a great gift, a touch of grace."

Jason was flattered. "Well, I've been blessed with certain skills. God has been good."

"You've been blessed to be a blessing," Arthur concluded.

Jason absorbed the compliment, quietly pleased. "Do you plan to be a pastor?"

"No sense of call as yet, but who knows? I worked in advertising for seven years—seven years of plenty for myself, seven years of famine for my soul. The ministry, though, might be too much the opposite. I'm unmarried, fortunately; I've saved enough to survive a few years while I figure it out."

Jason slowly sipped his wine, turning over an idea. "Have you ever considered that advertising men and clergymen actually have things in common?"

"Maybe." Arthur smiled patiently. "But continue."

"Well, think about it. Both are pitchmen. The advertising man sells tangible things, the holy man intangibles. I think intangibles are easier. You pitch the blue sky. No products to warehouse, no returns, no money back guarantees. If your tongue is golden and the pitch is good, you'll have them lining up to buy the world's one truly invisible commodity."

Arthur laughed easily. "Like the emperor's new clothes!"

"Some make a fortune at it…religion attracts its fair share of con men."

Arthur hesitated, assessing the remark. "Yes! Amen to that." He took a swallow of wine. "But the story can have a twist to it. If the holy man pitches the blue sky long enough, he can end up buying it himself. God has the damndest sense of humor."

Jason had overstepped, Hannah knew. He poured himself more wine. "I'm kidding you, of course. I'm heavily invested in that blue sky. I'm pulling your leg."

Smiling, Arthur said, "Your humor has more than a grain of truth to it. I appreciate it."

He was letting Jason off with grace. Noah chose that moment to wake up, and she rose quickly to see to him.

Arthur stayed for dinner and well beyond. Jason insisted on it and began calling him Art. They emptied three bottles of wine. The conversation transcended their usual level by a good measure. And it wasn't so much Arthur's words that made the difference--it was his listening.

Realizing with a shocked apology that it was after eight, Arthur gathered his things along with half a dozen brownies Hannah persuaded him to take. She carried the foil package for him to the front door, and since his car was in the public lot down the street, she walked him to it. The sun was dropping low, the sky washed with oranges and pinks.

"I stayed too long," he said off-handedly.

"Not at all. I just hope your paper doesn't suffer."

"No worry there…I think I've finished it."

"Really? I'd like to read it."

He stopped and put his things on the hood of a Land Rover while he looked for his keys. "Do you mean that? I'm desperate for a critical reading."

"Of course I mean it. I'm up to my neck in leisure time right now."

"Then, yes, I'll take you up on it…if you'll show me some of your poems."

Out of her came a melodramatic sigh. "I'll have to think about that." She handed him the brownies as he bent to tuck his laptop, blanket, and towel into the back seat. When he straightened up, they were only inches apart.

"I'll need to know how to get hold of you," he said, not moving away. She saw how richly brown his eyes were.

The kiss seemed perfectly natural. He'd intended just to brush her cheek with it, but she turned so their lips met and stayed there longer than either expected, embarrassing them in a pleasurable way. In a slightly reckless tone, she said simply "Wow."

"Couldn't have expressed it better." His half whisper was thrilling.

And then they both laughed, breaking the spell, exchanged cell numbers and goodnights. As he drove off, she stood watching until he turned toward town. Alone now, feeling alive in ways she hadn't in years, Hannah headed toward a sky of capriciously shifting colors.

Jason and Jenny were seated side by side at the beachside windows, watching the sun drop toward the brightly blazing water.

"Just in time," he said. "Another sunset, another day."

Hannah sat down beside him. The spectacle was something she rarely missed. It made a million-dollar cottage seem almost worth the price.

"Interesting evening," he said as the sun touched the line between sky and lake.

"I wasn't sure what to expect, but I enjoyed him." Hannah ventured this cautiously.

"He certainly has charm,' Jenny added.

Jason wasn't finished. He'd obviously been thinking about it. "Clever, charismatic, endlessly charming, honey dripping from his tongue—all the basic ingredients. I have to be honest, I wouldn't trust him as far as I could spit."

Hannah was stunned, blindsided by his assessment. What in the world had she missed?

"I thought you had fun," she said

Smiling sagely, he said, "That's the great trick—I did."

Jason left for home just after dinner on Sunday; he had a 6 A.M. surgery. Hannah was impatient for him to go. On Monday, she waited for a call from Arthur, but it didn't come. She tried texting him. By late Wednesday, he hadn't replied. She made the effort to gather a few poems to show him, though she felt uneasy and vulnerable doing it. On Thursday, while Noah napped, she drove into town and passed the seminary several times hoping to see him. She had no idea where he lived. The town was small and a Land Rover would surely stand out. She looked for nearly two hours but never found it.

****

Four years passed. Hannah quit library work, preferring the twelve classroom hours a week, nine months a year of teaching. On a Thursday evening, one she'd anticipated with excitement and anxiety, she slipped through the glass doors of Goodfellow's Bookstore where in less than an hour she would read and sign copies of her first book, *A Private Stretch of Beach and Other Poems*. Close friends and some colleagues had promised to be there, but she had no idea of any others who might show up. She knew her ex-husband Jason would not be one of them, nor would her sister, who was still struggling with the circumstances of the divorce. Hannah had suspected something for weeks during the late summer of Jenny's recuperation, until, on the evening of an unexpected class cancellation, she'd walked Into the cottage to find them tangled on a couch, the red surgery scar a raw line between Jenny's breasts. The humiliation and betrayal had nearly crushed her, but for her sister's sake, Hannah made no public issue of it.

Jason and Jenny had been married two years now. Hannah forgave her, but Jenny nursed a complicated, angry remorse that Hannah didn't understand. In truth, Jenny had done her an immense favor. Hannah wanted none of the property, and Jason had been fair in the settlement. The queen's role was her sister's now, and Hannah gladly relinquished it.

The reading area, a back corner of the store hidden behind the theology shelves, was set up with chairs. The lectern and sound system appeared ready for her. She let the manager know she was there, realizing she still had fifty minutes to kill. She was too full of nervous energy to browse the books, so she made her way to the coffee bar to wait it out with espresso. What she really needed was a bottle of wine.

She found a secluded table in a far corner and sat with her back to the room. She tossed down a folder of notes and a copy of her book, which she opened, attempting to look absorbed.

"Excuse me," someone nearby said. "Would you mind signing this for me?"

A man held out a copy of her book to her. The voice, vaguely familiar, drew her eyes up. Arthur Brown stood looking uneasily at her. He wore a casual silk shirt and sports coat. His brown eyes were still unnerving. For a moment, her heart hammered.

"Arthur? I can't believe it's you."

"Funny thing, I was shopping here yesterday and picked up this book of poems by a local author. Of course, I didn't realize Hannah Stuart was actually Hannah Marsh—at least until I spotted your photograph on the back cover."

She hesitated, wondering what to tell him. "I've taken back my maiden name."

"I guessed as much. I know now that you've been divorced a few years. I know the heart specialist remarried your sister. I've been living in Chicago, but it didn't take long to get the story."

"It's high on the list of local scandals," she muttered, inviting him to sit, which he did as she signed the book. "How are you, Arthur? You look very nice all dressed up. I've never seen you in anything but a bathing suit."

He laughed heartily. "I was thinking the same thing about you. Your bathing suits nearly torpedoed my thesis."

"The thesis I never read?"

He took a deep breath and exhaled. "I'm sorry about that..."

"I hope they let you graduate."

"I'm proud to say they accepted the paper, though with reservations. Too much independent thinking, one said. Too far out on the progressive fringe, another wrote. I agreed entirely. I was hoping for a charge of heresy, but no one went that far."

She smiled. "I intended to show you some of my poems."

"Well, I'm four years late, but I read them last night—all of them." He shifted his eyes to a nearby window. "I was touched, Hannah--in ways I can't even express. The title poem was actually painful to read. It has in it the reason I never got back to you."

"Has it? I'm not sure what you mean."

His eyes returned to hers. "I think you know as well as I do. We were a short hop from disaster. I did what I believed was right even though it wasn't what I wanted. If I'd met you even once more..."

She understood in an instant. All the confused hurt she'd felt about him had been wasted pain. Jason had been wrong. It was he (perhaps even she), not Arthur, who was not to be trusted, not even as far as she could spit.

Yet she was wary. Relationships had become risky to her, and she'd made a habit of protecting herself.

Arthur stayed for her reading and browsed the theology shelves while she signed copies. Afterwards, at his suggestion, they slipped into a nearby tavern for some white wine and fairly copious toasts. She'd sold a surprising number of books, and his enthusiasm about her success excited her. For a while she found herself basking in his radiance once more. When he told her that his decision to forego contact with her, hard as it was, had marked a turning point in his life, the admission tantalized her. It also sent up warning flags.

She stared at her hands, and then glanced at her watch. "Goodness. Forgive me, Arthur—but could we save that thought? I didn't realize the time. I still have papers to read for tomorrow."

"Oh—of course," he said, "I'd lost track completely." He locked her with his eyes…and a moment later, with a glowing, gracious smile, at last released her, unable to hide his disappointment.

At home, she undressed and tucked herself into bed, restless but relieved at the care she'd taken of her heart. Her large bedroom doubled as her office. On a broad oak desk she observed her computer and printer, orderly stacks of her writing and behind it student work in manila folders. Shelves surrounded her, neat rows of her books organized by author's last name. Her things were just so, just as she wanted them, just as she'd left them earlier. She opened a book of Thomas Hardy's poems, savoring the melancholy rhythms and delicate, devastating lines about love grown cold.

It seemed she had successfully packed up all disruptive thoughts of Arthur, even though he still had a habit of invading her dreams, sometimes in disconcertingly sexual ways. She'd concluded he was one of those bewitching, hit-and-run types who played women like musical instruments. After a brief struggle, and to her great relief, she'd managed to let the infatuation go.

And yet now, at midnight, as her phone began to ring, the sound raced through her veins like electrical current.

****

His charm, as it turned out, was real, though exasperating when he spent it on undeserving people. He had a more generous spirit than she. It was he who took the time to begin some healing with her sister, opening a door, they hoped, to Noah. Arthur was now an affordable housing advocate in Grand Rapids, fearless in his defense of the most vulnerable, and she had written a second book, helping move her up to department chair at St. Anthony's--though now that she was pregnant, she was thinking seriously of an indefinite leave. As an older mother-to-be, she could not imagine missing a single moment, a single joy.

Her ex-husband Jason, though a highly visible presence in the city, was as removed from her as a name in a yearbook. Once when Arthur asked her if she still felt pain about him, she told him honestly, "Why would I? Jason repaired my sister's heart; you repaired mine."

Arthur excited her as much as ever, but her body, thankfully, was calmer about it. Someday, when he was older and needing a boost, she would lie next to him in bed and tell him the story of her ecstasy on the beach.

SYBIL OF MALIBU

She lived in a house on the beach in Malibu. He'd had trouble finding it and arrived eight minutes late. Her manager invited him in, and (to make a point?) she kept him waiting in a small library thirty minutes before she appeared. Leo had seen her in a few movies, always brash and sexy, never the one who got the guy. She was older than he'd expected—late-40s or more—a bit drawn around the eyes and mouth, as if some surgery had already been done. Her house was surprisingly modest in size, furnished with furniture covered in what appeared to be African animal hides. She offered him a seat in a zebra skin chair.

"They're simulated skins, of course," she said. "I'm an activist." Her voice was low with an edgy kind of rasp. The Pacific side of the house was mostly glass, overlooking a narrow beach and heavy, rolling waves. He wondered if white shorts and a taut red body suit were her usual business attire.

Her manager Daniel stood at a kitchen counter pouring glasses of Perrier. He was younger than she was by at least ten years, dressed in linen pants and a flowing silk shirt, a slickly handsome GQ clone.

"Sybil and I both think your script is the best thing we've read in years." His voice was smooth and musical.

"I appreciate that."

"You're younger than I expected," she said, staring at him with the blue, unnerving eyes of a Siamese cat. "Your writing seemed older."

"Hmmm. Thanks." He smiled uncertainly, but she didn't smile back. His male lead character in this, his first script, was 65, more than twice his own age, and Sybil Malone (he'd learned from his agent), was ready to kill for the part of the female lead, a woman widowed in her late 20s. Leo, a nobody from Bloomington, Indiana, was exhilarated by the novelty of being treated as a writer of worth, even by an actress obviously too old and hard-edged for the part. This was his first working trip to Hollywood; he knew next to nothing about the business—a pretender who had somehow walked through the looking glass into a world as alien to him as Mars.

He'd previously published a first novel that didn't sell (in spite of some positive reviews}, several short stories in small magazines that very few read. Still, he remained a driven artist yearning for an audience, so he'd turned to screenplays at the urging of a friend now getting wealthy writing them. Without much struggle, he'd deserted half-formed notions of literary purity, quickly learned the mechanics of the screenplay from the friend, and turned out a script within four months. The process was worrisomely painless compared to the long slog of a novel. The friend read it, was impressed, introduced Leo to his agent who, equally impressed, had signed him and sold it within two months. It was all too easy, especially the money.

Leo was now a bona fide member of the Writers Guild of America. His name had appeared twice in *Variety*. A movie of his script was in development at MGM with a well-known director attached. He felt amiably smug but tried not to show it. He told no one in the business that his real job was buying and selling used textbooks in a Midwestern college town. In Hollywood he said simply (and only when asked) that he ran a bookstore near a university. It seemed acceptably literary. He had no intention of leaving the bookselling business since the mortgage on the place was his, he lived in an apartment above it with his girlfriend, and the prospect of moving to Los Angeles dismayed him. Writers could write anywhere, he reasoned. Those interested in his talent could fly him out when they needed him. If that didn't work, he still had a job, a home, and a relatively stable life.

She'd invited him to her house to look him over—this novice who'd written a part she coveted—and to pitch a story idea for him to develop in collaboration with her. Yet already she seemed disappointed in something. Was it his bearded, sheepdog look, his polyester shirt, his unexpected youth, ordinarily an asset in this business? As he looked out at the pounding waves, the floor seemed to roll slightly beneath him. When he'd told his director he was meeting Sybil Malone at her request, the director had mumbled something—possibly ironic--about her legendary charm. Leo had never asked what he meant.

She pulled on a white cashmere cardigan and buttoned it partway up the front. "What do you know about the world of punk rock?" she asked.

Leo considered it for a moment. "Practically nothing."

"Well…no matter. I know enough for both of us."

"We think you'd be right for this," Daniel said sincerely. "Your writing is more dense than what we usually see. It touches the heart but in a gritty, unsentimental way. You might be surprised that Sybil is interested in the lead in your film—did you know that?"

"No, I didn't," Leo lied. "I'm flattered."

"I like the character," she said in a surprisingly neutral voice. "The part would need rethinking, of course, but that's not really why we're here. I have an idea for a two-woman film, a punk rock singer and her manager. I play the manager. Do you know 'Punk Rock Girl,' by The Dead

Milkmen?" She grew more histrionic as she spoke. "The music is raw rage against a corrupt dominant culture. I envision poignancy in chaos, love emerging between the two women in the midst of drugs and debauchery--an unexpected sexual relationship between straight women. In my mind, it is very powerful material."

"Interesting," Leo said. "Very interesting." He was lying again. He'd seen glimpses of the outlandish spiked Mohawks, tattoos, offensive tee shirts, pink hair, and grotesque body piercings that had begun spooking the general public a few years before. Now it was 1983 and apparently the time, she felt, to make an artistic statement about it. "I just don't think I'm the best choice," he went on.

"I think you are."

"I don't know the subject. I have no passion for the music." Truth was, he hated it.

"No worry. I'll provide the passion."

"Hmmm. Well...go ahead, tell me more."

She resumed her scattered tale with panache, as if she were living it. The phone rang but she paid no attention. Daniel slipped away to the beach room, closing the door before answering. The haze that had hung above Los Angeles that morning now seemed to be drifting into Leo's mind, muffling her words so he heard only pieces, disordered and surreal. He watched Daniel talking, shaking his head, apparently upset.

"Somewhere there'll be a groupie scene, a party, with drugs and graphic sex...whatever we can get away with. And in the midst of it, the two women will wander away to another room and begin to discover their feelings for each other, feelings so much more real than—"

Daniel interrupted, calling her name twice before she came out of the spell she was weaving. Leo watched her face distort with anger.

"I'm telling my story, goddammit! **What**?"

Daniel stared sheepishly at his suede loafers. "They've signed Carlotta."

Her face turned gray as stone. "Like hell they have."

"The promises were bullshit."

She shrieked like a banshee, lifted a glass globe from the table in front of her and heaved it against a stone fireplace. It exploded in a thousand gleaming shards. Leo was dumbstruck. She turned to him with a ferocious glare. "Did you know about this?"

"About what? Who is Carlotta?"

She turned to Daniel. "The poor schmuck doesn't know. Welcome to Hollywood, honey, land of the knife in the back."

Leo took a deep breath to steady whatever was shaking inside. "What the hell is going on?"

"They signed Carlotta Ewing to the lead in your film," Daniel said, watching her nervously.

Leo, the clueless neophyte, knew only that Carlotta Ewing was a young actress who had recently risen to stardom.

She paced agitatedly. Her jaw tightened as she spoke. "Sorry, sonny, but your script is screwed. It's a charming screenplay, a small film, a character piece. Now Carlotta will turn it into a big, star-driven, multi-million dollar production. She'll bring in her own writers and by the time they get done with it, you won't recognize a goddam thing you wrote. Well, at least you'll make enough money to pay the psychiatrist you'll need afterwards." She laughed crazily. "Daniel!" she shrieked, but her manager seemed suddenly to have disappeared. "That cowardly bastard! This time I'm really firing him. I can hear him! Listen! That's his Mercedes—he's running from my wrath!"

Leo heard the car screech onto the Pacific Coast Highway, and, feeling panicked, possibly in some kind of danger, he rose from the zebra skin chair. "Look, I'm sorry. I had nothing to do with this. I really have to go."

She laughed again, came close, and stuck her face in his. "Like hell you have to go. We're still in a meeting. You're seeing me through this, you naïve fuck. Oh—and forget about my project. You don't deserve it. I can tell you're a one-shot wonder anyway. Just by luck, you got things right once but probably never will again. I've seen it more times than I can count. The one-shot wonders of Hollywood. I'll bet you're a one-shot wonder in bed, too."

"You don't know anything about me."

"Sure I do. I know your type. You're such a little boy. You're in a jungle, little boy, and you don't even realize it." She pushed him back into the zebra chair and sat on the arm of it, pressing her hip against his side. "I'm Sybil. I know all. When I first set eyes on you, I knew exactly what you were thinking."

He couldn't speak for a moment. "What was I thinking?"

"Your mind is uncomplicated. It was roaming all over my body."

"That's not what I was doing."

"You're lying. Sybil knows."

Leo leaned away from her hip and bare thigh. She was truly deranged. He took a desperate tack. "Well, look at you. How could I not notice?"

"Ah, there it is. Now we're getting somewhere. I'm curious--is writing a substitute for sex for you--sublimation, or something Freudian like that?"

"I never thought about it." His voice was dead flat with a faint tremor.

"I was expecting someone mature, someone who understood me, not a little boy." She snorted, leaped up suddenly, and went to a bar near the fireplace, crunching heedlessly through pieces of glass. She poured two Scotches without asking what he wanted, returned, and shoved one in his hands. "Here. We need a drink." She had the bottle under her arm.

"Thanks."

She drank the Scotch standing and without speaking, draining the glass in less than a minute and pouring another for each of them. She flopped into a chair across from him. A weary calm seemed to settle over her as she drank more. "I'm a sorry fucking nightmare," she muttered with sullen emotion. She wiped her wet eyes (real tears?) with the back of a hand, smearing her eye shadow. A long, unsteady inhalation followed, after which her voice sounded laryngitic. "Why are you throwing away your talent in this shithole business?"

He'd missed lunch and could already feel the alcohol blunting his brain; he slowly shook his head and didn't answer immediately. But her stare forced it out of him. "Who knows? A friend convinced me to try it, and, chop-chop, here I am. It was easy."

"Well, lucky you. Just don't expect it to be easy any more. It'll suck the soul right out of you."

He shook his head. "I'll be long gone before that ever happens."

Her grin grew tight, razor-thin. "You've got both feet in quicksand already, you dumb cluck." She closed her eyes. "And me? I'm in up to my goddam neck!"

She rose with a moan and made toward a bedroom at the end of a hall, the bottle and glass still in her hands. She kicked the door hard, and it crashed behind her. Leo waited. No sound came from the bedroom. Five minutes turned into fifteen. He felt traumatized, eviscerated, grieved, and somehow guilty. At last, silent as a mouse, he let himself out.

His film (well, hardly his any more) was made with Carlotta Ewing in the lead. It opened to bland, lenient reviews, far more merciful than Leo felt it deserved, and it was gone from theaters in short order. Leo 's name was first in the writing credits, followed by three others.

Though it seemed odd, he soon was hired to write another movie script, and then several more (for complicated reasons none made it to screen). They were challenging, profitable ventures for him but in the end a bit like building houses that no one lived in. Urged by his agent, Leo began doing some television (no longer the kiss of death it once had been), where the money and production were more dependable. Within two years, because he was now writing for a series with producing credit, he moved to Los Angeles. The show was a lightheaded but lucrative family sitcom with laugh tracks. To his bafflement, it would last seven seasons and go into syndication. Leo did find therapy helpful, especially when his long time girlfriend returned to Bloomington. The punk rock project, to his knowledge, never saw the light of day. He was able to keep abreast of Sybil Malone's career by following (always with a vague twinge) her infomercials for bone density drugs and reverse mortgages.

MRS. BARKER

What was supposed to be the best time of my life had turned into the worst. It was the summer before my sophomore year in college; I'd managed as a freshman to find my way out of engineering and into English and caught fire reading literature I'd neglected in the interests of science and math. I'd lost a scholarship as a result but gained a passion for a rich, dark, and complex world I'd somehow managed to ignore up to then. All of this seemed good—I finally knew why I was going to college. But that was only half the story.

Mrs. Barker weighed on my mind as I hefted Budweiser cases from the truck onto a dolly and then into the Tip Top Party Store, where my driver, Joe Saladino, was writing out an invoice for Popeye, the owner, whose neck was as thick as my waist.

"I see you got your college boy back," Popeye rasped. "Another summer of rest, Saladino?"

"The kid loves working with me, right, Henry?"

"Right," I said, rolling by him toward the beer cooler.

Joe was happy to let me do the heavy work—I was building muscle, and he was saving his 50-year-old back.

He was a decent guy, deeply uncomplicated, with a gut that advertised the product we delivered.

Mrs. Barker, a divorcee, lived with her three wild little boys in the house I'd grown up in. My parents had bought into a business 1200 miles south and taken the entire family with them. I stayed to go to college and keep the Budweiser job, the one I'd started the summer before courtesy of my father, a musician who owned a local bar he'd sold for a bigger one in Florida. The delivery job paid for most of my year at MSU, back then around $1500, including room and board. By the time of their move, early summer, they hadn't sold the family house, so they left my bed and one chair, and drove out of my life, deserting the place to me until it sold or rented.

Though I admitted it to no one, I felt utterly lost, orphaned, abandoned. It was melodramatic and childish, I knew—I was 19 by then. But my family was large and close, three younger brothers who irritated and amused me in equal doses, and two little sisters, 6 and 4, tail-enders whom I loved like my own children. I didn't realize until they were gone how tightly my life had been tied to family. I had one best friend from high school, now my roommate in college, but he stayed at school summers, away from his alcoholic father, and worked mowing the acres of campus lawns.

Our house, so full of life, was empty and haunted by ghosts groaning in walls, by echoing whispers that woke me in the night. I was alone and desolate. I'm guessing I must've had a small nervous breakdown, if there is such a thing, because suddenly I wanted to crawl in a closet and hide. I had a terrible time being social, even laughing. Small talk was agony. The strange loss of inner resilience scared me. I ached for my mother's cheery presence, for her cooking, for her dinner table clamoring with family; I longed for my father's piano filling the house with music, for all that anchored my life and sheltered me from a harsher world I was daily getting glimpses of…in my reading, in the unrest around me—mobs attacking Freedom Riders, atomic missiles in Cuba, a gathering war in Vietnam. My childhood at times struck me as a Pollyanna daydream.

The woman next door, Mrs. Oz, had a key my mother had entrusted to her, hoping she'd keep an eye on things. Mrs. Oz sat in her side window like an enormous toad, watching our house as her kids ran amok. The few times I brought a girl to the empty house, my mother heard about it. I pretty much loathed Mrs. Oz. Her husband was a window dresser whom she bullied. She was a busybody and worse--she would enter our house when I was gone and take my books without asking. When I told her those books were assigned reading for school (Hemingway, Fitzgerald, Steinbeck), she returned them, but with ragged covers and torn pages thanks to her kids and her own slovenly habits. At that point, I lacked the inner strength to call her on it. When September came at last, I packed my books and with relief returned to college, burying myself in my room and studies, rarely going out except to classes. My best friend, who partied at every opportunity, was concerned about me.

Not until mid-winter did my parents manage to rent the house. They couldn't afford to fly me down for Christmas break, so I filled in as a carrier for the post office. Nor did my parents have the means to make two house payments, so the renter, Mrs. Barker, seemed like a godsend. A rent check arrived in the mail on time for each of her first three months. But for the following three, nothing came at all, not even an explanation.

When I returned to town for the summer and work, my father wrote and asked me to find out what was wrong with Mrs. Barker. I was living in the Saladino's basement for $50 a month. I slept on a hide-a-bed in Joe's damp, blessedly cool, partially-finished rec room. In this dim cave I'd found a safe if not entirely habitable hiding place. The bathroom was upstairs, unfortunately, and Joe's wife liked to linger there. I sometimes peed in her laundry tub with the water running. When I slept (never without difficulty), I was beset by bizarre nightmares of wrinkling cloth and girls with withered lips, visions that—for no discernible reason--terrified me.

I ate on my own, mostly takeout, though now and then Joe came down with beers and cheese curls for both of us.

"You need a tv down here to keep you company," he'd tell me.

"I like my books. But thanks for the concern."

"At least get out once in a while," he'd say, lifting his Budweiser. "You can't just work and read, Henry."

"I'll get out soon."

Yet I stalled for several days before I drove over to see Mrs. Barker. I had an old VW bug that got me around in a hit or miss way. I parked in front of our weathered frame house with its front porch of rusted screens. Our driveway was full of tricycles and toys, so I stayed clear of it. The neighborhood was borderline crummy, with a Salvation Army Chapel half a block down. Their band was out on the street just finishing up a number.

Mrs. Barker was sitting on the porch, sorting socks, not expecting anybody. The sun had set, and a pink blush was fading from the sky. When I approached the door, she watched with apprehension. I said hello, but she didn't return it.

"I'm Henry White," I said. "This is my parents' house."

"Oh. Okay. I've been expecting someone to show up. Come on in."

She opened the door and offered me a rattan chair facing the matching loveseat she occupied. She wasn't at all what I expected--about 30, dressed in a thin summer dress, tall and attractive but angular and worn-down looking, as if the weight of the world was on her.

"I just got my boys to sleep. Want a beer?"

I didn't. I wanted to deliver my message and get out. But I said "Sure."

So she went inside. I took a moment to glance at the foyer and living room. The house was pretty much trashed. She returned with two cold brown bottles.

"My ex-husband sent child support for three months and then disappeared," she said, sitting down. "I should've contacted your parents but didn't know what to say."

"Maybe you could call them and explain."

"My phone is shut off."

I was embarrassed for her. "Sounds like you've got some troubles."

"I guess I do." She took a long swallow of beer. "I suppose you want us to clear out now."

I suddenly felt bad…and trapped. "Well…I didn't say that. My parents are understanding people, but it's just that they're making two house payments and it's tough."

She nodded, getting the point, and drank more beer. "Funny. I grew up pretty happy and carefree. A little wild, maybe…nothing all that bad, unless you ask my parents. But I never thought life would turn out so hard."

"I know," I said sincerely.

"You do? You're pretty young for things to be hard, Henry."

Something fluttered in me when she spoke my name aloud. I looked down at the concrete floor. It was the same epoxy gray I'd painted it four years before."I think sometimes I'm going crazy," she said abruptly, but then laughed.

I'd had that feeling way too often. I looked past her through the screen and saw Mrs. Oz in the window. Mrs. Barker turned and spotted her, raised her middle finger defiantly, and Mrs. Oz vanished from the window, outraged. "That damn nosy cow. She looks in my windows all the time."

I silently applauded. "She's the neighborhood witch. My mother gave her a key to the house, so watch out."

"Don't worry, I changed the lock when I first moved here. I caught her trying to get in."

I laughed. "Good for you, Mrs. Barker."

"Don't call me that. It sounds like some old lady. Call me Clare. I'm not that ancient, Henry. I only had my ten-year class reunion last summer. A few years ago I was a free spirit, just like you…like you should be. I was at the beach all summer long, usually in a bikini and driving boys to drink, if you can imagine."

I smiled uneasily. "I can."

She stared at me a moment and raised her skirt a little above her knees. We didn't talk for a bit. Then out of nowhere she asked me if I'd ever made love on a beach. Even though it was warm on the porch, I began trembling, and my voice shook as I admitted I hadn't. The truth was, that in spite of several earnest efforts, I was still a virgin. Whenever I heard, "We better stop," I'd stop, figuring it was something we both needed to agree on.

"Sounds nice," I said in almost a whisper.

"Yes, it's very nice…" and she drew me a picture. "…on the beach in the dark with the waves coming in and the moon shining down. You feel more alive in the open air… more naked, like your skin is brand-new and the moonlight is turning your body to silver. It can be a beautiful, beautiful thing, Henry." Her legs parted a bit. It was dark on the porch now, but in the shadows under her skirt I could see a thin strip of white. "Sit next to me," she said.

I hesitated. "Mrs. Oz…"

"Well, let's just go in."

So I followed her into the living room, and she closed the blind on the Oz side. "I'm sorry the place is a mess," she said. "I can't seem to get myself going some days."

"It's okay. Nothing that can't be fixed."

She stepped close and pressed against me, her hands on my hips. Though I was scared stiff, I paid attention to the feel of her breasts as they touched my chest, how the ridge of her sex pressed on mine. Upstairs, one of her boys cried in his sleep. I went to kiss her but discovered her pushing me back so we weren't touching.

"I can't do this," she said in a voice I could barely hear. "You don't deserve to be fooled with. You're a kind boy. It's not your fault I'm desperate. We'll leave as soon as we can."

I was confused, dizzy with a mix of lust and honest caring. "Don't leave. Let me see what I can do, " I said, regaining some composure.

"No. You don't owe me a thing."

"You and your family need to live someplace, Mrs. Barker. Let me try at least."

She moved closer, went up on her toes a little and kissed my cheek. "Okay, Henry. But I don't know what help you can be."

I drove home and thought about Mrs. Barker—Clare--and her boys. I tried not to think about her body. I tossed and turned half the night, wondering if she was still working me in some way. The next day was Saturday, my day off with nothing but empty time to fill, so I hauled myself out of the basement, went over to the house and sat for a while with her on a broken-down red couch where our broken-down brown couch used to be. I could hear the boys ramming around upstairs. Occasionally, one of them would look with curiosity down the stairway at me and then disappear. It was the same stairway my sisters had come down wide-eyed at Christmastime.

I asked her what she needed to do to make ends meet. I knew the rent was $125 and utilities weren't included. She had to work more, she told me. She was a waitress at a restaurant out on South Division, but she could only work two nights because of the boys--those two nights covered by a kind lady from the Salvation Army Chapel down the street. Clare said she needed a sitter at least two, maybe three more nights a week to make it. When I offered my free services for those nights, (wondering what the hell I was saying), she laughed and told me I was crazy.

"Why? I'm done working by four each day. You work from five to ten. The timing is right."

"You don't even know my boys," she said, full of doubt. "I'm telling you, they wear you down fast."

"I've got three young brothers, and two little sisters about the age of your boys," I told her. "I'm qualified."

She seemed to be wrestling with emotions and didn't speak. Finally, she took a deep breath. "You'd think I'd be able to ask my own family for help, but they moved away to Florida, like yours did, but without even telling me. They left me high and dry. My parents don't know my boys at all—only seen them once."

"How come?"

"It was Rick, my ex. They said he was a bad seed—a troublemaker. They wouldn't even come to the wedding."

"That's kind of rough."

"Well, turns out they were pretty accurate—Rick's a total train wreck, and I was too stupid to see it. I had to learn the hard way."

I hoisted myself up out of the couch and clapped my hands, hoping to look decisive. "Okay, we try things out next week. Just let me know the nights."

"You don't know what you're getting into, Henry."

"Sure I do. Maybe I'd better meet your boys now." I offered a hand and helped her to her feet.

"Try if you want. But you can get out of it any time," she said with a sigh. "Any time."

"Have some faith," I told her, so she called the boys down.

It was curious how things went. Jacob, the oldest and moodiest, didn't like me. He had a picture on his dresser of his dad and him sitting on a motorcycle.

"My dad's bigger than you," he said. "He could beat the shit out of you."

I could tell from the photo that I was way bigger than Rick, who looked short and wiry as a weasel, but I said, "Yeah, he probably could. Does your mother let you talk like that?"

"Sure."

"Well, I don't. So cut it out."

"You aren't the boss."

"I am till your mom gets home so shut up."

He scowled at me but didn't answer back.

Little Rick, the middle one, was slow catching onto basic things like getting dressed and tying his shoes, but he never stopped asking irritating, interesting questions: "How come farts don't make smoke? Why do we have two holes in our nose? How come Huckleberry Hound is blue?" On and on like that. I did my best. Jacob could take just so much of it before screaming at him "Shut your stupid mouth!" Little Rick seemed to be lacking in something, but I couldn't put a finger on what it was.

Billy was the three-year-old, a whiny perpetual motion machine who frayed my nerves the most of the three but would thankfully wear out right after dinner and fall asleep under the table or beside me while I read them a book. Jacob refused to read with us at first, but I knew he was listening. Eventually, he'd sit down on the floor, maintaining a respectable distance. Their favorite storybook was *Where the Wild Things Are,* and I didn't wonder.

They seemed fine with my cooking--simple crap like hot dogs, macaroni and cheese from a box, and the spicy chili I learned about from my roommate at college…all the basic food groups. Dealing with their noise, their constant meltdowns, their meanness in that first week—it all turned out harder than I ever imagined, especially after hauling beer all day. I wondered how Clare managed it all the time. They were undisciplined and resentful of orders, especially when I made them help out, but they hadn't had any of my advantages, like two good parents. They had one good one sometimes. Once they were asleep, I just felt like lying down and drinking beer, but instead I worked on setting the house in order a little at a time. It was good having something besides my own pitiful problems to focus on.

Clare had an old Ford sitting in the garage. It had died on her two months before, so she took the bus to work and back. I made her take my car because I wouldn't be using it. That got her home before 10:30. She always put gas in it, even though I didn't ask her to. She'd arrive to a clean kitchen and the boys asleep, and on the third night of my babysitting, she sat down and balled her eyes out. I drove home to Joe's basement that night and was asleep in half a minute.

On Saturday, I went over and told her I'd thought of a new plan. The boys didn't like the kind Salvation Army lady much because she made them eat vegetables and read them nothing but Jesus stories. I didn't especially like living in a basement, and I honestly liked my own house, so I told her, "What if I bought an air mattress, put it on the floor in the sewing room next to the boys' room upstairs, gave you the $50 rent I'm paying Joe, helped with utilities and food, and took care of the boys every night? I wouldn't have to go home afterwards because—guess what? I'd already be there!"

She gave me an incredulous look and sat thinking. "Well, what about Mrs. Oz?"

"Mrs. Oz…she'll have a field day. But I'll let my folks know what's going on before she gets to them. They're on to her. I'll tell them it's a business deal that benefits both of us--and them, too. And it's all on the up and up."

For the first time since I met her, I saw a glimmer in her eyes, as if some part of the weight had just tumbled from her shoulders. "You're too damn good to be true," she said.

I didn't have to think about an answer. "I grew up here," I told her. "And I could use a family."

It was then I think she began to understand me.

In a couple of weeks we'd settled into a routine with frequent setbacks. One evening I caught Little Rick whittling chunks out the rungs of the stairway with a jackknife. Jacob was nearby, watching him. I yelled so loud I scared them, stormed over and grabbed the knife. "Whose jackknife is this?"

"It's Jacob's," Little Rick told me.

"I let him use it," Jacob said as if daring me to do something.

I folded up the knife and stuck it in the pocket of my jeans. "Bad decision." I glared hard at him but didn't seem to intimidate him.

"Give me that knife back. My dad gave it to me."

"Then tell your dad to come and get it from me. You can't carve up my house."

"This is my mom's house."

"No, it's not. She's only borrowing it."

"It's her house."

"You boys carve it up once more, and I'll toss that knife in the river."

Jacob was nervous but half knew it was a bluff. In a week I gave the knife back, making him promise to keep it away from Little Rick and only use it outdoors. He grumbled his assent. Little by little he warmed to me. I knew he was embarrassed that he was seven and couldn't ride a two-wheeler, so I took him to the Salvation Army parking lot one Saturday and taught him in about an hour. He never said thanks, but I knew we had a bond after that. I offered to teach Little Rick, too, but he was in no hurry. "How come a two-wheeler stands up when it goes and falls over when it stops?" he asked. I knew enough physics to answer him, but I didn't.

The three of them still could drive me crazy, but there were compensations. The two older boys slept together in a double bed in my old room. Billy, the little guy, slept on a plastic-covered army mattress on the floor, slept like a stone but talked and cried in his sleep and sometimes wet the bed. We took to reading in the big bed, all four of us, and sometimes Clare would come home and find me sleeping in the midst of them with the book still open on my chest. She'd wake me up quietly, lift Billy onto his own bed, and we'd go down for a beer and some small talk, which I found no trouble at all with her.

I was surprised to discover she took the boys to the Salvation Army Chapel services every Sunday. I went along, of course, (I'd lived in the neighborhood my whole life and never once set foot in the place), in the process learning the main reason she went--the boys got whisked off to Sunday school for an hour and a half, and she could sit in the service and rest. The homilies by Captain McCann were mainly about God loving you no matter what lousy things you'd done, which was comforting, but then he'd get worked up and shout out a passage of scripture, shattering the peace in a jarring way. He needed some preaching lessons. I found the band pretty painful, but only because I was raised on good music. Clare never complained about it, and I noticed the people there were good to her. The place was a port in the storm for her and others, and it'd only taken me 19 years to find that out.

I checked out her car--the problem was just a dead battery, so I found a reconditioned one for $25, and from then on we were a two-car family. She thought I was a mechanical genius. I could see her begin to relax. She gained a little weight, and it looked good. She needed it. I discovered things about her I wasn't expecting, like how smart she was in ways. I was tired one night, trying to add up six rows of invoice figures, and she looked over my shoulder and said. "It comes to $3240.85." I snorted and went on adding six columns. The total turned out $3240.85.

"How the hell did you do that?"

"I don't know. I just can."

"Jesus, Clare," I said. "It's amazing. You should be working for the US Treasury, not serving meatloaf and mashed potatoes on South Division."

I discovered she read more than I did, mostly my books, since now she had some time. *The Grapes of Wrath* was her favorite—reminding her a little of her own scrappy life. She loved bad rock n roll, too. Thanks to my dad I was a high-tone jazz fan. She just laughed at my condescending comments and told me you couldn't argue taste in music. And she was right, of course.

One night Billy was upset and crying in his sleep, so I went up and lay down beside him on his army mattress, feeling his fears. Next thing I knew, Clare was standing above me in a robe, cursing under her breath, a thing I didn't often hear her do.

"Better get up, Henry," she said. "He's wet the bed and you, too."

I woke up enough to realize I was soaked through. Even my wallet was wet. I got to my feet, managing to say nothing offensive beyond, "Damn. He was tossing and whining in his sleep, so I got in to settle him down. It was just an accident. No harm done, Clare."

She got Billy to his feet, still nine-tenths asleep. She stripped off his pajamas as if she'd done it a hundred times, stripped the bed, and had him dried and dressed and tucked in again in about two minutes. "Get out of those things. I'll go down and run you a bath."

I carried Billy's wet stuff to the basement for her, then came back up to the only full bathroom in the house--just off the master bedroom on the main floor where she slept. She was running steaming water in the big old claw-footed tub, the one hardly anyone but my mother and little sisters ever used, at least as far as I knew.

"Get out of those soggy clothes," she told me. "I'll throw them in the wash right now. I'm sorry, Henry. It's pretty disgusting. He only does it once in a while."

She stood there waiting. I was self-conscious but went ahead and stripped off my shirt. I was tall and loose-jointed but at that time in the best shape of my life, so I didn't mind baring my upper body. I handed her my shirt, and she stood there waiting for the rest. When I hesitated at my belt, she said, "Should I wait outside?"

"Maybe so," I said, and she stepped into her bedroom. I stripped off the rest, opened my wallet onto the radiator, and handed her the soggy mess through a crack in the door. The tub was steaming; I turned it off and gingerly got in, lowering myself into water almost too hot to tolerate. In a few moments, though, it felt heavenly. I honestly hadn't been in that tub since I was a little kid with a rubber duck.

My dad had put a shower in the basement, and that's where the boys were expected to clean up. This tub was so big and the sides so high that I felt like some kind of Roman emperor. I heard the washing machine go on in the basement; moments later there was a knock on the door.

"Mind if I come in?" she asked.

"If you want," I told her uncertainly. She came into the room, keeping her eyes on mine.

"I stink of urine and cigarette smoke. Could I get in with you a minute?"

"Ummm, are you sure?"

She undid the tie on her robe and it dropped to the floor. She had nothing on underneath. Though she was thinner than she should have been--hipbones sticking out and her ribs showing faintly under round, pale breasts--she took my breath away. "I always thought this big tub was meant for two," she said and calmly stepped between my legs and sat down with her back to my chest. "I want you to wash me all over, even my hair, and then I'll wash you." She handed me a bar of soap, so I started hesitantly on her back, working up a lather, and soaped as far down as I could. Then I moved around to her front—more fascinating in every way—and my hands grew more assured. She purred when I got to some spots, so I'd linger there and keep returning until she was slippery with soap.

She said, "I saw you in the back yard mowing in just some shorts, so I knew your body was inspiring."

"Not half as inspiring as yours."

"I can feel your inspiration, Henry."

"I'm sure."

"Have you done this before?"

I hesitated, uncertain of what to admit. "In a bathtub? Not really. Nor on a beach."

"I mean any time."

"No," I said, because I couldn't lie to her. "But I've tried enough times."

She laughed, bent her head back and kissed me on the lips. "Well, tonight you better mark your calendar. Your trying days are over."

Going to bed with Clare was a college education. I worried from the start about getting her pregnant, but she said, "Rick used to knock me up just looking at me, so after Billy was born I got my tubes tied. No more worries." I was relieved but sad, too, sad that part of her life was already over and done. At times I would lie in bed beside her, wondering what a child of ours might have been like.

I learned everything about love making from a grown woman with passion and patience, not by trial and error from girls more scared and uneducated than I was. Clare showed me all the things she liked best, so I did them every time and did them first. Rick, she told me, only did what he wanted and nothing more. The truth is, I loved doing everything she asked me to. I touched and studied every inch of her body, stretch marks and all. She did the same with me, admiring my parts in ways they never have been since. I could have made love to her three times a day if the boys weren't around and she'd been up to it, but sometimes she came home from work tired and just wanting to talk about the day. I liked that, too. I slept in her bed on nights when I had to be up at five for the beer truck, so I was long gone before the boys woke up. Never, on those nights with her warm body touching mine, did I dream of wrinkling cloth or girls with withered lips.

I turned 20 in August, and she baked a cake for me and gave me a book of Robert Frost's poems. It sits on my desk to this day. The boys drew me funny pictures of the five of us on paper placemats from her restaurant. I still have those, too. An August birthday always bothered me. Summer was close to being over, school was soon to start, change was in the air. The summer I was 20 was the worst one ever for that feeling.

Clare told me she'd seen people outside the house taking pictures of it. Though we had no "for sale" sign in the yard, she figured it was real estate people--some buyer looking at the place. She wasn't distressed, but I was. I phoned my mother and found out the Salvation Army was interested in buying a half block of houses to tear down for a women's shelter, and our house was one. She also told me Mrs. Oz had called her about Mrs. Barker and me shacking up together. My mother had told her it was mean, lying gossip, that she already knew what was really going on (everything on the up and up), and never, ever to call her again. We'd wondered why we hadn't seen Mrs. Oz sitting like a toad in her side window. It was good to know my mother was still watching out for me—even from long distance.

September came, and my father called and said an agent would be closing on the house the end of October. I needed to let Mrs. Barker know so she could make other living arrangements. He asked me to thank her for making up the back payments, for clearing off the slate. He said she was a woman of integrity, and I agreed.

MSU started in late September back then, later than any other school. It meant I could work longer, but instead I quit two weeks early to spend more time with Clare and the boys. Jacob was in second grade now, in a school just two blocks away, and Little Rick was starting morning kindergarten. Billy went two days to a nursery school at the Chapel, so Clare and I had a little time alone. I knew the summer had been the start of healing for me, but I was afraid of losing more than I'd gained.

We were lying in her bed, having made love in a slow, lingering, melancholy way. "I have a plan I want to run by you," I told her.

"You and your plans."

"I want to take a year off school and help you and the boys get on your feet."

She laughed a little and kissed me with such warmth I melted into her arms. "Henry White, you aren't even legal age yet, but you're the best man I ever met. I do love you."

"I feel the same, Clare."

"So I won't even listen to such a sweet, dumb plan. I come with a load of baggage, Henry—like one of those dustbowl Okies in *The Grapes of Wrath*. Now's the time for you to go out and find your life, not prop up mine. I'll make my way. I always have. Don't do the same stupid stuff I did. You go to school this year and don't stop for anybody. Find out what your life is supposed to be. I know it'll be something good...maybe great."

I felt heartsick. "You're saying this is the end of us?"

"Of course it is. My love will still be there. Just like your family's love is always there even when they're so far away in Florida. Love's your safety net, Henry."

"Then what's your safety net?"

"You've been my safety net. You've seen me through my hardest time. That memory won't ever leave me."

She had little awareness, I believe, of all she'd seen me through, how the four of them had been my lifeline. "Who wants a memory to live on? I want you with me, holding tight like now."

"Nothing like this lasts forever," she said and kissed me again.

So she forced me out, and I went back to my room at school. For three straight weekends, I drove home to be with her and the boys. On the fourth, I found the house deserted, empty as a shell on the beach, and no sign of a note. The Oz house was deserted, too, and a house down the street was already being bulldozed. I drove by it. The naked basement walls looked as barren as a park pool after Labor Day.

I did hear from Clare once, maybe two months later. She sent a letter care of my parents, and they forwarded it to me. It was very short--said she was sorry for leaving without a goodbye, but it made it easier for her. The boys said hello. There had been some sort of reconciliation with her parents, and they were down in Florida now, living in her parents' trailer, and she could already tell it wasn't going to work. She signed it "Love, Clare"—the single bone she tossed to me.

Clare had been strong medicine for me and I, perhaps, for her, but it was way too dramatic to say we'd fixed each other's lives. Certain symptoms hung around in my head for the next five years or more, even when I began college teaching. Something inside of me stayed fragile but over time became controllable and one day disappeared.

The family house is only a memory now but still a holy place to me. When I think of it, it's Clare who comes to mind. She was right—eventually I did find my life. I want to believe she found hers, too.